Mistress

A *Pride and Prejudice* Variation, with Parts Not Suitable for Those Who Have Not Reached Their Majority

by Sophie Turner

Revised second edition

Published in the United States of America

Based on the characters and original plot from the public domain work, *Pride and Prejudice*, by Jane Austen.

ISBN: 1543211860
ISBN-13: 978-1543211863

CONTENTS

PROLOGUE

May 22, 1815

Near the town of Meryton, in Hertfordshire, two sisters who had always been particular friends were so fortunate as to live within three miles of each other. One was happily married, and while it would be impolite to say the other was happily widowed, it may be said that she was more content in her widowed state than she had been in her married one.

"My dear Lizzy," said the married sister, who was called Jane, to the other, "we are to have company at Netherfield soon – a small house party, only, but I hope you will join in our dinners, and perhaps a ball, if I am able to convince Charles that we should have one."

"My year is very nearly complete," replied Elizabeth, who would have rejoined society earlier, if she could have done so without injuring her reputation. "I have for some time been desirous of participating in society, and I would be very pleased to make my re-entrance at Netherfield."

"Oh Lizzy, I am so delighted you should say that," said Jane. "I must tell you, though, that Mr. Darcy is to be one of the party. I know you did not get on well with him, and I hope you shall be able to meet as polite acquaintances, at least."

"Jane, dear sister, it has been better than three years since I have last seen him, although he did write to express his condolences on the death of my husband, which rather surprised me. I cannot say I am looking forward to making his acquaintance again, but I shall certainly be polite to him. I do wonder, though, at his coming to Netherfield. I had thought the breach between him and Charles to be irreconcilable."

"Charles is much too amiable to maintain an irreconcilable breach," said Jane, smiling as though to indicate how well her own amiable nature matched that of her husband. "He and Mr. Darcy met at White's last year, and they have gradually renewed their acquaintance, with some apology – I understand – on the part of Mr. Darcy, who felt himself in the wrong for what occurred between them some years ago, although Charles says it was as much his fault as Mr. Darcy's."

"Well, I had not imagined Mr. Darcy capable of admitting wrongdoing in any matter, so I am quite surprised at what you say, Jane. I shall meet Mr. Darcy politely, as you ask, and perhaps if he is capable of admitting himself in the wrong, now, we shall get on better than we did previously."

Before the two ladies could converse further, the housekeeper, Mrs. Hill, entered the parlour and said, "Mrs. Collins, if you please, one of your tenants is in the kitchen and requests an audience with you."

Elizabeth rose, and smiled apologetically at her sister, who rose as well and said she should be going anyway; there were a great many preparations to make for the house party. Thus they separated, Mrs. Bingley to make her return to Netherfield Park, and Mrs. Collins for Longbourn's kitchen.

November 27, 1811

It happened so quickly, they did not even have time to send for Mr. Jones. They were recounting all that had happened at the Netherfield ball over breakfast when Mr. Bennet complained of a strange sensation in his arm. His wife said it sounded quite like her nervous attacks, which silenced him for a while, but Elizabeth could see he was truly not well. His countenance appeared pale, glistening with sweat, and she asked if they should send for the apothecary.

"Not yet, Lizzy. I think I shall just go and sit quietly in my library for a time," he said.

He rose, took a few steps toward the door, and collapsed, clutching his chest. He was surrounded by his wife and daughters, exclaiming in their shock and fear, and Elizabeth, who was as shocked and afraid as any of them but kept her exclamations to herself, was forced to push her way between Mrs. Bennet and Catherine to see if she could ascertain what ailed her father. He gasped and whispered, "Lizzy – " but could say no more, and Elizabeth focused her attentions on trying to soothe him, for his affliction seemed most painful. Minutes later, he was gone.

Elizabeth was not allowed the luxury of shock or grief, for her mother and younger sisters descended into hysterics, her mother worst of all, and someone was required to manage things, to order the servants to carry the body of their master to the parlour, to lay him out there and cover him. At first Jane was quiet, but clearly as shaken as the rest of them, although Elizabeth found that if she gave her sister a command, it would be followed, and that Jane seemed better when she had tasks to accomplish. As for Mr. Collins, he determined his proper function was to assist with prayer and sermonising, which perhaps soothed Mary a little, but was of little benefit to anyone else in the household.

Eventually, Mr. and Mrs. Phillips came to lend their assistance – Elizabeth longed for the presence of her aunt and uncle Gardiner, but they were away in Bristol and could not be expected back for days, even if they hastened their return. Still, some assistance was far better than what she had received before, and Elizabeth went up to the bedchamber she shared with Jane. She wished to rest for a few minutes and have a little time in privacy to finally adjust to what had happened, to fully feel her grief. She was not alone for five minutes before there came a knock at the door.

It was Mr. Collins. She understood what he was going to ask, and she was horrified. Her father was not even cold, much less buried. That he would choose this time of her greatest shock and vulnerability, that he would not even allow her half-an-hour of quietude before forcing her to think of where her family would live, was completely abhorrent to her.

In that moment, she hated him, and yet she knew she would have to marry him regardless.

November 30, 1811

Charles Bingley's countenance was not one formed for moping, and yet Bingley was doing this very thing as he stood over the sideboard and considered the breakfast selections. Darcy surveyed his friend and wondered if he had taken on an impossible task, in attempting to make Charles forget about Jane Bennet.

It had been easy enough at first. With the eager assistance of Caroline Bingley, the flaws of Miss Bennet's family had been noted, and to these flaws Darcy had added, gently, the lack of evidence that Miss Bennet held any romantic affections for the man who stood dangerously close to becoming her particular suitor. Charles could be rather easily convinced into believing these things, but things believed by Charles Bingley's head were not so easily absorbed by his heart, and this accounted for his moping over the sideboard.

This could be rectified, though, Darcy thought. He abhorred the idea of conspiring over anything, much less conspiring with Caroline Bingley, but he agreed with her that this was necessary, and that with a little distance from Jane Bennet, Charles would soon enough forget the young lady he had called his angel. In time, then, he might find another angel, one of more appropriate family and fortune.

Charles sat down with his plate, eventually, and the selections thereupon made it clear to Darcy that his friend's appetite had not been much affected, which he took as a positive sign. Time, time was all that was needed to make everyone forget of the Bennets, and time would be afforded to them here, along with every distraction London had to offer.

"I had thought to attend the Claytons's ball tonight," Bingley said. "Do you intend to go?"

"The Claytons are not the greatest *ton*, Charles," Darcy said, taking care not to note that this was so because they were still in trade, and Bingley was not so very far removed from it. The last thing he needed was for his friend to meet some pretty young tradesman's daughter, so that Bingley's vulnerable heart fell under the spell of someone even less suitable than Miss Bennet. "Why do we not go and dine at White's, instead, and have a night of cards, after?"

"Yes, I suppose that would be better. I do not really think my spirits ready for much in the line of dancing, anyway."

If Bingley was not in spirits for dancing, perhaps his heart was more severely affected than Darcy had thought. Still, his plan seemed poised for success through breakfast and the pot of coffee that followed it, taken leisurely in the drawing-room. Miller came in with the post, and there was a letter for Charles, which was studied silently for some time before he attempted to comment upon it.

"My God," Charles said, "Mr. Bennet has passed. There was some trouble with his heart, and apparently he succumbed to it."

"Charles, are you quite sure?" Darcy asked, for his mind was racing as to how this affected Elizabeth Bennet, and as he had determined to think no more of any Bennets, this was most troubling.

"Sir William Lucas wrote to me of it," Charles said. "He has been assisting Mr. Phillips and Mr. Collins with the preparations for the funeral."

"Those poor girls," Darcy murmured, although he thought only, *poor Elizabeth!*

"I think the same, Darcy. I think I should go to them – to Miss Bennet," Charles said. "I know you said you do not think she has affection for me, but everything has changed, and I am not sure that she did not – "

"Charles, I beg you, do not act hastily. Miss Bennet will only be more vulnerable in her present situation, for losing all her security in life. I expect she would gladly accept anyone that came to her and seemed likely to secure her a home. Is that all you require in a wife – gratitude, for putting a roof above her head?"

"No – I do not have *requirements* for a wife. You may be as cold and logical as you wish about marriage, Darcy, but I have a heart, and Miss Bennet has moved it – oh, how she has moved it! *You* convinced me I should not pursue her because of her family, and because she was not attached to me, but I find it does not matter to me if she is not so attached to me as I am to her. I – I love her. I do not want to live without her."

It was at this moment that Darcy understood he had lost Bingley. Before, when Charles had not understood the extent of his love, he might have been persuaded out of it. Now it was too late. His marriage to Jane

Bennet could only be avoided if she would refuse him, and no young lady in her right mind could refuse such an offer at such a time.

"I am going to go back to Netherfield," Charles said. "I am going to pay my condolences, and be of service to the family in any way that I am able, and when it is appropriate, I am going to ask for Miss Bennet's hand. For if such an exquisite creature is marrying me for my fortune, I will care not. If she does not love me so much as I love her, then I will seek to earn her love."

"This is precisely why we determined to separate you from Miss Bennet," Darcy said, unthinkingly.

"You *determined*? You mean this was planned? All of these seemingly casual conversations about Miss Bennet were the result of some determination between you and my sister?"

"Yes, Charles, we thought it best for you."

"Did no-one think perhaps I might be able to determine what is best for myself?" Charles shouted, growing a concerning shade of red in his countenance. "Do you all think I am a child, rather than the head of my household? A feeble-minded half-wit, that you must conspire around?"

"That is not at all what we thought. But a man in love may not think so clearly – "

"I am thinking clearly enough! I am thinking that if there is a woman in this world that I love, and she is a gentleman's daughter, and I can secure her hand, there is absolutely no reason why I should not!"

"Charles, think of what you are saying. Think of what you are taking on – not just Miss Bennet, but the whole family. Are you prepared to have the mother and the silly sisters living under your roof at Netherfield? Are you prepared to call on the aunt and uncle living in Cheapside?"

"I should not be ashamed of relations living in Cheapside when my own father lived the first half of his life within sight of his warehouses on the Tyne. You and my sisters may have conveniently forgotten he did not always reside in Scarborough, but I assure you, I have not," Bingley said. "As for Mrs. Bennet and her daughters, I am not so selfish as you, Darcy. If I can ease Miss Bennet's present distress by offering a home to her family, that will be pleasing to me, not abhorrent."

"You think me selfish?" Darcy asked, prepared to present Charles with any number of arguments to the contrary. Yet each of his arguments seemed to dissipate as soon as they formed, and he listened to his friend with growing concern:

"Of course I do, although if I must sum you up in one word, I suppose it would be proud, and I suppose I would say you have spent so long in pride of the Darcy name, and presuming what those who hold the Darcy name must do – and apparently what friends of those who hold the Darcy name must do – that you have always acted selfishly, and you have always looked down on those you consider beneath you. You do not want me to marry Jane Bennet because it would reflect poorly on you to have a friend make such a marriage. I am already tainted by *trade*, and my taking a wife with any such connexions will prove too much an embarrassment to you. Because this must have nothing to do with my own happiness – it must all be about *you*, Darcy."

"It was not – that is not why I discouraged the connexion," Darcy said, stung by what Bingley had said, and wondering desperately how to explain himself.

"Oh, is it not? Perhaps it is not why you discouraged the connexion. Perhaps you could not bear to see me happy, while you wallow in your own misery. Yes – misery. You will spend your whole damn life worrying over maintaining your position in society, and you will never do anything to pursue your own happiness. Now that I am presented with the choice, I have no interest in being like you. I will pursue my own happiness, and I will ask for Miss Bennet's hand, and I do not care if you do not like it, you arrogant arse."

Charles set his coffee cup down with crashing violence, then, the remnants of his coffee splashing onto the tea table. Any other man would have strode out immediately, but Bingley took out his handkerchief, rapidly mopped up the spilt drops of coffee, then stood and walked out of the room, ending his acquaintance with Fitzwilliam Darcy. The man who had until now been his particular friend watched his exit in stunned silence, desperately trying to conjure something to say to make him return. As a man who did not make close friends easily, Darcy felt the deepest desperation over losing one, and as the result of his own actions. He could not bring himself to say he had been wrong, however. That might, he realised, be further evidence of his pride.

He began a study, then, examining his thoughts, words, and actions in the whole course of his life, but particularly since his father had died, searching for selfishness and pride. In shame, he found them in abundance, and he sat there, alone, considering how he had come to err so grievously, and how he could affect the changes in his character he now knew he needed to make. This was not the only thing he considered, however, for he could not help but wonder what it would be like to do what Charles had spoken of: what would it be like to pursue his own happiness?

December 2, 1811

Elizabeth had dreamed often, in the nights since her father's death. She dreamed of happier times, when he was still alive, and in the mornings suffered the crushing disappointment of recalling all at once that he was gone. There would never be another evening of bantering with him at the dinner table, never another rainy morning whiled away with him in the library. She recalled, too, that Mr. Collins had supplanted him as master of the house, and she was betrothed to him, a thought that filled her with dread.

They were always a quiet party over breakfast, dressed in black and the spectre of what had happened in that room less than a week ago hanging over them. Occasionally, Mr. Collins would say something foolish, something insensitive, and Elizabeth would find herself overcome with anxiety. *I cannot marry this fool*, she would think, *but I must, I must.*

Elizabeth was suffering from the memory of a particularly vivid dream on this morning, and when she had eaten what little she could stomach, she excused herself and went quietly to the library. Here, the memories of her father were strongest, and here she could sit, undisturbed, and mourn. She should have gone to the parlour, with her mother and sisters, for they were still receiving any callers who had not yet paid their condolences. But Elizabeth did not think she could face another day of such sympathies – mostly sincere, but marked with too much curiosity – as they received from their neighbours.

She did not sit, instead making her way along the bookshelves, quietly fingering the spines. Elizabeth knew every title in this room, although she had not read nearly all of them; there was something soothing and familiar about studying them all again. Everything had changed, except these books, this collection her father had cherished and done much to build during his lifetime. When she had progressed halfway around the room, the door opened without so much as a knock, and Mr. Collins came in, saying:

"There you are. Selecting a book, no doubt, but you should not require of any of these for some time. When I go to Kent to take my leave of Lady Catherine, I will stop in town to make some purchases to form a collection for you and your sisters. Your moral education has been lacking, but we will see that rectified soon enough," he said.

Elizabeth merely stared at him, and felt all of the equanimity she had gained that morning receding, supplanted immediately by distress.

"Regardless, I came to find you because Mr. Bingley has come to pay his condolences, and you should be present in the parlour." He turned to leave, and Elizabeth felt herself required to follow him, wondering what Mr. Bingley's presence should mean.

Lost among the chaos of her father's death had been a letter from Caroline Bingley to Jane, informing her that the Netherfield party were following Mr. Bingley to town while he attended to some business, and indicating Miss Bingley thought it likely that the party would remain there the whole winter. It had been read eventually, however, and served to create a further dejection in poor Jane's spirits. Mr. Bingley's presence in the parlour showed his sister to have been wrong in her indication, but *how* wrong, Elizabeth could not know. She endeavoured to turn her mind to what it might mean, for it was too unpleasant to think of what Mr. Collins had said in the library – that he should control her reading – although she could not do so for long, for Mr. Collins spoke again:

"Miss Elizabeth, before we go into the parlour, I should note that in the future, I would prefer it if you arrange it with me before you enter the library. I shall have a great deal of important business to attend to within there, as master of the estate, and I should not like to be interrupted," he said. "However, once you have finished the course of reading I set out for you, if you do wish to choose a book, you may let me know in the morning, and I am certain we can find a time within the course of the day that is convenient for the both of us."

"My father always allowed us access to the library at any time we wished it," Elizabeth protested.

"I do not like to speak of such things so soon after that melancholy event," he said, "however you must acknowledge my right as master of the house to arrange things as I wish them. And your younger sisters have been allowed a faulty degree of indulgence, which must be curbed. It will be your duty as my wife and as mistress of the house to aid me in this."

"That I might endeavour to do," Elizabeth said, "but I do not understand why that should limit my access to the library."

"As I said, we shall arrange things," he said, then turned to walk toward the parlour.

If more time had passed since her father's death, Elizabeth might have felt more anger at his statements and his dismissal of her, and responded in turn. Instead, however, her frayed emotions could only allow the tide of dread to rise still higher, and it was with tears in her eyes that she entered the parlour and greeted Mr. Bingley. He gave her the condolences it seemed he had already given the rest of the family, and was then informed by Mr. Collins of the betrothal. To this his reaction was shock, and when he spoke, it was to say, "Oh – it is to be a long engagement, no doubt."

"We shall be wed on December the 18th," said Mr. Collins, curtly. "Surely you see the impropriety of Miss Elizabeth and I residing under the same roof for the duration of a longer engagement."

Charles Bingley's manners were too polite for him to present any of the rebuttals to this statement that Elizabeth herself had attempted to introduce, that it was customary for a widow and daughters to be allowed a goodly period of time before an heir took custody of a house, that Elizabeth could have gone to live with her other relations for an appropriate period of mourning, that it would look almost as poorly in the neighbourhood for the daughters of Longbourn to go into half-mourning so quickly as it would be for a man and his betrothed to live under the same roof without the presence of her father. Elizabeth's arguments had all been swept aside by her mother, whose nerves had ceased their troubles almost immediately after she had learned her daughter was betrothed, and therefore her own future was secure. Mrs. Bennet was eager to see that future fully secure, and Mr. Collins was eager to begin his married life, and neither had given any merit to Elizabeth's pleas to mourn for longer.

"And how are your family, Mr. Bingley? Are they in good health?" Mrs. Bennet asked, perhaps to change the subject, but in such a manner that Elizabeth cringed.

"Yes, my sisters and brother are in good health."

"Have they returned to Netherfield as well?"

"Ah – no. Mr. and Mrs. Hurst are to remain at their house in town through the winter, and Miss Bingley has gone to Scarborough."

"Scarborough!" cried Mrs. Bennet. "At this time of year?"

"Yes. We have an aunt there who required of her companionship, and is likely to continue to do so for at least a year," Mr. Bingley said, rather curtly.

There was little else Mr. Bingley could speak of following this, and so for some time more he did not speak, and merely gazed at Jane, who lowered her eyes and blushed, but with a faint, wistful smile directed towards him. Elizabeth sat there watching him, willing him to ask Jane for a private audience, willing him to do that which would allow Elizabeth to break her engagement. She would do it, she thought – if she was certain Mr. Bingley would propose, she would do it as soon as she could.

He made no such requests, however, and after the silence had lasted long enough for it to become awkward, he rose and told them that if there was anything he could do to be of assistance in such a time, they must let him know of it immediately. *Yes,* Elizabeth thought, *yes, there is, you can offer for Jane, and save me.*

December 5, 1811

Darcy heard no more from his friend. He spent the days following the breach in quiet reflection, continuing to be most affected by what Bingley had said, and ashamed of his past behaviour. He did not know if Charles had sensed his tendre for Elizabeth Bennet, and if therefore his comment about Darcy's pursuing his own happiness had been meant specifically, and not generally. Darcy thought about this – this alien concept of doing what he wished, without a thought of connexions or society, of asking the loveliest creature of his acquaintance to marry him. Yet if Charles thought these things of him, what must *she* think?

Still, he considered it, until one day, there was an announcement in the papers, short, simple, and incredibly wounding. It was not the one he had been expecting. "Miss E. Bennet, of Longbourn, in Hertfordshire, is betrothed to Mr. W. Collins, vicar of Hunsford, in Kent."

Oh, Elizabeth, what have you done? was his only thought at first. Yet it was clear enough what she had done: she had acted to secure a home for herself and the remains of her family, and accepted the offer of that odious parson that held Lady Catherine's living. Charles must by now have made his return to Netherfield, but not his offer, and poor Elizabeth had sacrificed happiness for the security of what remained of her family.

Darcy thought, in that moment, of going to Hertfordshire, of staying at an inn, if Charles would not have him at Netherfield, of making, in essence, a counter-proposal to her. Surely she would prefer him to Mr. Collins! Yet every reason to order his trunks packed and his carriage readied seemed to be followed by two reasons why he should not do so. The mother and the silly sisters could be set up in a separate establishment, somewhere in Derbyshire but not *too* near to Pemberley. To ask her to break her existing engagement would be substantial, but she was a woman, and could do so if she decided in Darcy's favour. But, acting on the perceived impossibility of a marriage between them, he had been guarded with his affections; any proposal from him would likely come as a surprise to her. Thinking of this returned his thoughts to conjecturing as to her opinion of him. If it was poor – if she would refuse him, if she would choose that horrid man over him – it would be his undoing. He thought of how it would be, of riding from an inn to Longbourn, of requesting a private audience, and the myriad ways in which she could refuse him.

It would be better to write to her, he thought. Putting his proposal in a letter would enable her to spend some time in deliberation between her two offers, to be informed of his affections in a manner that would be better done than what he would likely manage in speaking. And if she did choose to refuse him, whether out of preference or out of honour in keeping her present engagement, at least he would not have to hear her speak it. The shattering of his soul could occur in private, in the comfort of his study, with a decanter of brandy at hand.

Darcy gathered his writing things, and after spending the better part of the morning and a quire of paper on various drafts, finally arrived at:

"Dear Miss Bennet,

"Please accept my sincerest condolences on the death of your father. I believe you and he were close, and I am sure this makes what would already have been a difficult time all the more unbearable. Having lost both of my own parents, I can say that time will heal the wound somewhat, but never completely. I still feel their absence, even now, and believe I shall for the rest of my own life.

"Having seen news of your engagement in the papers, I should now congratulate you upon it. However, I cannot, for Mr. Collins has secured the very hand in marriage that I myself desire, and while I abhor breaking a commitment, and expect you do as well, I am going to request you do just that.

"I admire you greatly, and I have felt my affections towards you growing for some time, and wish I had declared myself sooner, before another offer could be made to you. As I now find myself second, I will not attempt to compare myself with your betrothed, but will make the case for myself as best I can.

"Pemberley brings in more than 10,000 pounds every year, and sometimes nearer 11,000. Of that, I had thought 700 pounds an appropriate amount for your pin money, but that may be increased if you think it insufficient for your needs as a married woman. Your jointure, on my death, I would settle at 1,200 pounds per year, so you would have a sufficient amount to set up your own establishment. I do regret to say that Pemberley does not have a dower house, so this may be necessary. I would also set up an establishment for your mother and younger sisters, and would ensure Mrs. Bennet and any of your sisters who do not marry are kept in comfort for the whole of their lives.

"You would have your own bedchamber and dressing-room, both at Pemberley and my London house, and no expense would be spared in decorating them to your taste, as well as any updates you desire within the remainder of either house. Pemberley is a large house, but my housekeeper, Mrs. Reynolds, has held her post for fourteen years and is a most diligent and trustworthy woman, so you may decide for yourself what proportion of your time you wish to spend in household management.

"I would hope for a marriage in which your affections matched my own, but I fully understand they may not, at the time of your reading this letter. I would ask only that you allow me to do all I can to grow them over time. I await your response, and remain –

"Your most humble and obedient servant,

"FITZWILLIAM DARCY"

Once he had read it through several times, and determined it to be what he wished to say, and of appropriate tone to be proposing marriage to a young woman who had just lost her father and accepted the hand of her cousin, Darcy then turned his mind to how to get it to her. It would not be appropriate to send it to her directly; the best thing to do would have been to send it to Charles, and ask that his friend give it to her discreetly. As that was not an option, however, he eventually decided to send it under cover to Mrs. Bennet. He did not think that woman liked his company, but he also did not think she would turn down the possibility of her daughter marrying into a greater income. Indeed, he thought, she might be his greatest ally at Longbourn. Thus another letter of condolence was written, to Mrs. Bennet, informing the woman that it covered a proposal of marriage for Miss Elizabeth Bennet. Wishing to spare the family the expense of receiving this packet, he took it to a neighbour to have it franked, and gave it to a servant to post. Then there was nothing to be done but wait.

December 18, 1811

Mr. Bingley had not called on them again. It could not be told whether this was because he did not wish to, or because shortly after Mr. Bingley's visit, Mr. Collins had abruptly decided they should no longer be at home for callers. Mr. Collins's reason for this was that they were in mourning, and anyone who intended to pay their condolences should have done so by now.

The only communication they had received from Mr. Bingley had been a letter to Mrs. Bennet, kindly offering the use of one of his carriages for the wedding day. Mr. Collins had neither the present income nor the inclination to purchase a new carriage for his bride, and so he would make the trip to the church in Longbourn's present equipage, and the Bennet ladies would divide themselves between the Gardiners's carriage and the one that had been sent from Netherfield early in the morning.

Elizabeth could see all of these carriages, waiting in the drive. She had been standing by the window, gazing out, as her mother and younger sisters left the room, leaving only Jane to remain with her.

Jane came to her, and embraced her tightly, saying, "Oh, Lizzy, I know it is not what you wanted, but I hope it will be a good marriage."

The embrace had left wrinkles in Elizabeth's gown, the deepest shade of lavender silk she had been able to find, but she cared not. The dread of the last few weeks had been replaced with something more, something worse, a sort of dizzying panic.

"Do you need a moment to yourself, Lizzy?"

"Yes, please."

Jane left her, and Elizabeth found her panic now manifesting itself in the strongest desire to run away, to escape her fate. Jane would let her pass, surely, and she could be down the back staircase and out in the fields before anyone else realised something was amiss. She could be gone, and free – free to do what she wished and read what she wished, never to be controlled or touched by that pompous man. And yet she felt the impossibility of this. Where would she sleep? What would she eat? Where would the money come from, for these books she wished to read?

She was trapped. She knew she was trapped, and all she could do was wait in this room, until Jane finally knocked on the door and told her they could not wait any longer. Jane and Mr. Gardiner – who was to give his niece away – were the only ones in the carriage, and they rode to the parish church in silence.

That dizzying panic never left her. The service seemed to go far more quickly than was possible, and Elizabeth, who had always been of a strong constitution, spent much of it wondering if she was going to faint. But she did not, and then it was over, and she was exiting the church with her hand on her new husband's arm. She was exiting the church as Mrs. Collins.

There was to be no wedding breakfast, with most of the family now in half-mourning and Mrs. Bennet required to see through her whole year, and so there was a strange mingling of all of the guests outside the church. Elizabeth broke away from Mr. Collins and went to converse with her neighbours, in no hurry to return to Longbourn. She was speaking to Charlotte Lucas when she saw Jane and Mr. Bingley, off to the side of the crowd. Bingley was holding her hand and Jane was nodding, and Elizabeth felt certain they had reached an understanding.

To think of what might have happened if they could have done so earlier was far too painful for Elizabeth to contemplate. Nor could she think with happiness towards her sister's situation – not yet. At present, she had a very specific set of unpleasant thoughts to dwell upon.

December 20, 1811

Darcy might have spent his days after the sending of his letter to Elizabeth Bennet entirely worried over her reaction, and what he should find in her response, but for the news from his steward three days after he had sent it that one of his tenants had died. Richardson could have handled the matter as regarded the tenancy, but it was the sort of event Darcy felt his presence necessary for, and so he had ordered post horses for a journey north.

He had found there enough to occupy his mind, so that sometimes many hours passed before he could wonder whether Elizabeth Bennet's response would arrive that day, forwarded on from town. If the death of a tenant could ever be called easy, this was one of the easier ones to deal with – Mr. Stratton had been getting on in his years, and his widow was no more than five years younger than him. Stratton had left behind a comfortable fortune for his wife, and still more could be expected, upon the sale of his cattle. Yet those cattle required a buyer – ideally the new tenant – and Mrs. Stratton a home, for she had no family living that could take her in.

A place in Kympton was soon enough located for her, and Darcy interviewed several candidates to take on the tenancy, eventually finding one with sufficient fortune to purchase all of Mrs. Stratton's cattle, who had the additional qualities of being a kindly young man, and one a little guilty of supplanting a widow in such a way. Young Mr. Baleman assisted the widow in moving her possessions into her new home, and promised he should call upon her every few days in such an earnest way that Darcy felt certain he had made the right choice for the tenancy.

He would have made his return from Pemberley entirely satisfied, therefore, except that no letter from Elizabeth Bennet had ever been forwarded there. During the ride back to London, with matters of his estate no longer occupying him, Darcy began to fear he would not receive a response. He thought over his letter, and wondered if it was too businesslike, not affectionate enough. He wondered if merely asking for her hand in marriage when she was already betrothed had been abhorrent to her – so abhorrent she did not even think it worth a response. He wondered if instead her lack of a response had been founded on her opinion of him, an opinion based on his behaviour in Hertfordshire, which he now knew to be nowhere near what it ought to have been.

And he wondered if her response had simply been misdirected in the post, or his own letter had gone astray, or he had been wrong about Mrs. Bennet's willingness to give his offer to her daughter. Misdirection of one letter or another could be rectified, and Darcy held out hope that a letter *had* been delivered at the London house, but it had arrived near enough to his expected return that Miller had decided it should just be held there. If that had not been the case, he would have his carriage readied again to go to Hertfordshire the next day, and declare himself in person.

He arrived to find no letter, and considered making the journey to Hertfordshire then, but it was far too late in the day to attempt a call at Longbourn, and so he determined it better to go early the next morning. He passed his time with a quiet dinner, and then retired to his study to catch up on the last few days' papers. It was there that he saw the wedding announcement.

He was shocked, at first – he had not thought things should progress so fast as they must have, with the Bennets in mourning. They should not have progressed so quickly, and his first reaction was anger – anger that his own plans had been so thoroughly destroyed, that Elizabeth had been required to marry so quickly, rather than being allowed to mourn her father.

Yet the anger merely delayed the inevitable, which was the realisation that regardless of the cause, regardless of how very wrong it was, Elizabeth was now married. With this realisation, his thoughts turned to despair, for his despair upon understanding that Elizabeth was now irretrievably lost to him was complete. She was lost to him, and whether it was by choice, or by lack of knowledge that another option existed for her, he alone had been responsible. *Oh, Elizabeth! Poor, lovely Elizabeth, to be locked in matrimony with such a man!*

Darcy amended his orders, now, that the journey should be a return to Pemberley, that it should be delayed until after Christmas, and that Georgiana and her companion should prepare their things as well. For that was his only desire, now, to take his sister and return home.

It was too late to make any improvements as a lover, but he could improve himself as a brother, and as a man. He could become a man who would have been worthy of Elizabeth. There might not be any promise of happiness in that, but there would be satisfaction, at least, in correcting his ways, in better doing his duty. That was all he had to live for, now.

CHAPTER 1

June 26, 1815

Aside from church and meeting with her tenants, Elizabeth had not been in society for the better part of a year, and she felt both eager anticipation and a little trepidation as the carriage took her and the remaining Bennets to dinner at Netherfield. The remaining Bennets were her mother, of course, and Mary and Kitty; Lydia had married Lieutenant Denny, the natural affections she had felt greatly magnified by the promise of moving out from under Mr. Collins's roof. Denny now held an ensigncy in the regulars, purchased in part with funds provided by Elizabeth, and he was quartered at Deal with his wife, having thankfully made it through the late war with no injuries.

The curbing of her younger sisters's indulgences had perhaps been the only beneficial change at Longbourn that Mr. Collins had instituted. Allowances had been required to be strictly adhered to, boarding school had been threatened, and in the end Catherine had become far more reasonable, and Lydia had at least left in a respectable manner. For a time, Mary had, unfortunately, become even more severe under Mr. Collins's influence, but even she had eventually seemed to understand what a poison he had been upon the household, and most particularly on his wife. The Miss Bennets had both been invited to live at Netherfield, for a time, but had returned to Longbourn after the birth of little Charles, a relief to Elizabeth, if not them, for things had been even more difficult at Longbourn with only her mother and Mr. Collins there.

Both Catherine and Mary had seemed happier, with Mr. Collins removed from the house, but they could not be described as fully happy. Elizabeth hoped that with herself now out of mourning, she could give them more chances for happiness: more opportunities for Mary to exhibit, and more society and perhaps a few beaux for Kitty, for Elizabeth was a bit surprised her younger sister had shown no eagerness about following Lydia into matrimony, although perhaps the right man had not yet come along.

Tonight, however, Elizabeth would focus on her own happiness; she would give herself over to the enjoyment of being in society again, for even if Mr. Darcy was to be among the guests, surely there would be others who were amiable and good company. The introductions were made in the drawing-room, a rather long string of them, for what had begun as a small house party had become Charles Bingley thoroughly filling Netherfield with his friends. It was only after the introductions were complete that Elizabeth saw Mr. Darcy, standing at the edge of the room much as he had used to do. He looked older; she supposed she did, too, but he seemed to have gained much more than three-and-a-half years of age. His complexion was more tanned than when she had known him last, as well, although it was nothing extraordinary for a man who spent a good amount of time out of doors. What surprised her more was his expression, which she had remembered as being aloof and proud. Now it seemed to her more aloof and melancholy, but then he surprised her still more by smiling at her, and making his way over to where she stood.

"Mrs. Collins," he said, giving her a bow so deep she wondered if he was mocking her.

"Mr. Darcy." She gave him a curtsey in equal proportion; if he *was* mocking her, she would mock him in return. "Thank you again for your condolences on the death of my husband. It was good of you to write."

He acknowledged this statement, and inquired most civilly about her health and that of her family. These she gave a favourable answer to, and then asked after his own health and that of his sister. To this he replied that they were both well, and he had just been visiting his sister, in Gibraltar.

"Gibraltar!" exclaimed Elizabeth, before she could help herself. That Mr. Darcy's sister had somehow come to live in such a place was so incongruous she could scarcely believe it. She made to begin apologising for such an outburst, but he spoke first, saying:

"You are surprised, of course. She married a naval captain, and he was posted to the Mediterranean, so she chose to take a house there, to be nearer to him."

Elizabeth was even more astonished to hear this, for marrying a naval captain did not seem the sort of thing the proud young lady that had once been described to her would have done, nor something her proud brother would have condoned.

"My congratulations to her. I hope she is pleased with the married state?"

"Yes, very pleased. She – she had been disappointed once in love, so I am glad to see her so happy, now. I do wish she did not live so far away, however. Pemberley is not the same without her."

Here his countenance once again took on something of sadness, and Elizabeth wondered if it was loneliness that gave him such an expression. Having volunteered this information about his sister and yet mentioned nothing of a wife, Elizabeth presumed he had not married. She recalled he had been betrothed to his cousin, Anne de Bourgh, but that young lady had lost her life to a lengthy illness. Mr. Collins had read of it in the papers, and spent nearly a fortnight bemoaning the loss of a young lady of such quality, each day adding a great many lines to his ever-growing letter of condolence to Lady Catherine de Bourgh, one her ladyship had acknowledged with the briefest of replies.

Mr. Darcy's betrothal to Anne de Bourgh had seemed an arranged marriage, to Elizabeth, but perhaps there had been true affection; it was the only thing she could think of that should cause his present expression, beyond the absence of his sibling.

"Was it not dangerous, with war once again broken out?" she asked, seeking to divert the subject.

"I had sailed there before Napoleon escaped, thankfully, but it did mean my stay was of longer duration than was expected. Eventually my brother-in-law was able to find me passage on a homeward-bound man-of-war. I cannot say it was the most comfortable journey I have ever made, but I felt quite safe with seventy-four guns between myself and the French."

"It must have been so interesting, too, to travel on a ship of war in such a time. I would like to hear more of your voyage sometime," Elizabeth said, seeing that everyone was beginning to line up to go in to dinner. "I have travelled so little in the past few years, so I must take my voyages vicariously."

"Of course. I would be happy to oblige you."

Only as she walked away did Elizabeth realise she had voluntarily engaged herself for another conversation with Mr. Darcy at some point in the future. Yet he had not been so disagreeable as he was in the past – in truth, he had conversed so pleasantly she could hardly believe he was the same man she had known before. But then, people could change in the course of several years: she most certainly had.

Although Mrs. Bingley had provided an excellent meal, Darcy could hardly eat, in his present state of excitement. Elizabeth – *glorious Elizabeth!* – was just up the table from his seat amongst the unmarried ladies and gentlemen. She was there and looked as lovely as ever, in the palest lavender dress, laughing and conversing with those beside her. Upon learning she was once again a possibility due to her widowhood, Darcy had wondered if he had spent the past few years making her more wonderful in his mind than she truly was, growing increasingly deeper in love with an imagined Elizabeth rather than the real one. But she was every bit as he had remembered her, and he found new reasons for a further deepening of his love, for there were details and nuances to her that he had forgotten.

Oh, those torturous early days, after reading of Mr. Collins's decease. How Darcy had longed to go to her, to declare himself. It had been Georgiana who had counselled patience, after he had opened his heart to her. Georgiana, who had regained her confidence and her happiness, who had been newly betrothed, and mature enough to be giving him advice. Nothing should be done while Mrs. Collins was in mourning, except to send a letter of condolence. He had hoped, perhaps, that his letter might become the beginning of a correspondence between them, but her response, while polite, had left him no opening; there was nothing within that could be responded to.

So he had waited, and tried to determine some natural way in which he could be returned to her acquaintance. In that, his encountering Charles at White's, and making his apology and the first overtures of renewing their friendship, had been the deepest blessing. Their friendship was not what it once was; it had been renewed with caution, and still felt a delicate, awkward thing. Yet it had been renewed, and Darcy was grateful for it, even beyond its providing the opportunity for him to be here. How impatient he had been in Gibraltar, upon receiving Charles's invitation to the house party at Netherfield. Of all things, to be kept from his second chance by war!

He was there now, however, and he would seize this second chance, although he would keep Georgiana's counsel and go about things patiently. If Elizabeth had received his proposal, she could not have spoken to him tonight in the manner she had, without any degree of awkwardness. Darcy had to presume, then, that she was unaware of his affections, for he had done nothing to indicate them during his previous acquaintance with her. Gradually, he would do so now, and seek to understand her own. She was a widow, and he could not yet know what the state of her heart was; perhaps she had come to love Mr. Collins. Elizabeth glanced down the table at him, and he smiled. She returned the smile, and even this simple thing gave him hope.

Darcy made an attempt to apply himself to the food, so as not to be caught looking at her too often. When next he did look in her direction, he found her frowning, and wondered at what could have caused this. She did not look at him, this time, and eventually he returned his attention to his neighbours at the table, and to his food.

Too soon, the ladies made their exit from the dining-room, although at least this gave him a better look at her figure as she left, and he found it every bit as pleasing as it ever was. He was not the only man there who found Mrs. Collins pleasing, however; he soon learned Mr. Althorpe was most vocal in his praise of the young widow's looks, but with much agreement from the other single gentlemen, and for the first time Darcy realised he might well have competition for her hand, a thought that filled him momentarily with paralysing fear.

"She ought to marry soon," Mr. Althorpe was saying. "A woman, trying to manage that estate on her own – she'll run it down in no time. It wants a man's management."

"She seems to have done well enough with it in the last year," Darcy said, with his heart pounding, for he hardly liked speaking with a new acquaintance, much less confronting one.

"I am sure that is only because she kept with whatever procedures her husband implemented. It will be once she starts getting womanish ideas in her head, and acting upon them. That will be when she destroys her own income. Unless, of course, she marries me."

This prompted laughter from all the men around him, save Darcy, and he wished Charles was seated closer to him, for surely Bingley would have assisted in the defence of his sister, if he had overheard Althorpe.

"And where is your estate, Mr. Althorpe?" Darcy asked, knowing it was not likely Althorpe, the younger son of a viscount, would have one, and it was very possible he never would.

"Haven't inherited it yet," Mr. Althorpe said, pouring himself more brandy. "Fine little property, from my mother's side of the family, but it would be preferable to have Longbourn while I wait, particularly when it comes with such a fine-looking wife to warm my bed."

"Might it not be said, then, that Mrs. Collins has more experience in running an estate than you?"

The men laughed again at this, one of them saying that Darcy had Althorpe there, and thankfully the subject moved away from Mrs. Collins following this. From the occasional glares Darcy received from Mr. Althorpe, however, he felt certain he had just made himself an enemy. Yet he was glad he had done it, even if he had been discomfited by it; he did not like the thought of Elizabeth being spoken of in such a manner.

It was a relief, when the butler came to tell them that tea was ready in the drawing-room, but Mr. Althorpe, being nearer the door than Darcy, made his way thither more quickly, and Mrs. Collins was his object. Darcy watched, fuming, at the man's making every effort to render himself agreeable to the woman he had demeaned earlier. To his surprise, however, Darcy was rewarded not five minutes later, when he watched Elizabeth disengage herself from the conversation, and make her way over to where he stood.

"If you are at leisure, Mr. Darcy, I wonder if I might hear from you about your journey," she said, quietly.

"Of course," he said, trying to quell his feelings of delight and triumph so they would not reach his countenance. He led her over to an open sofa, and then proceeded to provide her with an account of his time in Gibraltar and his return on HMS Achille. Normally, speaking of visiting with Georgiana would have been a topic to sadden him, reminding him that his closest relation had moved so far away, leaving Pemberley even emptier than it had been and depriving him of the company he had come to enjoy more as a brother than a guardian. Elizabeth gazed at him with kind sympathy whenever he drifted into wistfulness, however, and such attentions from the woman he loved soon pushed any thoughts of loneliness from his mind. She showed herself fully engaged in all he spoke of, nodding at his descriptions and asking questions to glean further details.

"Oh, I have entirely monopolised your time!" she exclaimed, when it became clear that some of those who were not staying at the house were calling for their carriages.

You may monopolise my time forever, Elizabeth! he wanted to say, but did not.

"Not at all, Mrs. Collins. Indeed, I thought to provide more of my time, if you wish it, to come and look at Longbourn's books – to offer my advice on the estate." He did not know if she would take this offer, or even if she thought of herself as needing advice, but he did wish to give his assistance, and this was the thing he was best suited to assisting her in.

"Oh, yes, because a woman cannot run an estate! Surely I must require your *advice*," she said, furiously.

A sharp, stabbing pain in his chest. Were his chances already ruined?

"Of course not. Someone so clever as you should have no difficulty in running an estate," he said. "I – I know what it is to be given such a responsibility at a young age, and at least in my own case, I did not have anyone to turn to, that I could ask for advice. I had always relied on my father for guidance, and when he was gone, I found I had his responsibilities, and no longer the benefit of his counsel. I only meant that if you desired my advice, or simply wished for someone to talk over matters with, I would be pleased to give any assistance that I may. I apologise – I never meant to demean you."

Although given in panic, Darcy's speech appeared to be effective, for her countenance softened before she said: "It is I who should apologise. Your offer was very kindly meant, and I am sorry I spoke so sharply to you. Mr. Althorpe said something to me during dinner, and I suppose I am still a little sensitive over it."

He found himself relieved, both that they were returned to understanding each other, and that Althorpe had already revealed his true self to her.

"Pray do not worry yourself over it, Mrs. Collins. It cannot be easy, to be in your position."

She nodded. "I would like your advice, Mr. Darcy, if you are still willing to give it."

"Of course."

"Would tomorrow be convenient for you to call?"

He replied that it was, now very well pleased that he had offered his advice, and then she took her leave to go and see to her carriage's being called.

Elizabeth was still changed for bed by one of the maids; she had lasted less than a week under Hill's services in the mornings and evenings before the exclamations of her mother over how far she had come down in the world as a poor widow had achieved their desired effect. Elizabeth was not overparticular about such things, and anything that won back a little of her mother's goodwill had seemed a useful thing at the time. Mrs. Bennet had been relieved, at first, at Elizabeth's accepting Mr. Collins's hand in marriage – it had been the only thing to put a stop to the hysterics that had ensued following Mr. Bennet's death. Yet Mrs. Bennet had not entirely thought through that this meant her least-favourite daughter was to supplant her as mistress of the house, and even now, she continued to find new and inventive ways to chafe over this.

A particular contention of Mrs. Bennet's was that she had been required to move to what had been a guest bed-room, losing the use of her dressing-room. But in addition to not wishing to give in to this complaint as she had far too many in the past, Elizabeth had resolved to keep it, for that room had been her only refuge during her marriage. In that time, she had attempted to have some of the furniture removed, to be replaced with a little bed, but it had been made clear to her that adopting such an arrangement would not be acceptable until she had borne an heir. Since her widowhood, she had considered making good on those plans, and sleeping there, for the master's bedchamber was a room that held many unpleasant memories for her. But to do so would have been to show herself as weak to the household she now headed, and so she had merely ordered the furniture rearranged in the master's bedchamber, primarily to move the bed, and had redecorated that room in as appropriate a manner as she could while in mourning. The servants at Longbourn had accepted their mistress's sewing of new bed hangings and linens in black fabric as an activity of her mourning. Elizabeth's only care had been to make the bed look different, and if black was required to do so, she would do it. Now, she thought, she might choose something new, something bright and cheerful. Now, she was allowed to be cheerful, instead of keeping her smiles and good cheer hidden.

It was wrong, to be so pleased that a man was gone from this world, and yet Elizabeth could not help it. When it had happened, when one of the men from the local hunt had come galloping back to Longbourn to say that Mr. Collins had been unhorsed, and died there beside the fence he had fallen upon, her knees had given out, and it had rapidly become common knowledge in the neighbourhood that the widow Collins had fainted, upon learning of his death at such a young age. Yet Elizabeth had collapsed in *relief*, not grief, and it had been difficult, in the following weeks and months, to play the part of a mourning widow. She had mourned the man in her actions, but could not mourn him in her heart, or her mind. Not the man who had ordered her about, with no respect for her thoughts or wishes, who reminded her mother and sisters regularly of his *largesse*, in allowing them to stay there at Longbourn, a man who treated his servants and tenants so poorly.

Elizabeth shook her head. She tried not to think about those days. She desired only to remember the past as it gave her pleasure, and there was little pleasure to be remembered from her married life. She would much rather think of Mr. Darcy, and what an agreeable turn he had taken, conversing with her for so long and so easily, and forgiving her with every politeness when she had spoken so harshly to him. He seemed completely altered, and for the better.

He was still the man who had wronged Mr. Wickham so severely in the past, however, and Elizabeth was not sure that a man who could commit such a wrong could wholly recover from his inherent character. Yet Mr. Wickham had run off to Gretna Green with Mary King, and Elizabeth was forced to admit that such an action was not at all compatible with the sort of character a clergyman ought to have, and so perhaps there had been some justification for Mr. Darcy's refusing the living. Then again, Elizabeth had been in mourning, when Wickham's courtship of Miss King had occurred; perhaps there had been true love between the two of them, and if there was, Elizabeth could better forgive an elopement. She, of course, had given up any claims on Mr. Wickham's heart with her engagement and marriage.

She was willing to believe that perhaps there was more to the story of the living than she had been told, and she supposed she would have more opportunity to understand Mr. Darcy's character, if he was to call and give his advice regarding the estate on the morrow. This she was looking forward to more for the advice than the man giving it, however much he had changed; Charles and her uncles had assisted her with financial and legal matters since the death of her husband, but none of them had any sort of agricultural experience. Elizabeth did not know how much Mr. Darcy knew of such things – Pemberley was such a large estate, it was possible he had several people working for him, and bothered himself little with the details – but surely he must know *something*, to have offered his advice.

Elizabeth considered her estate and its tenants as she went about the room extinguishing the candles, the last done carelessly, so that it smoked a little as she climbed into bed. This was the place where she made the most effort to forget about her married life, and had the least success. Mr. Collins had not been a considerate man anywhere, and the bedchamber had been no exception.

Sometimes when she closed her eyes, Elizabeth thought for a moment she could still feel the ghost of him touching her. A stout man on his wedding day, Mr. Collins had bade his wife to keep a good table, and had availed himself of it thoroughly, growing more and more corpulent, his fat, sweating belly slapping against that of his wife as he pumped in and out of her. This Elizabeth remembered most vividly, despite her every attempt to forget it. She remembered the foul odours emanating from his body, the horrid taste of his mouth when he kissed her, and most of all, the pain, not just the first time as she had been promised, but every night. A pain substantial enough that when Mr. Collins had made her go to town to see an accoucheur, to explain why she had yet to conceive his heir, she had set aside her embarrassment and told the physician of it. He told her the act was not meant to be pleasant, for a female, and prescribed sweet oil for the pain. She lied to her husband, and said it was supposed to help with the production of a child.

The oil had lessened the pain a great deal, but a child had never come. The Longbourn entail had expired with Mr. Collins's generation, and so when he had bequeathed all his worldly possessions to the fruits of his wife's womb, or failing this, his wife, those possessions had included Longbourn. Elizabeth had freedom, now, as well as security, and never again needed to endure what she had in this place.

She shuddered, and turned so she was facing the empty half of the bed. This was how she preferred to sleep, so that if she dreamt of her married life – and she did, often – she would wake and recall that it was over, reassured by the emptiness of her bed.

CHAPTER 2

June 27, 1815

Darcy awoke early, and so filled with eager anticipation that he determined to go for a ride before breaking his fast, so as not to turn up at Longbourn at an inappropriate hour. He rode there, as well, at what seemed the proper time, yet soon enough cursed his self-inflicted delay, for Mr. Althorpe appeared to be returning from Longbourn.

"Not home!" Mr. Althorpe called out to him.

This wounded him more than it should have, for Elizabeth had told him to call today. Then he realised she might not have been at home specifically for Mr. Althorpe, given how she had been spoken to by him at dinner. So Darcy rode on, and found Mrs. Collins was indeed at home, and would receive him in her library.

There was a masculinity to this room that made Darcy suspect she had made little alteration to it, perhaps in remembrance of one of its past occupants – most likely Mr. Bennet, for the furniture was too old to have been installed by Mr. Collins. It made her appear all the more feminine to be seated behind such an immense desk, and this, in turn, made him think of what it would be like to clear the desk of its contents and lay her down upon it, loving her as his wife.

Such thoughts would be the worst sort of distraction, if he was to have a discussion about business with her, and so he banished them from his mind, bidding her good day and asking her how she was that morning. His pleasantries were followed by her response that she was well, and then the equivalent inquiries on her side.

"So – how shall we begin?" she asked, once he had responded.

"Why do we not have a look at the books, first? Unless you have specific questions?"

"I do not," she said. "It is the questions I do not know to ask that trouble me. I am hoping perhaps you may help me learn of some of them."

Darcy seated himself in one of the chairs in front of the desk, and turned the great leather-bound volume around so he could read it. Eventually, likely realising the session would not be so useful to her if she was reading upside-down, Elizabeth came around to his side of the desk, and seated herself in the chair beside him.

"Do you check the balances, or does your steward?"

"I do not have a steward. Mr. Collins went through four, during his lifetime, and the last left shortly before his death. I never replaced him."

"You manage the entire estate without the assistance of a steward?" he asked, incredulously. Pemberley was larger, of course, but the thought of trying to manage it without Richardson's help was most overwhelming.

"You probably think that foolish. Everyone else seems to."

"I would not say foolish – I think it incredibly difficult. Perhaps it is I who should be applying to you for advice."

She smiled faintly, and he returned to studying the accounts before him, moving through a variety of handwriting until he reached that of greater delicacy. There was more care apparent in each of these entries, and it remained consistent from the earliest days of her management to the last entry. Having quickly looked over the whole of the book, Darcy returned to the earlier entries, and examined them in more detail, asking her questions as they came to him, and finding that once they had begun discussing the estate she did discover some of her unasked questions. He was able to answer some of them, and for the others, to at least discuss possibilities with her. Conversation flowed freely between them, interrupted only by Elizabeth's periodic desire to write down her notes on something they had discussed.

"I would need to see the field in question," he said, in response to one of her queries. "If you like, we may go there now."

"Tomorrow, perhaps, if you are available? I have already taken up too much of your time."

"It is nothing," he said. "And it cannot be too long a ride. Shall I ring the bell to have them saddle your horse? My groom has mine outside."

"I do not ride," she said, quietly.

He recalled her having walked the three miles to Netherfield all those years ago, to visit her sister. At the time, he had thought it due to a horse's not being available, not that she did not ride at all. Since her elder sister had arrived at Netherfield on horseback, he concluded something must have caused Elizabeth to dislike the activity even prior to its causing her husband's demise.

"How do you visit your tenants?"

"Sometimes in the carriage, if the horses are not needed. Usually I walk, though."

"I recall you were quite a walker, but it must be exhausting to do so to conduct most of your business."

"It is not too bad. I like that I am free to walk as I please, now." Her countenance turned guarded after she said this, and Darcy realised she had just revealed something of her married life, and it had not been good.

"I drove my phaeton here from town," he said, wishing to turn the conversation back in a more pleasant direction. "What would you say to driving out tomorrow, to see the field?"

"I would like that very much," she said, and she forced a smile. Darcy could tell; he had a great deal of practise in forcing smiles, and he wondered what unpleasant memory must have lingered, to require her to have to do so. Surely if she had not wished to drive out with him, she would simply have invented some excuse.

Elizabeth walked him to the entrance-hall, but upon hearing her mother and sisters in the parlour, he said he wished to greet them. He had intended to do so at dinner the night before, but had managed nothing more than a bow from across the drawing-room, although he had no regrets over how he had been primarily occupied within that room. His request seemed to surprise Elizabeth, but it did not seem the surprise was unpleasant, and he was shown into the parlour to make his bows to Mrs. Bennet and her two daughters.

"I know it has been some time," he said to Mrs. Bennet, "but please allow me to now give my condolences in person on the death of your husband."

"Well! Thank you, Mr. Darcy, that is very good of you. Although you did not give them in any other manner," Mrs. Bennet said. She spoke far too artlessly for her to be attempting any sort of concealment involving his letter, and Darcy now felt certain she had never seen it.

He felt the familiar ache in his chest again. Mrs. Bennet had not received his letter, which meant her daughter had never received the one it covered. Elizabeth had never known she had a choice. He took his leave of her, then, and was required to force his own smile.

CHAPTER 3

June 28, 1815

Elizabeth had worried after agreeing to drive out with Mr. Darcy that his phaeton was one of those high-perch variations she had seen on those few occasions she had been to town in the last few years. Yet while the equipage in Longbourn's drive looked fashionable, it was not terribly high, and felt sturdy enough when he assisted her in.

It felt intimate, too, for rather than having a man up on the back, a groom was to follow them on horseback, and Elizabeth wondered how it had come to be that mere days after being returned to his acquaintance, she was riding out in an open carriage with Mr. Darcy. Proud, disagreeable Mr. Darcy! Yet he had been very agreeable, these past few days. They had spent hours in the library yesterday, and it had pleased Elizabeth to find that he spoke to her as an equal, one estate owner to another, and that his advice, when given – and given delicately – had been excellent.

"Are you comfortable. Mrs. Collins?" he asked, gathering up the ribbons.

"Yes, very."

With hardly more than a few murmurings and some movement of his hands, he set the horses moving, asking as they settled into a neat little trot if the pace was comfortable for her. She replied that it was, and then passed her time in observation of his skill in driving his team, which was considerable, and yet without any ostentation. Quietly, he would speak to one horse or the other, quietly, he would adjust his ribbons, holding what looked to be a well-fed pair capable of much greater speed to their current pace.

Even at that pace, they made quick work of what would have been an hour's walk for her, and Elizabeth pointed out the field she wished him to examine as they approached. Mr. Darcy pulled the horses down to a walk and then a halt beside the field, the groom jumping from his mount to hold all three animals. Mr. Darcy then offered his arm, to help Elizabeth down from the phaeton, and encouraged her to retain it as they climbed the stile and entered the field.

It had always been the poorest on the Longbourn estate, with clover, grass, oats, barley and turnips all generally failing to grow, except in a few scattered patches. Elizabeth had discussed what was to be done with it with her tenant, Mr. Wendell, and they had decided to allow it to rest for the year, Elizabeth forgiving a proportionate amount of Mr. Wendell's rent. Even fallow, the field looked poor, with grass, weeds, and wildflowers growing in stunted little patches.

Mr. Darcy knelt and took up a handful of soil. "It looks well enough, but clearly something is the matter with it."

He looked about the field, but was prevented from any further investigation by Mr. Wendell, who came running out to meet them.

"This the new steward?" he asked. "I'd be mighty pleased if he has any ideas o' what to do with me field."

"No, Mr. Wendell," Elizabeth said, and she thought Mr. Wendell could not be entirely blamed for thinking Mr. Darcy was the new steward, for he was wearing sporting clothes, and Mr. Wendell was not the sort of man who could tell at a glance that they were of the highest quality. And Mr. Darcy *was* presently digging at the ground with a branch he had found nearby. "He is a gentleman visiting with the Netherfield party. He has been managing his own estate for many years now, and offered his advice."

Mr. Darcy rose, turned to face Mr. Wendell, and requested an introduction, but once Elizabeth had given it, he looked confused over what to do about the present dirty state of his hands. Upon being offered an equally dirty hand by Mr. Wendell, however, he shook it. Mr. Darcy then asked a few questions about how various crops had done in the soil, and looked about the field, contemplative, before setting off at a good pace toward the other side of the field. There, it was bounded in part by a hedgerow, and in part by a grove of trees, and it was the grove of trees that appeared to be Mr. Darcy's destination, Elizabeth and Mr. Wendell trailing behind him. Mr. Darcy reached for a fruit on a lower branch of one of the trees, pried it off, and produced a pocket knife, cutting it open with a slow, satisfied smile.

"Black walnut," said he. "I have not seen it before, but I am almost certain of it. My father warned me about it – the wood is valuable, but it is toxic to livestock, and, I presume, to plants. A friend of his had an estate where some generations ago it was thought fashionable to plant trees from the Americas without any understanding of their qualities, and I believe the same happened here."

"You mean these trees have been makin' me field sick? All these years?"

Mr. Wendell asked, with a pleading look towards Elizabeth. Longbourn's timber belonged to her, and could only be felled at her command.

"We shall have them down, as soon as we can," Elizabeth said. "It sounds as though they promise to bring in a goodly amount if the wood is so valuable, and for your trouble, Mr. Wendell, we shall put some of it towards an improvement on your farm. What would you recommend?"

"I been worried about the roof on me barn," Mr. Wendell advanced, hesitantly.

"I think that an excellent investment," Elizabeth said.

They made their walk back across the field at a slower pace, Elizabeth feeling a bit of wonderment that such innocent-looking trees could have put it in its present state.

"Black walnut," muttered Mr. Wendell, shaking his head as he walked, seemingly in the same state as his landlady. "You sure he i'int the new steward? Or mebbe ye can convince him to take the job?"

Elizabeth laughed. "I assure you, he is not, Mr. Wendell, nor could I ever convince him of such a thing. Mr. Darcy has his own estate to manage, far larger than Longbourn, and we are very fortunate that he has given us some of his time."

They took their leave of Mr. Wendell, regained the phaeton, and set off at what seemed precisely their pace of before, to make their return to the house.

"How long do you think the field will take to recover?" Elizabeth asked.

"I do not know. It might be a year, it might be several. You could try burning the field and then planting clover, to restore the soil, but if the ground is poisoned, I am not sure it will help. If the clover does take, I would not graze any cattle – "

Mr. Darcy ceased speaking, then, because the horse the groom had been riding upon off to the side of the phaeton had reared up nearly vertically, dumping its rider unceremoniously on the ground and galloping off. Darcy reined his own horses in immediately, and to her shock, gave the ribbons over to Elizabeth.

"Will you hold these, please? Just pull straight back if they attempt to move."

"I – I – yes." Elizabeth took them from him nervously, but without saying more. It seemed petty to protest over being afraid to hold the horses when Mr. Darcy's poor groom was lying prone on the ground.

"Tom! Tom! Are you hurt?"

"Only me pride, I think," came a voice from the ground. Tom sat up, then, and was assisted to standing by his employer. It did seem a little more than his pride was wounded, for he leaned on Mr. Darcy's shoulder, limping as the two of them walked over to the phaeton. "Bee stung 'im, I think. Can't think of anything else to make Archer spook like that. If'n ye don't mind, I'll just rest a minute an' go after him."

"Nonsense, Tom – you will not catch him as you are. If Mrs. Collins does not mind, we will return you to Netherfield and send for the apothecary. Mr. Bingley will have some men that can be sent off in search of Archer, and I am sure he shall turn up somewhere," Mr. Darcy said. "I could not face your parents if something happened to you because you went limping off after a horse in a county unknown to you."

"I do not mind," said Elizabeth tensely, still clutching at the ribbons, although the horses had not moved.

"Oh! – Mrs. Collins – I am terribly sorry," Mr. Darcy said, and left Tom on his own to make the last few steps to the phaeton, as Darcy rushed to take up the horses at their heads. "You may let go of them now."

Elizabeth did so, and then decided to step out of the phaeton, a little shaken by all that had occurred. Solid ground – ground she had not fallen upon, or been turned over onto – felt a relief to her.

"I do not mind," she said, again, "so long as we may take a moment, before we set out."

"Of course. Would you mind also if Tom drove, so he may sit? I will stand at the back."

"Aw no, sir, I can't do that, drive beside the lady with you standin' at the back. Ain't right."

"Until the apothecary sees to your leg, you will not be standing at the back of any carriage," Mr. Darcy said, firmly.

Elizabeth would readily have volunteered to walk, so neither of them need stand at the back of the carriage, but she did not think this option would have been preferable to either of the men. They drove back to Netherfield as Mr. Darcy preferred, therefore, where Mr. Jones was summoned to look at Tom's leg, and a group of both grooms and gentlemen – who saw it as an opportunity for sport – were mounted to search for the horse. Mr. Darcy was not among them, however, for he would return Mrs. Collins to Longbourn.

"Are you well, Mrs. Collins? This has all been rather more excitement than I had been hoping for, in our drive."

"I am well, thank you," Elizabeth said.

"I fear this will prove a setback to my wishing to teach you how to ride."

"You wished to teach me how to ride?"

"I did, although perhaps it was presumptuous of me to think you do not know how. Perhaps you do, and do not prefer it?"

"I have had some instruction, and it was enough to make me determine I wanted no more, even before certain events proved to me how dangerous it may be, and continue to do so. Pray do not attempt to make a horse-rider out of me, Mr. Darcy. Your efforts will be in vain."

"Very well, Mrs. Collins. May I at least convince you to take another drive with me in the phaeton? I assure you, today's events were most unprecedented, and I would like for you to experience a more pleasant outing."

"I shall," Elizabeth said. "However, there was one positive aspect to today's outing – you have thoroughly solved the problem of Mr. Wendell's field."

"I hope I have," said he. "Only time will truly tell."

CHAPTER 4

June 29, 1815

Darcy had always awoken early, and over the last two mornings, he had taken to remaining in bed for a little while, and indulging his growing fantasy. In it, Elizabeth was his wife, but still seated behind that immense desk in her library at Longbourn. He would enter, and she would rise, saying, "there you are, my love."

He would kiss her passionately, hungrily, and her hunger would equal his. It would have been some days since he had seen her; perhaps he had made the trip to Pemberley, while she remained at Longbourn. He would revel in her curls beneath his fingers, soft and smooth, and her hot, delightful mouth on his. Then he would run his hand down her back, and feel her lovely bottom, her firm, slender thighs.

Perhaps it would be Elizabeth who picked up the estate's book and the materials for the letter she had been writing, setting them down on a bookshelf nearby. She would draw him back to her, and put her own hands on his arse, pulling him even closer, feeling his desire. Then she would lay back on the desk and look at him, those beautiful eyes dark with yearning, her hands held out to him in invitation.

There could be no invitation better than this, and he thought of how he would lift her skirts up, nearly feeling the muslin beneath his fingertips, and then thinking of how she would look with her skirts bunched about her bosom, heaving under her stays. He would lay his hands on her legs, now, caressing silk and bare thigh before his hand found her most pleasurable places and made her writhe at his touch, emitting the most delicate noises in her ecstasy. Sweet, glorious Elizabeth, now inviting him to take his own pleasure, to slide his cock within her.

His hand was a poor substitute for that most secret place of the woman he loved, but it did suffice, with a handkerchief to capture the results, for he did not like the idea of Netherfield's servants knowing this was how he spent his mornings. His own man, Mason, was at least exceedingly discreet, although even Mason's having to deal with handkerchiefs soiled in this manner was tremendously embarrassing to him. Everything about this felt embarrassing and most ungentlemanly, but it would make it easier to be around Elizabeth later in the day without distraction, without becoming impatient, and he had used that end to justify the means.

Patience. As deeply as he desired her, mind, body, and all, he must be patient. Everything depended upon it. Georgiana had been right to counsel it. Georgiana, who had been most slowly and patiently courted, until finally receiving the proposal that had made her so tremendously happy. Georgiana, who had written in her last that she was in the family way. His sister, more than ten years his junior, would have a son or daughter before him.

At least the woman he desired a family with was again a possibility. It was impossible to think of this without wondering over Elizabeth's ability to bear children. She had been married long enough that there *could* have been a child, but whether this was caused by indifference, stillbirth, miscarriage, impotence, or barrenness could not be told, and it would be a very long time before he might be intimate enough with her to speak of it. It was possible that Bingley could have furnished him with this knowledge, but even in the old days, when they had been such close friends, Darcy did not think he would have queried Charles on such a topic. And in the end it did not matter – he would rather try and fail to have a child with Elizabeth than marry any other woman on earth. He prayed that she would accept him, and if she did he would pray that they were blessed with children, but if only the first of these prayers was answered, it would be more than enough.

Darcy rose, to wash his hands. Patience. Despite the disaster of the previous day, Elizabeth had agreed to another drive in the phaeton, and he would be a model of patience. He had his second chance, now, and he must be exceedingly careful with it.

As they had no planned destination for the day, he proposed they drive around to see some of the other farms, and Elizabeth agreed readily to this. Having already seen the worst of Longbourn's fields, Darcy now saw the best, and he found little to be impressed by, knowing Pemberley's land so well as he did. But Elizabeth spoke of having only just implemented a four-field rotation on many of the fields – her father and Mr. Collins seeing little use in it, and therefore not encouraging their tenants to adopt it – and he thought the fields would see steady improvement, now.

Elizabeth, whom Mr. Althorpe thought incapable of running Longbourn, was clearly doing better than either of her predecessors. Darcy thought back to the reward she had offered Mr. Wendell yesterday, to repair his barn roof with the proceeds from the sale of the black walnut trees that had been poisoning his soil. It was a good offer, one that had pleased Mr. Wendell, and yet one that would benefit the estate in the long term – a roof leaking at the wrong time could ruin much of a harvest. It was precisely the sort of thing he would have done, and Darcy was very pleased to see that although she might not be so experienced as him in estate management, their instincts were similar.

He was pleased, too, that she had asked after Tom's health immediately upon seeing the groom once again mounted on Archer, Tom having been cleared to return to his work by Mr. Jones, and the horse, thankfully, having been found uninjured. Care and responsibility for one's servants and tenants was perhaps the one thing Darcy's father had instilled in him that he had not managed to corrupt in his pride. It was the one thing he had always understood the importance of, and he was glad to see Elizabeth understood it as well.

Most of her tenants did not expect to see their mistress riding about in a phaeton, and it took a little time before they realised it was she and doffed their caps or touched their forelocks to her, but when they did so, it was with evident cheer. She was respected by her tenants, at least.

There was one man, however, who made no obeisance at all, although he stared at them sullenly, so that it was clear he had recognised her.

"Mr. Boyce," Elizabeth said. "He is the one whose rent is five years in arrears."

Darcy recalled there having been such a case when they went through the estate's books, but he had assumed this to be due to some hardship.

"Why, precisely, is his rent five years in arrears?" he asked.

"Because he is a large and irritable man, and he refuses to pay it," Elizabeth said. "He was the cause for several of the stewards leaving – Mr. Collins required them to collect the rent due, and his manner of refusing them was quite intimidating. I went to see him once and tried persuasion, but that did not work, either."

"Did no-one ever think to take legal action?" Darcy asked, still incredulous at the thought of a farm being five years behind in rent, and on an estate that could ill afford it.

"I – I did speak with my uncle Phillips about it," she said, defensively. "He thought it would not look good to the neighbourhood if I did anything while in mourning."

"I am sorry – I did not mean you, Mrs. Collins," Darcy said, seeking to keep his tone level so as to reassure her, and angry at himself for speaking without thinking. "This should not have been a problem you inherited."

"Surely you have seen that my late husband had no talent for estate management, and my father – my father would not – " she trailed off, and Darcy waited to see if she would continue, which she did, in a wavering voice: "I am sorry. My father had his flaws, but it was easier to acknowledge them when he was still alive."

"Of course," he said. "It is natural that you would wish to remember his better characteristics."

She nodded, and after they had driven on in silence for some time, said, "Would you – would I ask too much to request that you come with me to speak with him? You are right that I should begin legal action, but I think it only right that he be given some final ultimatum before I do so."

"I am at your disposal," he said, glad she had requested his assistance, both for what it meant for their burgeoning relationship, and because he did not at all like the idea of her going to see such a man alone.

"Thank you," Elizabeth said, with a lighter countenance. "Perhaps you shall work another of your black walnut miracles."

Darcy knew himself well enough to know that it was not so likely he would work a miracle where dealing with a difficult person was involved, but he turned the phaeton around, anyway. Mr. Boyce had gone into his barn, by the time they returned to the farm, and Tom dismounted more gingerly than he had the day before, to hold the horses as Darcy helped Elizabeth down from the phaeton. He offered her his arm as they walked deeper into the barn, and Darcy came to understand why she accepted it with what seemed particular eagerness when he had a better look at Mr. Boyce.

It was a rare man that was taller than Darcy, but Boyce was one such man. He had a good four stone of additional bulk on Darcy, as well, and much of it appeared to be thick muscle. Boyce was a great big bull of a man, with a bull's manners: upon being greeted very civilly by Elizabeth, and Darcy's being introduced to him, he only grunted, and his face took on an expression that seemed nearer a sneer, than anything else.

"Mr. Boyce, I wished to speak with you again about the rent," Elizabeth said. "I do not require it in full now, but I would like to see some indication of your good faith."

"Ain't got it," Boyce said.

"We have all been very patient with you, but you know I would be well within my rights to throw you off of your farm," Elizabeth said.

"Then throw me," Boyce said. "I'd like to see a bitch like you try, and then you can see where I'll throw you."

"How dare you speak to your mistress like that!" Darcy exclaimed, his face hot with anger. "You impudent fool!"

Darcy did not have size or strength on his side, but he did, fortunately, have speed, and he ducked as soon as he realised Boyce intended to punch him, dodging this first blow. Darcy had spent a goodly amount of time at Jackson's Saloon in his younger days, and he raised his own fists instinctively, even as he understood the futility of attempting to fight a man of Boyce's size. The best he could hope for was to use his agility to avoid injury until he could find some way to protect Elizabeth and end the fight. This he did, ducking and leaping aside as Boyce made several more attempts to strike him, until Darcy finally sighted what he had been looking for – anything that might be used as a weapon – and grabbed a pitchfork from against the barn wall. He stepped over to where Tom appeared to have done the same, with a shovel, and they put themselves between Boyce and Elizabeth.

"Think what you are about, Boyce, to be assaulting a gentleman," Darcy said. In anger, he considered adding that he would gladly see Boyce swing by his big, thick neck, but thought better of it. He was not sure if it was his words or his pitchfork that prevented Boyce from making another attempt on his person, but one or the other was effective.

"This ain't over," Boyce said, although it was he who exited first, out a side door, as red in the face as Darcy must have been.

Darcy was glad of it, so he could turn his attention to Elizabeth and the horses – *good God, she had been left to hold the horses again.* Tom must have sensed her discomfort around horses at some point, and he, too, made to take hold of the horses nearest him, which turned out to be the pair on the phaeton. Darcy took up Archer, and resolved he would tell Tom that he had done right in seeking to protect Elizabeth, for the lady was in far greater danger from Mr. Boyce than from holding three generally well-behaved horses.

"I am sorry, Mrs. Collins – once again we have made you hold the horses," he said.

"Under the circumstances, I am glad that you did. And they were all very gentle," Elizabeth said. "Even Archer."

Darcy scratched Archer behind the ears, to aid in calming his remnant anger. "Poor Archer, you are getting quite the reputation here in Hertfordshire, and all for something you could not help."

Tom turned the phaeton around, and Darcy helped Elizabeth regain it, climbing in beside her. It was a relief, to return to the road and be free of Mr. Boyce's farm, although Darcy now thought the man to be a much larger problem than he had before.

"Mrs. Collins, please promise me you will take up legal matters immediately. That man disrespected you in every possible way, and attempted bodily harm on someone accompanying you. I am glad he attempted it on myself, and not *you*, but he cannot be allowed to remain at large in this neighbourhood."

"What do you recommend?" she asked, in a wavering voice. She had been as disturbed by the events on Boyce's farm as he had, then.

"Have him arrested for debt, and do not allow him to be released until he has paid all of what he owes you, which he never shall. I doubt a man such as him has been setting aside what should have been paid in rent."

"I would consign a man to living the rest of his life in prison."

"Were it any other man, that would be something to think carefully over, but in Mr. Boyce's case, I would rather see him imprisoned for debt than any other crime he is capable of committing. I beg you to do this, Mrs. Collins. I would not rest easy knowing that man was still your tenant."

"I will," she said. "Will you – will you assist me in the matter? I have no idea how to go about such a thing."

"Nor I, but I have men in town who will know what to do, and I will write to them express as soon as I return to Netherfield," he said. "Does Boyce have a family? If so, I presume you will wish to make provisions for them."

"I would," she said, "but thankfully he does not. I hate to think of how he would have treated his wife, if he had one, and I believe I would have been even less reluctant over seeing him imprisoned for the rest of his life, if it meant she was to be free of him."

Would he have treated her as Collins treated you? What did you suffer, Elizabeth, that you are now free from? he thought, but he only nodded to acknowledge her statement, wishing all the while that he could think of the right thing to say to her.

They continued on for some time in silence, before Elizabeth said, "Mr. Darcy, thank you, for assisting me. I do not know what I would have done in such a situation, without you and Tom there."

"Had it not been for me, you would not have found yourself in such a situation," said he. "My temper got the better of me, when I heard him speak of you in such a way. You showed much better control than I."

"I have a good deal of practise in having men not respect what I say," she replied.

Darcy opened his mouth to protest that he did respect her thoughts and opinions, very much, that indeed he attended most closely to everything she had to say, but then he realised she was not speaking of him. She had that guarded look about her face again, and Darcy thought she meant her late husband, rather than those who said now that she could not run the estate, although perhaps she meant both.

"Then that is a shame," he said, "for I have always found what you say to be very much worth listening to."

Darcy could just catch a glimpse of tears in her eyes before she turned away, as though to look at the fields on her side of the phaeton. He wondered if he had gone too far, in saying this, if he had failed in patience yet again that day, but then she murmured a thank you, and he thought he had done right.

CHAPTER 5

July 1, 1815

It was exceedingly rare for a day to go by where Elizabeth did not see Jane, but it had been some time since Elizabeth had spent any time with her elder sister outside of company, and just as long since she had seen her nephew. As they were two of the people dearest to Elizabeth's heart, she planned to go to Netherfield well in advance of dinner, so she could have some time to visit with them.

She had intended to ride thither in her own carriage, sending it back so her mother and sisters should have a ride to dinner, but Mr. Darcy had called that morning with a response to his express regarding Mr. Boyce, and had offered her the alternative of riding over in his phaeton. Elizabeth had accepted his offer, although a little hesitantly, as this was now the fourth day in a row she would ride with him in the phaeton. So as to allow him another attempt at a wholly pleasant outing, she had gone out with him again yesterday, and that drive had indeed been pleasantly uneventful.

"Thank you for allowing me to ride with you. I suppose this will be my only opportunity to be out of doors today," Elizabeth said. Even she had readily admitted that she could not go out walking by herself as she usually liked to do, nor even with one of her sisters, while Mr. Boyce was still free. Already, she was feeling restless over being required to stay inside.

"My horses and I are at your disposal, on any day you wish to go out," Mr. Darcy said. "We should continue to avoid Boyce's farm, of course."

Elizabeth brightened at this, both for the opportunity to spend time outside, and because she did enjoy his company. "That is very good of you, although I fear Mr. Wendell will begin to think you are my coachman, and not my steward."

He laughed. "Let Mr. Wendell think so, if he chooses – I am happy to be of service to you."

They rode on in agreeable silence after this, until Mr. Darcy reined his horses to a halt at the entrance to Netherfield, and assisted Elizabeth down. She carried a valise containing her dinner dress, and he reached out his hand toward it, saying, "May I take that for you?"

"Oh, I am perfectly able to carry it, but thank you."

"I have no doubt you are able to carry it, but I will look to be an abominable sort of gentleman if I enter the house beside you with my own hands empty, so I beg you will reconsider."

"I suppose that is true," Elizabeth said, smiling, and she handed him the valise.

Upon their entering the house, he handed off the valise to a footman, told Elizabeth he hoped she enjoyed her visit with her nephew, and then indicated his intent to go to the library. Elizabeth climbed the stairs to the nursery, and upon entering that room was very glad she had not arrived wearing her dinner dress, for the younger Charles Bingley tottered over to her and gave her legs a slobbery embrace.

Leaning over to pick him up, Elizabeth swung him around in a circle, to the child's giggling delight, and exclaimed, "And how is my little nephew Charlie? How is he? How is he? His aunty Lizzy has missed him so very much!"

Her actions elicited no response other than giggles from the child and smiles from his mother, who had been watching over him from a chair placed beside his toys; Jane liked to spell her nurse for an hour or two each day. Elizabeth felt it, then, that stabbing wave of jealousy, that feeling of envy that sometimes overcame her, regardless of how much she loved her sister. Jane had every happiness: a husband who loved her and whose love she returned, a beautiful little child, and someday more to follow. What Elizabeth had was less happiness, and more relief.

She had wanted a child so badly – not for the reasons her husband did, but because she knew she could love a child unconditionally, and be loved in that same way in return. She had wanted a child, and yet feared that child might be taken from her, had feared Collins would have no more respect for her as a mother than he had as a wife. So she had prayed for the child most particularly after her husband's death, had prayed she would be one of those widows left in the family way, even if it meant her child would inherit Longbourn instead of her.

That had not been her lot, however. Elizabeth would have to choose a favourite, among the many children she presumed Jane and Charles would have, and that favourite would become her heir. That favourite child could not be Charles, as delightful as the boy might be, for as the firstborn son, he would either inherit the majority of his father's fortune or his estate, if

Charles Bingley did ever choose to purchase one.

Little Charles Bingley was a sweet child, however, and having been embraced most thoroughly by his aunt, he was placed on the floor. He seemed discontented by this, however, and held his hands back out to Elizabeth, saying, only, "Wizzy! Wizzy!"

Elizabeth laughed heartily, and made no endeavour to correct him, picking him up and swinging him around several times more, to his increasing giggles. This time, upon being set on the floor, he seemed content to play with his toys, although periodically he brought one over to his aunt for inspection.

"He seems to be doing so well, Jane," Elizabeth said, once she had praised a toy horse and given it back over to the child.

"Oh he is, Lizzy. I think he grows every day."

"You mean Wizzy, do you not?" Elizabeth asked, prompting giggles from Jane not so very different from those of her son.

When Jane had calmed, she said, "I am glad you can maintain your humour, Lizzy, given the situation with Mr. Boyce."

"Oh Jane, I know you worry, but I would rather I not be reminded of that man."

"I know, Lizzy, but I worry for you and my mother and sisters, there on your own at Longbourn."

"We have the male servants, and Mr. Darcy has had his groom sleep over the last two nights, so we should have more about us. Mr. Boyce might attempt something, but I do not think he shall succeed."

"How long must you put up with this threat of him?"

"Not so long, now," Elizabeth said. "Mr. Darcy had a response to his express, so we may set Mr. Boyce's arrest for debt in motion."

Speaking of Mr. Boyce returned Elizabeth's thoughts to Mr. Darcy, and she only just refrained from shaking her head over the absurdity of his involvement. If Elizabeth had been told a week ago that Mr. Darcy would soon be wielding a pitchfork and standing between her and an angry tenant, she would have laughed hysterically. Poor Mr. Darcy! He had offered to assist her with the estate, but could not have predicted what this would have gotten him into.

She was thankful that at least he had not responded in the hot-headed manner she expected many men would have, and attempted to fight a man like Boyce. He had provoked Boyce, of course, but Elizabeth could not bring herself to fault him for demanding that a man respect her. What a strange world this had become, one where Mr. Darcy defended her both with words, and a pitchfork. Elizabeth nearly giggled over the thought, but maintained her countenance, for Jane was speaking:

"Mr. Darcy has been very diligent in his assistance."

"Oh yes, he has been so helpful!"

Jane sighed, and was temporarily prevented from saying anything more by little Charles, who tugged insistently upon her skirts. Upon seeing that he had no intention of leaving, she picked him up to hold him in her lap, and said, "Lizzy, I do not know if I should say anything."

"I hope you will say something now, Jane, or I shall spend the whole evening wondering what it was you did not say anything about."

Jane frowned. "It is about you and Mr. Darcy. His attentions towards you have not gone unnoticed amongst our party, particularly that you have gone out riding in his phaeton every day. I know you are a widow and have greater freedoms, but I hope you will be careful with what you are about. I would hate to see your heart broken."

Elizabeth laughed. "Jane, this is not some romantic courtship. I promise you, his purpose has been to help me with the estate. I expect he will do the same for Charles, if your husband ever does choose to make his purchase."

"I am not so sure of that, Lizzy."

"Oh no, he can have no interest in me in that way," Elizabeth said. "Do you not remember? He only finds me *tolerable*. I will say he has been much kinder than I had expected, though, to help me as he has. I will endeavour to request less of his assistance, though. I do not wish for people to talk – I presume Mr. Darcy dislikes being the subject of gossip as much as I do."

"Good, Lizzy, thank you for listening. This is not to say that I would not be very supportive of the match if his intentions are – "

"Jane, dear, do not entertain impossible subjects," Elizabeth said, embracing both her sister and her nephew. "Now, I think I shall go change, before you begin imagining me as the Prince Regent's next particular lady, or something equally absurd."

Elizabeth made to leave the nursery, but then halted in the doorway, realising there would be no better time to ask about something she had been developing an increasing curiosity about, and so she turned around: "Jane, what was it that happened, between Charles and Mr. Darcy?"

"Mr. Darcy did something he should not have done, and when Charles learned of it, he chastised him quite thoroughly."

"Do you know what it was that Mr. Darcy did?"

"I do, but it hardly matters now."

"Jane, are you going to leave me to die of curiosity? Will you truly not tell me?"

"I will not," Jane said, firmly enough that Elizabeth knew it would be useless to attempt to work on her sister any further. "Mr. Darcy has taken great pains to re-establish his character as a result of what Charles said, and I do not think what he did then should influence our opinions about the man he is now. Certainly you have seen the change in him – you were his severest critic back then, and now you clearly enjoy his company."

"I see what you are doing here, Jane, but I shall be immune to your attempts to raise the subject again. I do enjoy his company – as a friend," Elizabeth said. "I have no desire for anything more, and I am sure he does not, either."

Elizabeth strode out into the hallway, searching her mind for any evidence that Jane was right, that Mr. Darcy's intentions towards her *were* romantic. There had been nothing at all flirtatious in his manner, however, nothing that indicated any desire beyond lending assistance he was very qualified to give to a widow who was the sister of his friend.

Still, Jane *was* right that Mr. Darcy had changed for the better, and Elizabeth thought he deserved praise for making a conscious effort to do so, and succeeding so much as he evidently had. Towards her, he had been far, far kinder than she would have expected any man to be, and what he had told her two days ago in the phaeton, that he found what she said very much worth listening to, had very nearly made her burst into tears. There were some parts of her heart that were still very much wounded, and she never would have expected Mr. Darcy, of all people, to aid in healing them.

There was an unfortunate proportion of disagreeable company to be found in the drawing-room, when Elizabeth had changed into her dinner dress and come down, for Caroline Bingley had joined the house party, finally deigning to leave London, and Mr. Althorpe was one of the few gentlemen to be found there. He did, of course, make his way over to Elizabeth, and she determined that these attentions, at least, must stop. She had tried more subtle hints to let him know she did not desire his company, but they had not been taken.

He told her of that day's sport, and then, when this failed to impress her, of the hunt for Archer, when it had been him that had captured the runaway horse. This Elizabeth listened to in spite of herself, for having been acquainted with Archer very nearly as much as she had been acquainted with any horse.

"The horse seems to have been forgiven for causing such a disturbance," Mr. Althorpe was saying. "I fear for the poor groom, though."

"Do you?"

"Oh yes, you should have heard Mr. Darcy tear into him, poor lad. I think I shall hire him on, if he loses his position over this."

"You think that likely?"

"Very likely. Darcy has been hard on most of the servants here – they are all afraid of him, his own servants most particularly." He produced a snuff box, proceeded to flick it open one-handed in an exaggerated fashion, took a goodly pinch, then continued: "I always say, you can tell a lot about a man in the way he treats his servants."

Elizabeth had at first been amused by this account, one she knew from watching Mr. Darcy interact with Tom to be completely untrue, but now she began to grow incensed, and thought she could not listen to much more. How could Mr. Althorpe think she would believe such things about Mr. Darcy? Did he not realise she understood what he was about, and could see this was merely a blatant attempt to puff himself up by slandering the man Mr. Althorpe must have considered his competition?

"Oh," Elizabeth said, aloud. Oh, she had been so young and foolish then! She had listened to everything Mr. Wickham had said to her without questioning its veracity in the slightest. Now, hearing Mr. Althorpe speak, and knowing his account to be untrue – and knowing Mr. Darcy to be as kind and generous as he was – she saw the error of her thoughts back then, and was ashamed.

"Yes, Mrs. Collins?"

"I am sorry, Mr. Althorpe. I was just reminded of some lies another foolish man once told me," Elizabeth said, curtseying and taking what she hoped was her final leave of him.

She seated herself at the edge of the room, requiring a little quiet time for reflection, and thankfully found she was able to have it. Jane had called Elizabeth Mr. Darcy's severest critic, and while he had apparently made efforts to improve his own character, Elizabeth was now required to admit that she had misjudged him, back then, and she feared she found him a better man now because she had thrown off her past prejudices, rather than any change Mr. Darcy had invoked in his own character. So much had happened since then, but not so much that she could not feel shame over her past mistakes.

Equally concerning, however, was that Mr. Althorpe thought Mr. Darcy a romantic rival. Elizabeth resolved that once the matter with Mr. Boyce was complete, she would stop taking up so much of Mr. Darcy's time. She should have committed to doing so immediately, but the thought of turning down his offer of daily rides in his phaeton, of being trapped inside Longbourn until Mr. Boyce was no longer a threat, was too difficult to bear.

Whenever Mr. Boyce was arrested, however, there should be no more reason for her to be taking up so much of his time. She would let him enjoy the Netherfield party and be a man of leisure, rather than her always drawing him into her troubles. Regardless of *his* intentions, if it had been noticeable to Jane and Mr. Althorpe, it must have been noticeable to the rest of the house. She had enjoyed Mr. Darcy's company very much, and would miss not having so much of it, but Elizabeth did not want his kindness to be repaid in gossip and rumours.

Elizabeth looked up, then, and found the object of her thoughts entering the drawing-room, and looking very well that evening. While Mr. Althorpe could rightly be described as a dandy, everything about Mr. Darcy's dress was exceedingly understated, and yet clearly of the highest quality. She chastised herself, then, for the last thing she should be doing after her conversations with Jane and Mr. Althorpe was contemplating Mr. Darcy's manner of dressing. Still, when he gave her what seemed a particular glance and smiled, Elizabeth could not help but return his smile fully.

CHAPTER 6

July 5, 1815

Darcy could no longer indulge in his fantasy in the mornings. After spending each night in a shallow, worried sleep, he would wake at dawn, seized anew with the fear that Mr. Boyce had made some sort of attack on Longbourn in the night. Then he would remain in his room in a state of nervous tension, waiting for the only thing that could alleviate his worries – Mason's knocking on the door and entering with a message from Tom that all was well. Darcy wished, desperately, that it could be him instead of Tom offering his added protection to the women of Longbourn. Yet while a servant could easily enough be loaned to the house, Darcy's leaving Netherfield to take up residence there would surely have set tongues wagging.

They were close to the arrest at least, he reminded himself, rising and pulling on a dressing gown so he could pace the room. Mason found him thus half-an-hour later, and the valet made his knock, entered, and gave his employer a knowing look as he said, "Tom says all is well at Longbourn House, sir."

"Very good. Thank you, Mason." Darcy wondered just how much his servants had guessed regarding his affections towards Mrs. Collins – whether they understood he wished her to become his wife, and therefore their mistress. There could hardly be a man more discreet than Mason, however, and that knowing look was likely all the clue Darcy was to get towards comprehending how well his valet understood his romantic intentions.

Mason dressed him, and then Darcy left the man tidying up the room, himself going down to breakfast. If there was any advantage to his rising even earlier than he usually did, it was that he was easily the first to arrive for the meal, and could usually break his fast well before the later-rising, more unpleasant members of the house party made their way in. On this morning, he breakfasted with no-one, as it turned out, although Netherfield's servants had learned his ways and had a pot of coffee at the ready when he walked in. This suited Darcy quite well, and he slipped out of the house and down to the stables; he would go for a brief ride to pass the time, then make the drive to Longbourn.

Elizabeth was ready for him when he completed the latter; she came out wearing an exceedingly fetching bonnet, although Darcy suspected his opinion of the bonnet had everything to do with the countenance it framed. He assisted her up into the phaeton and then climbed in himself, quietly checking the case beside him on the seat before he took up the ribbons and told his horses to walk on.

"Where do you wish to go today? Out toward Oakham Mount, perhaps?" Darcy asked. Yesterday she had asked him if he would drive her into Meryton in a tone of some embarrassment, as she was of the hope that a book she had ordered had come in.

"Oh, Oakham Mount sounds very nice," Elizabeth said.

Darcy set his horses trotting down the lane thither, then asked, "And how do you find *Waverley*, so far?"

Elizabeth's embarrassment, he had learned, was in exposing herself as a novel reader, but it had been alleviated by his assuring her that he very much enjoyed novels as well, and while he had not yet read *Waverley*, he intended to, and would be interested to learn her opinion.

"I have not progressed very far, but I am enjoying it. It is much easier to be stuck indoors when one is absorbed in a good book."

"I entirely agree, and it should not be too much longer now, before Boyce may be arrested."

"I hope so – even with my books, I hardly know what I should have done if not for our drives. I believe I would have gone crazy, trapped inside that house. I cannot thank you enough for giving me so much of your time."

There was something peculiar in her tone, when she spoke of being trapped inside *that* house, and Darcy glanced over at her sharply. He could not make out anything more of her meaning by her countenance, however, and when he spoke, he endeavoured to do so lightly. "It is nothing. You may repay me by loaning me *Waverley* when you are done."

"If I can loan *you* a book, I shall consider that quite an accomplishment."

"I fear someone has been telling you tales of the library at Pemberley. It is larger than that of Netherfield, certainly, but it – "

"No, no, you must not demean your library. I have imagined it as a most delightful room indeed, and I do not wish to have my imagination contradicted. And I have heard it said that you are always buying books."

"I should not say *always*."

"Well, then, make your confession – how many books have you purchased this year?"

Darcy began a count, lost track at three and twenty, and finally said, "Upwards of twenty, I believe."

She laughed heartily. "And still the other half of the year remaining. No, sir, I will not allow you to demean your library."

"I *was* going on a long sea voyage," said he, defensively.

"Oh, if I feel trapped inside a house, I fear I should have gone mad on board a ship. I know you could walk about on the deck, but still, I do not know how you bore it."

"The same way one bears any journey, I think – for the promise of what is to come."

"Yes, of course, to see your sister. And then to return to your library at Pemberley," she said, with a teasing smile.

No, Elizabeth, it was to return to you – to finally have my second chance after those painful years of heartache, he thought, but did not say.

Darcy's lack of a response brought a lull in their conversation, but they had long since reached a point of comfort in each other's presence that precluded the need to be constantly talking. They reached Oakham Mount, a sight Darcy found rather underwhelming, having been reared on childhood tours of his native county. He did not share this with Elizabeth, however, and instead listened sympathetically to her lamentations on how she would have liked to walk to the top as he turned the phaeton.

They returned quietly as well – it was a beautiful morning, and Darcy could see she was enjoying it as much as he was. Her enjoyment must have been greater, though, for Darcy's opportunities to be out of doors were not so limited as hers were presently. He kept his team trotting on at a steady pace, until he was shocked to feel Elizabeth's hand clap down upon his knee, as she gasped, "My God, it's him!"

Darcy had only a moment to blush, a blush he glanced over and saw echoed upon her own countenance as she removed her hand with a glance of high consciousness, before they were both required to turn their attention away from embarrassment and towards what had caused her to make such a rash gesture: Mr. Boyce was riding a horse across the field that sided the lane. Darcy could not know what the man's intentions were. They were nowhere near his farm, but Boyce could have just as easily been taking a shortcut to Meryton as he could have been riding about, seeking to do harm to his mistress.

Darcy determined it would be safest to assume the worst, and once again laid his hand down upon the case beside him, which contained a brace of loaded pistols. He did not seek to open the case – not yet – but he felt some reassurance in having them if the need did arise, and it might, for their present course would intersect that of Mr. Boyce.

"Do you think he means to chase us?" Elizabeth asked, breathlessly.

It was precisely the right question to ask, for it required Darcy to assess the situation, and in his assessment, to rationally talk himself out of any concern. He had a brace of pistols, as did Tom, trotting along behind them, and unless Boyce had a gun he had yet to brandish, there was little the man could do to harm them in their present situation. Having made this assessment, Darcy said, with the confidence he did truly feel, "That might be his intent, but he is not going to outrun my bays with *that* horse."

"Perhaps – perhaps you could show him how very fast your bays are. A – a canter, at least, and if you think the lane good enough, you could – you could spring them."

"Are you certain?" Darcy asked, and when she nodded, he said, "please hold on, then."

He waited until Elizabeth's hand grasped the side of the phaeton, and then quietly gave his horses leave to canter. The bays had been held to a much slower pace than they preferred for much of their time in Hertfordshire, and they shot forward in unison. Darcy watched Mr. Boyce as they did so, attempting to calculate when they would cross paths with the man, and then he glanced over at Elizabeth, for she had begun to speak about the fineness of the weather, but in a hollow, unnatural voice.

Darcy returned his attention to his horses momentarily, found them solidly committed to the path, and then looked more closely at Elizabeth. Her hand was rigidly locked upon the side of the phaeton, and whether this was because of the pace of the horses or the presence of Mr. Boyce, he could not tell. If Boyce had done anything to further worry him, Darcy might have truly sprung his cattle, but Boyce merely trotted toward the lane.

When they reached the point where Boyce was as near to them as he would come – thanks to their present pace, still far enough away for Darcy to have no need of the pistols – Elizabeth startled him by calling out, "Oh, you were right, Mr. Darcy – this is most exhilarating!"

Whether or not Mr. Boyce believed her ruse, Darcy could not tell. As they passed the man, Darcy looked at him carefully, and found Boyce's expression marked with an angry insolence. It concerned him deeply, and Darcy hoped his own expression was clear enough, and told Boyce of his thoughts: *If you attempt to harm her, I will kill you, if I need to. I will do whatever is required to keep her safe.*

As soon as they were out of Boyce's sight, Darcy reined the bays down to a trot and glanced over at Elizabeth, asking her if she was well. She had not spoken at all, since her exclamation as they had passed Mr. Boyce, but she replied in a tone of cheery overconfidence that she was perfectly well, and he worried for her.

He asked once again when he drew the phaeton to a halt in the drive at Longbourn, and once again received an answer in the affirmative. When he took her arm to help her down, however, he felt a tremor, and there was nothing more he wanted than to take her in his arms and hold her. That a woman he had always found possessed of such courage was put in this state was unbearable in itself, but he wished she would have been willing to speak of her fears with him, and could only hope that someday they would be intimate enough for her to do so.

Darcy returned to Netherfield a bit shaken himself, but found there the promise that such encounters should not be oft-repeated: he was given a note by one of the footmen informing him that the arrest had been issued, and the men he had hired were waiting to speak with him at the White Hart in Meryton. His every desire was to go to the inn immediately, but Darcy instead required himself to ask the servants where Mr. Bingley had gone to. He was informed that Charles was playing billiards, and made his way to that room to find Bingley engaged in a contest with Mr. Finchley.

This suited Darcy very well, for Mr. Finchley was a barrister, and he had provided some preliminary advice on the situation with Boyce. Therefore, Darcy did not need to pull Bingley aside as he explained that Boyce's arrest for debt was imminent, and Darcy expected he would need to be excused from dinner – Charles might merely say he had been detained on a matter of business.

"Do you wish me to come?" Charles asked.

"No, there is no need," Darcy said. "I have hired three Bow Street runners – if they cannot manage to arrest him, I do not know who can."

"Darcy," Charles said, with a little glance towards Mr. Finchley, "If any expenses have been incurred beyond what my sister has paid out, they should be incurred by me. Mrs. Collins is *my* sister – you should not be hiring Bow Street runners for such a situation."

"I was the one who provoked Boyce," said Darcy. "If I could have borne all of the expense in seeing him put away, I would have."

Darcy considered this as he rode to the White Hart. He meant what he had said: he had been unhappy that Elizabeth had been required to bear the not-insubstantial costs of the arrest warrant, and if he could have hidden these costs from her, he would have. She had made it clear that she expected to pay for such things, however, and over time he had come to understand that to withhold these costs would have been to insult her. As she saw it, they were the necessary costs of the Longbourn estate, and they must be borne by her, its owner.

The runners, however, Darcy had quietly enlisted on his own. The local bailiff would have made the arrest eventually, but even before the morning's events, Darcy would have preferred matters be handled quickly and efficiently. Now, he did not think he would be able to sleep until the man had been locked up.

Such were his thoughts upon entering the White Hart. He glanced reluctantly at the door to the assembly-room, thinking of the miserable evening he had spent there so many years before, and then turned his attention to the innkeeper, who was informing him that a party had been awaiting him in the private parlour. Gratefully, Darcy accepted his direction and entered the parlour to find a man of Boyce's size rising to bow to him. There were two other men of similar bulk in the room, and for a moment, Darcy thought three runners was perhaps overkill. Then he remembered he did this for Elizabeth's safety, and wondered whether he should have hired four.

"Jacob McKinnon, sir," said the man who had bowed. "We have the warrant for Boyce's arrest, and we can move as soon as ye wish. We had thought to catch him first thing on the morrow, if'n that is amenable for yourself."

"I – actually – I would prefer it be done tonight, if at all possible – "

A momentary silence followed, and Darcy attempted to sort through how to explain what had happened that day and how it worried him, as well as what his relationship to Mrs. Collins was.

"A'course, sir. If'n ye wish it be done t'night, I think we should be able to do so. D'we have your permission to take Mr. Boyce within his house?"

"Yes, of course. The house *is* Mrs. Collins's property."

"Very well, sir. Should be easy enough, t'catch one man in his house at night. D'ye wish to go wi' us?"

For a moment, Darcy was very tempted to say that he did, but then he was struck with a vision of the runners surrounding Boyce's farmhouse, and finding the man was not within, that he was instead bent on causing mischief at Longbourn. No, his place, if she would allow it, was within Longbourn, where he could ensure Elizabeth's safety.

"No – I shall wait at Longbourn with Mrs. Collins."

"Yessir. Then when we have him, we'll bring him to Longbourn. Ye tell us we have the right man, and Mr. Boyce'll be off to his new home in the Marshalsea."

"Thank you, Mr. McKinnon. Please make it so, and I hope I shall see you at Longbourn in a few hours."

Elizabeth had been severely rattled by the events of the day. When she had come into the house after alighting the phaeton, she had hardly known whether it was the threatening presence of Mr. Boyce, or the pace she had urged Mr. Darcy to take in the carriage that had caused the loss of all her equanimity.

A little reflection had led her to understand that it had been Mr. Boyce who had frightened her; she still did not trust horses, but she trusted Mr. Darcy as a master of the creatures. She did not know why Mr. Boyce had shown himself to them, but despite her attempts to show her lack of care regarding his presence, she still found herself seized with the deepest of worries over his appearance that day. She had remained safe only because she had been with Mr. Darcy in the phaeton: if she had been out walking, Mr. Boyce could have done her any measure of harm.

Elizabeth shuddered again at the thought of it, and was suddenly roused by the sound of the door bell, which further agitated her spirits by the idea of its being Mr. Boyce himself. But this idea was soon banished as useless and impossible as regarded Mr. Boyce's aims, and her spirits were very differently affected, when, to her utter amazement, she saw Mr. Darcy walk into the hall.

In an hurried manner, he made an apology over his appearance at such an hour, and explained that Mr. Boyce's arrest for debt was imminent, and he wished to pass the evening at Longbourn until the deed was done, if she considered it acceptable. Elizabeth answered him with warm gratitude, and asked if he would join them for dinner.

This he accepted, and as he went into the drawing-room to wait, Elizabeth found herself pulled aside in the hall and accosted by her mother: "Lizzy, you cannot have a man like Mr. Darcy to dine with such a table as you keep!" Mrs. Bennet whispered, furiously. "Not a bit of fish, I should wager, for a man who likely has two or three French cooks at least."

With some mortification, Elizabeth considered the menu for the evening, and felt that for once her mother was correct – that it would seem lacking to a man such as him. She had endeavoured since the death of her husband to instil economy on everything at Longbourn, including its dinners, although she did plan for more when company was to dine. Never had she thought she should be caught out in her frugality by an unexpected guest.

"I shall speak to Hill and see what can be done." Elizabeth whispered in reply.

"You had better hurry," said Mrs. Bennet, then she turned and entered the drawing-room, saying in a much louder tone: "Oh, Mr. Darcy, it is so good of you to look after us – such a horrible situation with that Mr. Boyce."

Exceedingly agitated, Elizabeth ran to find Mrs. Hill and urged the housekeeper to see what fruit could be got out of the kitchen garden to at least round out the second remove, then she attempted to calm herself as she joined the party in the drawing-room. Her spirits were somewhat soothed by taking up Mr. Darcy's now-familiar arm to go in to dinner, and by his most gentlemanly reaction to what was placed before him upon the table. At one point, he praised the jugged hare, and Elizabeth then had the mortification of her mother's naming it as a favourite of her daughter's. She blushed most thoroughly – Elizabeth had few, if any, favourites when it came to food, and jugged hare was not one of them – and chanced a glance at Mr. Darcy. He seemed to sense her discomfort, and said nothing more of the food upon the table, instead asking her if she had made any progress on *Waverley*.

She had done so, and spoke in a most distracted manner on her impressions of what she had lately read. It was a tenuous topic, but one that held until the second remove, very well supplemented at the last moment with an array of summer fruits, and from there they continued on to the book's setting, speaking of Scotland and the Jacobites.

This was far from the first time since her husband's death that Elizabeth had reached the end of a family dinner with a gentleman among her party, but once again she found herself unprepared. Distracted by the food, she had not thought to have port and brandy brought up from the cellar, and she hurriedly asked her butler to do so now. Elizabeth wondered at herself – it was not like her to be so worried over what she served her guests, and she could only attribute it to her mother's criticism and her agitation regarding Mr. Boyce.

"There is no need to bring up anything else," Mr. Darcy said. "I should be perfectly happy to come through and take tea with you all in the drawing-room."

He rose and walked out alongside Elizabeth, and she said, "I must apologise over the dinner. If I had known you were coming, I would have planned for more – "

"You must not apologise over the dinner you gave to a man who showed up at your door uninvited," he said. "And in truth it is far more than I am generally accustomed to."

Elizabeth gave him a look of scepticism.

"I do not use the dining-rooms at Pemberley unless I have guests for dinner," he said. "My housekeeper spends a goodly amount of time soothing my cook's poor nerves over my tendency to request a cold collation – or worse yet *sandwiches* – in my study."

She laughed, but as they entered the drawing-room, she could not help but wonder over this lonely bachelor existence of his, having sandwiches for dinner in his study. That could become her someday, she realised – her mother would pass, at some point, and if Kitty and Mary left home it would indeed become her, dining by herself. At least Longbourn was not so large as Pemberley – the larger the house, Elizabeth thought, the emptier it must have felt, and a house with multiple dining-rooms must have felt very empty indeed. And the Bingleys would not allow her such loneliness; she would never be alone so long as Jane and Charles lived so near. Perhaps, even, once she had chosen her heir, she could request that the child come to live with her, and keep her company.

This was a comforting thought, and Elizabeth was glad of it, for she still felt the lingering tension of wondering whether Mr. Boyce had been arrested by now. Mary offered to play the pianoforte for them, and although her playing was no better or worse than usual, Elizabeth was more grateful for it on this evening, for it provided a distraction.

Eventually, the door bell rang again, and Mr. Darcy rose to go to the entrance-hall. Elizabeth followed him there and was startled to see her butler hand him a pistol that had apparently been held for safekeeping; she waited in a state of high tension as Barnes opened the door. This revealed a large man, and upon seeing Mr. Darcy, the man said: "'Tis done, sir. Led us a merry dance of it, but we got him."

"Very good," Mr. Darcy said, and made to follow the man out to the drive.

Elizabeth followed as well, and when Mr. Darcy noticed this, he murmured to her that she did not need to come; he was merely going to identify Mr. Boyce so they could be certain they had got the right man.

"No, I want to. I hardly know how to explain it, but it is important that I see him. I need – closure, I think, is how I should describe it."

"Of course," he said, and offered his arm.

In the drive was a waggonette, and sitting shackled within was Mr. Boyce. When he saw Elizabeth, he turned his head to look at her fully, eyes glinting murderously in the moonlight. Elizabeth summoned her courage and found it did not fail her as she looked him fully in the eye, but she knew she could not have been so courageous if he had not been restrained, if there had not been several men seated around him, and of course Mr. Darcy's very tall and very solid presence beside her.

"It is him," she said, firmly. "That is Mr. Boyce."

"Very well, ma'am," said the large man. He climbed up into the waggonette and ordered its driver to leave.

The relief came over Elizabeth slowly as she and Mr. Darcy walked back toward the house, but by the time they entered, she was fully rejoicing in the return of her safety and freedom.

"Oh," she sighed happily, "I am going to go on such a long walk tomorrow. And you, Mr. Darcy, will be free again to pursue your own leisure, instead of always shuttling me about."

He was silent, and Elizabeth feared he thought her ungrateful – she *had* sounded terribly ungrateful, she realised, and she rushed to say, "It has been so good of you, though, to drive me out so often as you have, and to aid me with the arrest. I cannot thank you enough – I shall endeavour to make my way through *Waverley* as quickly as I can, for I owe it to you."

His countenance appeared very serious, and Elizabeth recalled Jane's warning all in a rush. For a moment, she feared he was going to make some sort of declaration, but then he smiled and said, "Do not rush your reading on my account. You know already that I have brought ample books to occupy myself."

Elizabeth returned his smile, inwardly teasing herself for having nearly been led by Jane. "Of course you have."

CHAPTER 7

July 10, 1815

Darcy handed Tom the ribbons with a pleased countenance. His instructions had been to have the old pony phaeton at Pemberley freshly painted and sent down to Netherfield, and for the gentlest carriage-trained pony that could be found in London to be purchased and also brought here, and his instructions had been complied with exactly.

"He will do perfectly, Tom. Let him rest a little, and then I shall drive him over to Longbourn."

Tom walked the pony off, and Darcy turned to find Charles standing in the stable yard and looking peculiarly at him.

"Rather small for you, is he not, Darcy?" Charles asked.

"He is not intended for me. He is intended for Mrs. Collins. I am sure you are aware she does not ride, and it is not sustainable that she conduct her estate's business on foot."

"Darcy, I must say something. You have been at Longbourn nearly every day since you arrived here – you go out driving with Mrs. Collins with some frequency – and now this. What, precisely, are your intentions towards her? She is my sister, and I will not see her treated ill."

How Charles had changed, these past few years: he still had not purchased his own estate, and seemed content to lease Netherfield, but he had borne the responsibilities of husband and father, and they had matured him. Gone was the old lingering puppyishness of when he and Darcy were particular friends, and while the amiability was usually still there, at present it had been replaced with something very near sternness.

"I intend to marry her, if she will have me," Darcy said.

"Why?" Charles asked, with a sceptical countenance. "Because she is an heiress?"

"No, Charles, of course not. How could you possibly think such a thing?"

"Why should I not think such a thing? You were not nearly so enamoured with her three-and-a-half years ago. What was it you said, at the Meryton Assembly? She was *tolerable*, but not pretty enough to induce you to dance, I believe."

Darcy felt his heart sink at the reminder that he should ever have said such a thing about Elizabeth. "I had hardly looked at her when I said that, and I did not know her then. Mrs. Collins would not be half so beautiful without her wit, and that I only understood once I had conversed with her. I assure you, it is many years since I have considered her as one of the handsomest women of my acquaintance."

This statement, and the manner in which it was uttered, seemed sufficient in convincing Charles that Darcy was motivated by love. Bingley shook his head, and sighed. "Have you been in love with her all these years?"

"I have. If I had better followed your advice about pursuing my own happiness back then, I might have asked her properly. We could have been married all this time, and hopefully as happy as you and Mrs. Bingley."

"You asked her, then?"

"I wrote to her. I now suspect, though, that she never saw my letter. I sent it under cover to Mrs. Bennet."

"Oh, Darcy, we both failed her – my poor sister. If you would have sent it to me, I would have found some way to get it to her. If I had even suspected you loved her, I would have written to you of how rapidly she was to be married."

"You and I were not on speaking terms, then."

"I would still have done whatever I could to forward your hand, rather than that of Mr. Collins – for her, as well as for you. I was aware, even then, that I had overreacted."

"You must not think that. You told me what I needed to hear."

"Perhaps, but I have a great many regrets over my actions during that time. If I had been able to promote your marriage to Elizabeth, even if I had made my offer to Jane at my earliest opportunity, I could have spared Elizabeth so much suffering. She was terribly unhappy in her marriage, Darcy. I had not been well-acquainted with Collins before he inherited Longbourn, but Jane says he had always been a pompous man, and attempting to run the estate turned him absolutely domineering. The accident – it is horrible to be glad over a man's death – but it came as a relief to all of us."

Darcy felt grief for Elizabeth pulling at his heart, but said only: "That accident was my second chance. I will spend my life endeavouring to make her as happy as I can, if she will let me."

"Then you have my blessing, Darcy, and I hope that she shall," Charles said.

Darcy held out his hand, and Charles took it as though to shake it, but then said, "Come, let us embrace like old friends," and did so, clapping Darcy on the back.

It was a comforting thing, to Darcy, to see his friendship with Charles further mended, but he was pleased with the conversation for other reasons. He had been wounded by what had seemed her immediate dismissal of his company, following Mr. Boyce's arrest. They had hardly stepped into the entrance-hall before she was announcing he would not need to drive her out any longer. After a moment's reflection, he had understood her better. *His* mind had immediately gone to the loss of her companionship, but hers had been turned towards the regaining of her freedom, and releasing him from what she had thought to be a burden. And now he thought he understood an additional motivation for her doing so – if Charles had noticed his attentions towards her, it was likely others had as well. A young widow still wearing grey and lavender was likely to be concerned for her reputation.

Darcy had set the procurement of the pony and phaeton in motion long before the evening of Boyce's arrest, but he was particularly glad he had done so now. They would ultimately give her greater freedom, but would also allow him more time alone with her, so long as she could be convinced to accept them and to let him to teach her to drive. If there were rumours, he hoped it would help with them and not hurt, for it would give her the ability to drive out independent of him or any other man, save a groom to attend her. Darcy did not see this as counterproductive to his aims, however. The pony and phaeton could be kept for her particular use if she did agree to marry him. And if she would not accept him – or if it took a very long time – it was important to him that she have this, for it would better ensure her independence and safety if he was no longer in the neighbourhood.

After Mr. Boyce, he found these things far more important than his own courtship: even if she never accepted him, even if things never reached the point of his proposing, he needed to know she was safe, and well. It was when he had first understood this that he had also understood his love for Elizabeth had deepened, over the years. When he had written his proposal to her, he had wanted her for his own. He still wanted this, badly, but even more, he wanted her to be happy, to never suffer what both she and Charles had hinted she had suffered during her marriage to Collins. If all worked out as he hoped, it would be him that endeavoured to make her happy, him that did everything he could to please and protect her as her husband. But her happiness, her safety, her security – all of these things were more important than his hopes. He had been a selfish being once, in practise, if not in principle, but he was not that man any longer; he was now a man who would give everything for Elizabeth, and he could only hope she would take it. If she did not, at least he would still have the Elizabeth of his fantasies, and the smiles of the real Elizabeth when he was fortunate enough to be in her company. For he would never stop loving her – a love this deep could never be recovered from.

When the pony, Chip, had rested sufficiently, Darcy took the umbrella they had been using as a trial, and placed it on the seat, then clambered awkwardly into the phaeton. It would be the perfect size for Elizabeth, but it was ridiculous for anyone of his height, and he hoped he was not seen by many in their house party as he turned the pony and made to leave the stable yard. He was not so fortunate, however, for Caroline Bingley was dressed in a most ostentatious riding habit and riding a chestnut gelding up and down the lawn just outside the yard.

"Mr. Darcy, good day to you," she called out, and trotted up to the phaeton, a curious expression upon her face as she looked over Chip and the equipage.

Unfortunately, Caroline Bingley had been returned to Darcy's acquaintance along with her brother. Darcy had been surprised, at first, to learn she had not managed to ensnare some man in matrimony, for she had immediately resumed her attempts with him. He had later learned, however, that Caroline Bingley had been required to pay a rather deep penance for her role in separating Bingley from Jane Bennet: she had been sent off to live with an aunt in Scarborough for two years. Darcy had his suspicions that Bingley would have left her there but for the thought of the aunt's eventually dying and leaving Charles and his wife with the responsibility of a spinster sister. Caroline had, therefore, been allowed to leave Scarborough and endeavour to make herself a match.

If her behaviour at the house party was any indication, she was pursuing her options in an aggressive fashion, for Darcy was far from the only gentleman she had flirted with. She still seemed particularly attached to him, however, and he hoped she did not think he had remained single all these years on *her* account. He watched her approach and waited for her over-curious query about the phaeton, and for her to volunteer to accompany him wherever his destination might be. He waited in vain.

"I see you are going out for a drive – I hope it will be pleasant. Some of us are going to go for a long ride – Louisa, Mr. Althorpe, Sir Benjamin, and I believe a few others – but poor Garnet has not been outside of Hyde Park for so long, I wished to ensure he was sufficiently warmed up," she said, turning her horse back toward the stables. "Good day to you, Mr. Darcy."

Thus, a little perplexed and perhaps a bit embarrassed over his conveyance, but none the worse aside from this, Darcy wished her a good day as well, congratulated himself on his escape, and set the pony trotting down the road.

The presence of a strange equipage in Longbourn's drive must have been announced within the house, for Elizabeth came out with her hands upon her hips, asking, "What is this?"

"This is Chip," Darcy said, jumping down from the phaeton and then remembering the umbrella. Tom had followed him on Archer, leading Darcy's own horse for the return journey, but he stayed mounted, and so no-one was holding Chip as Darcy began his demonstration. He ran at the pony, waving his arms, making such sounds as could usually be counted upon to spook a horse. He opened the umbrella right before Chip's face and waved it around over the pony's head, and all the while Chip looked at him placidly, if a little curiously.

Elizabeth, meanwhile, was laughing with her head thrown back at his antics, and Darcy thought it had been worth the cost of the pony if just to amuse her so thoroughly. Seeing he had stopped, however, she turned serious, and said, "Mr. Darcy, I told you not to attempt to make me a horsewoman."

"You said not to make you a horse-rider. You said nothing about driving, Mrs. Collins. Would you turn away the sweetest-tempered pony that ever was, without even trying him? Without even coming over to make his acquaintance?"

Resigning herself at least to this, Elizabeth came over to where they stood, hesitantly reaching out to stroke the pony's nose. She erred, in doing this, although with Chip it did not matter.

"Approach him a little from the side, next time," Darcy said, gently laying his hand on her shoulder, and encouraging her to move to a better location, one which did happen to be nearer him. He ignored the thrill such closeness brought him, and continued, "We have yet to find that which will startle him, so it is of little matter to Chip, but it is good to get into the habit. Horses cannot see just before their noses, so for you to touch them without their seeing your hand approach is just like someone sneaking up behind you or I, and tapping us on the back."

Elizabeth nodded, and recommenced stroking the pony's nose. "He is very sweet, I will give you that, Mr. Darcy. But I cannot accept him from you, nor the carriage."

"Mrs. Collins, there can never be said to be *no* risks, when horses are involved, but they could not be minimised more, with this pony and this phaeton. The wheels are low – if you do someday encounter that which startles Chip, it is only a little jump to safety. You may conduct your estate business without needing to walk anywhere, so you need only walk when you wish to for your pleasure."

"I – it is a fine idea, and one I might consider, but I meant that I cannot accept such a gift from you. People will talk more than they are already."

So her concern *was* for her reputation, then. Darcy was glad to have this confirmed, rather than the alternative, and said, "If that worries you, then try him for a time – I will teach you to drive him – and if you find you wish to keep him, then I will sell him to you. The phaeton, as well."

Elizabeth had not stopped stroking the pony's nose, and Darcy thought this boded well for Chip, and for himself. She looked over the phaeton, and seemed to consider the possibility seriously. She sighed. "Very well Mr. Darcy, I will give Chip a trial."

CHAPTER 8

July 24, 1815

"Whoa now, Chip." Elizabeth pulled the pony down to a walk, and smiled with the pleasure that came from having mastered something new, and in her case, having mastered something she had not thought she would ever attempt.

It had been several days since Mr. Darcy felt compelled to run alongside the phaeton when she clucked the pony up to a trot, which Elizabeth felt relieved over; it must have been terribly exhausting for him to be running so much as he had while teaching her, and yet he had remained good-humoured through it all, even in those moments she was sure she must have been a frustrating student.

Mr. Darcy. No-one could accuse him of romantic intentions, now that he had done this for her. Yes, the thoughtfulness of it was stunning, and Elizabeth was wholly touched by it, that he had been able to find a pony with such a sweet disposition that even she – who had never been able to forget an unfortunate experience during her childhood – was unintimidated by him. Yet to find her a pony and a phaeton that no-one taller than her could fit comfortably in, and to train her to drive herself, was to put a decided end to their drives together in his own phaeton, and indicated most thoroughly that his intent had only been to provide assistance.

Still, she had enjoyed these sessions with him, and hoped she would continue to have some contact with him, some opportunity to continue their friendship. The party at Netherfield would be breaking up soon, culminating in the ball Jane had indeed been successful in convincing Charles to host – although Elizabeth did not think it had taken any true convincing at all.

Mr. Darcy lived in Derbyshire, and Elizabeth was rarely in town, so she was not certain how often they would see each other following the ball. He and Charles seemed to have further repaired their friendship, however, and so she hoped she might see him a guest again at Netherfield.

Elizabeth jumped down from the phaeton and smiled to her instructor before making her way to Chip's ears and scratching him in the one spot that could garner a significant reaction from the pony, who leaned his head into her ministrations.

"You are going to spoil him," Mr. Darcy said, dismounting his horse, for he had played the part of her groom as she had driven a small portion of Longbourn's grounds, a test of her skills, and one she had passed.

"He deserves to be spoiled!"

"Perhaps he does."

"He is a true gem, Mr. Darcy. I do not know how you found him, but you must now let me know the cost."

"That is not how gentlemen conduct business, Mrs. Collins – naming costs in the open air. At the very least, we should speak over it in your library, but these things are best done over correspondence, as furtively as possible. I will have my man send you an invoice."

"I am not a gentleman."

"True, you are a lady, and that is all the more reason for us to go about this in as roundabout a manner as possible."

Elizabeth laughed, and saw she would not make any further progress with him on this particular topic at present. "I shall protest if you attempt to gouge me, Mr. Darcy."

"I hope you will find me very reasonable," he said, and gave his reins over to Tom, so he could walk with her and Chip back to Longbourn's stable.

There, Chip was given over to the coachman, Rodney, who had quickly realised the pony was the only animal in the stable his mistress truly cared for, and therefore deserved to be given proper deference. Elizabeth would not be the only person to spoil him, she thought, as she watched him disappear into the stable to be untacked and rubbed down.

Mr. Darcy offered her his arm, and they walked together back to the house.

"Thank you," Elizabeth said, softly. "I know I was resistant, at first, but this – this was the most thoughtful thing anyone has ever done for me. To know I may conduct my business as I need to, without fear of injury, nay, with an animal I thoroughly trust – it is what I needed, but would never have thought to ask for."

"I am glad – that was my aim," said he.

"I fear, though, that I shall be losing my instructor soon. Are you for Pemberley, after the ball?"

"Yes, I believe so. I may conduct a little business in town, first."

"It must be lonely at Pemberley – without your sister," Elizabeth advanced, hesitantly.

"It has been, when I am at home, although I do have responsibility for my servants and my tenants," he said, then added, "that sounds rather empty, when I say it aloud. I am merely their employer."

"I do not think it sounds empty. I believe a good master, or a good landlord, is a bit like a father. That is how you seem to Tom, at least. You treat him as though he is family."

"Tom is the son of one of my tenants – their family have held the farm for many generations."

"Please do not call it empty, then, to take responsibility for men such as him in the way that you do."

"I shall not, then, but it is not the same as – as it was when Georgiana was at home," he said. "I had thought to have a house party later in the year, and better fill Pemberley. I hope you might be available to attend?"

"I would like that. I have travelled so little in the last few years, and from what you have told me of Derbyshire, I would very much like to see it."

"Very well, then – you must look for your invitation in the post," he said. "I do not suppose you have known much loneliness in life. Not with such a large family as yours."

They had reached the house, but Elizabeth indicated the path to the garden, and they walked on.

"It is possible to feel alone amongst others, when those who understood you are gone."

"Your father?"

"Yes, and Jane. At least she had not gone far." Elizabeth's eyes filled with tears, and she was surprised to find him reach over with his free hand and cover hers.

"You and your father were very close, were you not?" he asked. "The loss of a parent can never be easy, but that must have made it all the more difficult."

"Yes, we were very close. I knew, of course – I knew that someday I would lose him, but I did not think it would happen so soon. Although in truth, the difficulties of our situation outweighed the difficulties of the loss, when it happened."

"Of course. I am sorry – I spoke without thinking," he said, withdrawing his hand.

"You need not apologise. I do wish the loss could have been my focus, at least for a little while," Elizabeth said. "I wanted to mourn my father for longer, but he – but it was determined best under the circumstances that I marry quickly."

"I would have – I would have thought some arrangement could have been made to allow you that time. You *should* have been allowed time to mourn."

Once again, Elizabeth struggled to contain her tears, seeking to divert the conversation once her voice was steady enough to do so: "You have known the same loss, of course, twice over. How old were you, when your parents died?"

"Seventeen, for my mother, and two and twenty, for my father. Each loss was difficult in its own way, but I believe my father's was the more difficult. I was fortunate, if such a thing can be called fortune: his illness was of slightly longer duration, and thus I had a little time to prepare."

"How does one ever really prepare for such a thing, regardless of how much time one has?"

"You are right: you can never be truly prepared. I felt that acutely, in the beginning. To have lost forever the person whose company I enjoyed, whose advice I had relied on, was difficult enough in itself, but added to that was finding myself bearing the burden of his responsibilities. For that, at least, I was glad to have some little warning."

"I understand you. When my father died, it was so unexpected. Everything and everyone in the house was all in chaos. I wanted to cry – I wanted to have time, just to comprehend what had happened – but someone needed to take charge of everything."

"And it was you, of course, who carried the responsibility for your family in that situation, as you do now."

"I did, for a time," Elizabeth said, bitterly, "but my responsibilities ended on my wedding day."

"I understand yours was not a happy marriage," he said, quietly.

"In that, I bore some fault, too. Someone less headstrong than myself might have attempted persuasion, or even manipulation, to bring about her wishes, but I hated that Mr. Collins would not listen to me, and the more I argued with him, the more he diminished my role." Elizabeth could not believe she had shared such a thing with him, something she rarely even spoke of with Jane, and yet she had no regrets in saying what she had. She had thought Mr. Darcy reserved, but in truth, his quiet demeanour made him a very good listener, and he always spoke with what seemed an astute sympathy, when he did speak on delicate topics.

"Do not put the blame on yourself, Mrs. Collins," he said. "You were placed in an impossible situation, and Collins was a fool if he would not listen to you."

He had again spoken so as to nearly overwhelm her, and Elizabeth wondered how her opinion of him could ever have been what it was. Still, she had shared as much as she was willing to, and did not want to continue the conversation in this line any further, so she took a deep breath, attempting a cheery tone as she said, "It is in the past, now. Even my half-mourning is complete – I am so looking forward to the ball. I suppose you are not. I recall you were not very fond of dancing."

"I would wish to dance with you, if you have not filled your sets."

"I have not even begun to fill them."

"Might I have the first, then?"

"Certainly."

Elizabeth was pleased to know she would have pleasant company for the first set, and felt fairly certain Charles would ask her for the second. Beyond that, she thought it likely she should have to endure the company of the single fortune-hunters – hopefully Mr. Althorpe would continue his present distance. It would be noted, she thought, that she would lead off the ball with Mr. Darcy, and it was very possible he would ask her to dance again. Although he seemed easier in company now, there was a lingering awkwardness to him sometimes that made Elizabeth wonder if he preferred her company because she was more familiar to him. She was glad he was comfortable in her presence, but it would be best for their reputations if she did not dance a second set with him, she thought, as he walked with her back to the house.

CHAPTER 9

July 27, 1815

A private ball at Netherfield was preferable to a public one, but Darcy still disliked much of what came with it: the crush of people, the jostling of his person in said crush, the endless greetings and niceties all made him long for a quiet evening in Pemberley's library. Still, he did have one thing to anticipate at this ball – Elizabeth had promised him the first set, and he intended to ask her for the supper set as well. In so doing, he would push things just the slightest bit farther along, but not too far: patience, he must remember patience.

It had long since been clear that this painstakingly slow courtship could not be completed by the time the party at Netherfield broke up, and he had been tremendously glad to have Elizabeth agree to join in a house party at Pemberley. That he would now need to hold a house party at Pemberley, to determine the acquaintances he should invite beyond the woman he wanted to be mistress of the house – and then play host to them for some weeks – was a further draining thought, and so he returned his mind to Elizabeth.

What she had said about her half-mourning being complete – had that been meant for him? Or had it simply been a statement meant to put such a terrible time behind her, one it had clearly pained her to speak about? She had confirmed, when they spoke in the garden, those things he had already suspected about her marriage, and he had ached for her. He did not understand how a man could be married to such a woman without fully appreciating her, how Collins could attempt to suppress such a lively mind rather than delighting in it, and these thoughts had turned his sentiments from ache to anger, although he had taken care to hide this emotion from Elizabeth.

Darcy had hated that propriety dictated he call her Mrs. Collins even in that time, that her very name must have been a reminder of all that pained her. He prayed she would change it to Darcy, hopefully before the year was out, and he was glad she had been willing to speak to him of her marriage, even just a little, for it indicated a new openness between them, one he hoped to build on when she came to Pemberley.

Oh – Elizabeth! He caught sight of her in the entrance-hall, leading her mother and sisters, something Mrs. Bennet seemed greatly displeased by. Elizabeth looked glorious, though, finally wearing white, delicately embroidered white muslin that became her better than anything else possibly could have done. Darcy emitted a ragged, shaky breath, and thought of the day when he hoped to hold the figure in that dress and kiss her as thoroughly as he had always wished to kiss her.

Elizabeth was in high spirits upon entering the ballroom. The effect of wearing whatever she chose, of an evening ahead of dancing, had been even stronger upon her than she had anticipated, and not even her mother's comments could dampen her spirits.

She saw Mr. Darcy, standing at the edge of the room and looking discomfited. Rather than judging him for it, though, as she had used to do, she was struck by the sense she sometimes felt about him, that she wished for him to come to see her, to single her out amongst the crowd – and then he did.

"You look very well this evening, Mrs. Collins."

"Thank you, as do you."

"Shall we go in?"

He offered her his arm and they went forth, finding the ballroom a little less crowded than the entrance-hall had been. The crowd thinned a bit more as those who cared less for the dancing made their way to the refreshments and the card-room, and then Jane and Charles were walking about and letting everyone know the dancing was to begin.

Elizabeth and Mr. Darcy took a place behind the Bingleys, who led off the dance, and it was not until they turned that she saw Caroline Bingley and Mr. Althorpe further down the line. She chuckled, and noticing this, Mr. Darcy followed her gaze.

"I think I have not seen two people who deserve each other more," he said.

Elizabeth chuckled more thoroughly, and said, "You are absolutely right. There is enough vanity between the two of them that if they can remember to flatter each other, rather than themselves, they will be the most content couple in the world."

The dance separated them then, and when they came back together, he said, "Are we speaking enough for your taste? I believe one of us was supposed to comment upon the number of couples in the room, was that correct?"

"Do you remember that?" Elizabeth asked, smiling, and glad he could teaze her over it, for she could not say her comments from the last Netherfield ball had been made with her opinions of him in the correct place.

That was the day before everything – no, she could not think of it now. On that day, she had been comparably happy, and on this day she intended to be far happier. She was thankful the dance separated them again, so he would not notice her face had temporarily saddened, and by the time she was returned to him, she was in better spirits.

"Perhaps I may, then, ask if you prefer faster dances, or slower," Elizabeth said. "I seem to recall you liked a reel."

"I seem to recall you did not."

"Oh, but I do, at the proper time."

They continued on in this manner until the dance ended, and he went to fetch her a syllabub as they waited for the second in the set. To her surprise, Jane called a reel for that dance, and Elizabeth felt certain Mr. Darcy had requested it, before or after his retrieving of the syllabub.

Elizabeth *did* enjoy a reel, and she was surprised to see Mr. Darcy was very good at it, although she supposed he would not have sought to teaze her at the cost of his own embarrassment. She finished the set breathless and giddy from the dance, and he led her from the floor.

"Did you only do this so you would not have to put up with so much of my conversation?" she asked, laughing. "I suppose I should merely be glad I am *tolerable* enough these days to tempt you to dance."

Elizabeth spoke without thinking; they had been teasing each other over the past for the whole set, and she did not expect his reaction to this particular comment. His face turned ashen, he murmured a request for her to excuse him, and immediately fled her company. She felt a tightening in her chest: she feared she had wounded him, and she desired nothing more than to find him and restore his friendship.

She tried the terrace first – if it had been her in his place, she would have wished to get some air. He was not there, however, and Elizabeth feared that as a member of the house party, he might have taken that perquisite of fleeing to his own room. She recalled his penchant for books, however, and thought it a good possibility that he had gone to the library.

He was there, alone in silent contemplation before the window, looking out into the twilight. Even in the dim light, Elizabeth could see his posture was one of sadness, and she closed the door behind her and approached him quietly.

"Mr. Darcy, I am so sorry. I meant only to teaze you."

He turned to look at her, and Elizabeth found even deeper regret over her comment, to have pained him so, before he said, "Did you overhear me speaking all those years ago, at the Meryton Assembly? Or did Charles tell you of what I said?"

She replied that she had overhead him.

"What must your opinion of me have been?" he cried. "How horribly I acted, in those days!"

"My opinion was not good then, I will own. But since then it has completely altered," she said, laying her hand over his on the windowsill. "You are the most kind and honourable man I know. I am very glad we have renewed our acquaintance."

His expression lightened, and Elizabeth was pleased she had succeeded in soothing him.

"You mean this, truly?" he asked.

"Yes, I do."

"Elizabeth, there is one way in which I have not altered. I am still in love with you – most ardently."

Elizabeth inhaled sharply. In those first moments, his declaration shocked her, but then she realised it should have been long apparent to her. All of this care and concern for her, all of this thoughtfulness, could only have come from love. The deepest love, if she was to judge by the expression in his eyes.

Instead of seeing his attention for what it was, she had denied it, to Jane, and more critically, to herself. She had wanted it to be impossible for him to be courting her, so she could continue to enjoy his company. For she would have put an end to the courtship, if she had thought it a courtship. She would have put an end to it long before falling in love herself, for now that she gave herself the freedom to examine her own feelings, she knew that they, too, were love.

She knew then that she had erred, terribly. She had misled herself, but far worse, she had misled the best man she knew, and now she would have to break his heart. Elizabeth withdrew her hand from his, tears already forming in her eyes.

"You do not return my affections," he said, flatly.

"No, I do – I do return your affections," Elizabeth said, weeping. He gave her his handkerchief, and his thoughtfulness even at this time made her weep all the more.

"But something is troubling you."

"It is the question I believe you were going to ask if I returned your affections that troubles me."

"That you marry me? Elizabeth, I assure you I had no intentions of confessing what I just did on this night, still less of pressuring you into a decision you may not be prepared to make. But yes, my intentions have been marriage."

"I wish – I wish deeply that my own intentions were different. I would never have wanted to cause you pain when you have been so kind to me. But my marriage was one of such misery that I vowed I would never marry again."

"It would be different, I think, with someone who loves you," he said, hesitantly.

It would be, Elizabeth realised. Mr. Darcy would respect her thoughts and opinions, as he did now. Their marriage would be a partnership, one grounded in friendship and love. She felt at that moment the strength of her trust in him, in her own feelings towards him, and had very nearly convinced herself that it *could* be possible, that she *could* marry Mr. Darcy. Then she recalled the most significant of her reasons, for vowing never to marry again. She was reminded of the suffocating weight atop her, of the scent, of the pain, and she shuddered.

"You are cold," he said, removing his coat and draping it over her shoulders. The evening air coming through the open window had only the slightest hint of a chill, but Elizabeth made no attempt to disagree with such solicitousness.

He *was* leaner than Mr. Collins, much leaner, and of an athletic form, she thought, now that she had been afforded a closer look at his figure than she ever had before. He seemed a man who was very fastidious in his grooming, which should mean he bathed more often. The pain would be the same, though, she thought. Then she glanced down at his breeches, and thought it likely the pain would be greater.

To her mortification, he had caught her glance, and she rushed to say, with a terribly hot face: "I found the marriage bed very unpleasant – it is not an experience I can bring myself to repeat."

He contemplated this for some time, then said, "If I give you my word, that I will not require you to share my bed, would you then agree to marry me?"

"Mr. Darcy, you cannot be serious."

"I am completely serious. I know what it is to live without you, Elizabeth. If that is the sacrifice I must make so you will be a part of my life, then I will make it."

Elizabeth was overwhelmed at the depth of his love for her, that he would offer her a celibate marriage, even as she knew that what he offered was impossible. He must desire children – an heir, at least – and he must also have a man's natural appetites. What he offered now with every good intention must someday displease him, and if she became his wife, his word now would mean nothing then, if he determined she must take up marital relations. She could not bring herself to trust any man enough to take such a risk, even Mr. Darcy.

"It is incredibly generous of you to offer, but I could not do that to you. I am sure you desire heirs, and I could not bear to have you come to resent me because I cannot continue your line," she said. "Even if I could bring myself to share your bed, and I do not think I can, I was never in the family way, in the whole course of my marriage."

"It does not follow that the fault in that was on your part," he said. "However, I do not want you to consider that, if it troubles you. I give you my word as a gentleman that it would not be required of you, and beyond my word, I would put it within the marriage contract."

Elizabeth shook her head, gazing at him mournfully.

"Is there nothing I can do to persuade you?" he asked, in a most desperate tone.

"I fear not," Elizabeth said. "If there was any man I would ever consider marrying, it is you. But I would be less than the wife you deserve."

"If your objection is on my behalf, I wish you would allow me to decide for myself, Elizabeth. Have you not wondered why I never married? Why I have remained single all these years? I did so because my heart remained bound to you, and no other. So if you believe you are freeing me to go off and find some other wife, some wife you feel more deserving of me, I will not allow you the luxury of such thoughts. You are consigning both of us to remain alone."

Elizabeth's tears had lessened, but this statement brought them back with even greater force, and she felt him gently lay a hand upon her shoulder.

"I am so sorry," he said, in a raspy voice. "I have gone about this terribly. I did not wish to upset you so, nor to pressure you, when I know things have been so difficult for you. May we just – may we just not decide anything, for now? Take a little time – indeed, take as long as you need – and consider what I have proposed."

She nodded, although she feared her answer would never change. Although she was afraid this would give him false hope, perhaps, she thought, he needed a little time spent between hope and doubt, for it was easier to transition into disappointment from doubt. If he was not yet ready to have the door completely closed on all possibility, Elizabeth understood this, and sympathised deeply with it. Still, she did not want to leave him with too much hope that she would change her mind, and she said, "If my answer is no, may we – may we still continue our friendship? I value it deeply."

"You may have as large a portion of my life as you wish, Elizabeth – it is all yours for the taking," he said. "But I would need some time away from you at first, I think. It would not be easy for me to recover from such a wound, and I believe it would be too painful to see you, for a time."

"Of course. I understand." The tightness had returned to Elizabeth's chest, and she knew this time there was nothing she could do to alleviate it – save agree to marry him. Silently, she removed his coat from her shoulders, handed it to him, and left the library.

Far too distraught to return to company, she thought to flee upstairs and sit in Jane's dressing-room until she was calm enough to return to the ballroom. She was not so fortunate as to avoid encountering anyone, however, and the person she did encounter was one of the last people she would have wished to see.

"Can you believe that oaf Sir Benjamin trod on my frock?" Caroline asked, fanning out the skirt of her dress, which, if it had been ripped by Sir Benjamin Ketteridge's foot and then repaired, carried far too much trim for any evidence to be noticeable. "Oh, poor Eliza, whatever has happened to you? I suppose your pursuit of Mr. Darcy has come to an end, too. You ought to have learned from me and gone after a superior man, instead. I am sure you think yourself an heiress now, and able to snare Darcy, but I suspect neither of us has enough fortune to tempt him. I believe he seeks a replacement for Anne de Bourgh, and Longbourn is hardly Rosings Park."

If Elizabeth had encountered Jane in the stairwell, she expected in her present state she would have burst back into tears. Caroline, however, had roused her anger, and she stood up straighter, saying, firmly, "Whatever Mr. Darcy is to me, I will not listen to you impugn his honour, Caroline."

"His honour? You do know he treated Charles in an infamous manner, do you not?"

"And he has apologised and been forgiven, so do not think you can change my opinion of him," Elizabeth said. "I have nothing more to say to you on the subject of Mr. Darcy, so you may as well return to the dancing."

"Well!" Caroline sneered, and began to descend the stairs. "I wish you good fortune in your pursuit, Eliza, but it is bound to end badly. Unless you wish to become his mistress – that, I suppose, he might allow, and perhaps that is just the thing for a country widow like you."

Elizabeth thought of any number of furious retorts for this, but held firm to her promise to say nothing more on the subject of Mr. Darcy. She did continue up the stairs to Jane's dressing-room, but remained only long enough to attend to her toilette, ensuring her countenance did not bear the signs of either her anger or her tears, then she returned downstairs. She might have liked to hide herself away for longer, but between her and Mr. Darcy, one of them should be seen in the ballroom, lest it be thought they had slipped away together. As she had been the one to wound him as she had, it was only fair that she be the one to return to company. She walked over to where her sisters were standing, and found Jane greeting her in some agitation.

"I wondered where you had gone to," Jane said. "Would you mind staying with Mary and Kitty for a little while? Mama said she wished to greet Lady Lucas, but she has not returned, and I need to check on supper."

"Of course – I shall stay with them."

Jane departed, and Mary seated herself quietly; her preference had never been for a ball, although she had been looking forward to her opportunity to exhibit during supper. Kitty, it seemed, was engaged for the next dance, for as the current one came to a close, Mr. Finchley approached to claim her hand.

Kitty went off with him, but with less enthusiasm than she had done in her younger days – gone, it seemed, were the days when Kitty had gleefully danced every set at every ball. She had grown up, Elizabeth thought, perhaps faster than she should have, in such a household as she had known. Perhaps, though, she had grown up enough to contemplate marriage with someone like Mr. Finchley, who had both a good income and a good temper – a very suitable match for Kitty.

Elizabeth's thoughts in this line were interrupted by Sir Benjamin, who approached, and asked for her hand in the dance. She was thankful to have her role as chaperone to give as a ready excuse as to why she could not. This would end her dancing for the evening, but her spirits were too agitated to be enthused by the prospect of dancing – nor was there any purpose in it, for she was certainly not seeking any *other* offers of marriage – and so she did not mind.

Sir Benjamin, it seemed, did mind, for he returned soon after with Mrs. Bennet in tow, that lady saying, "Oh, my dear, Lady Lucas and I got to talking, and I had no notion I was preventing you from dancing! As I told Sir Benjamin, I should not object to his dancing with *any* of my daughters, save Jane, of course, for why should he dance with her, when she is so well married?"

With her reason for declining eliminated, Elizabeth could no longer avoid the dance, and she and Sir Benjamin joined at the bottom of the line. He was not such an oaf as Caroline had made him out to be – Elizabeth had suffered through far more miserable partners – but her thoughts were not on him as she made her way through the set, and if he *had* stepped on her dress and required her to leave the ballroom again, she would not have minded.

Elizabeth was not certain if she was ready to reflect on all that had happened in the library, but she found reflection imposed on her whether she desired it or not. First in her queue of memories must be that declaration of Mr. Darcy's, that of his longstanding ardent love, one he had provided ample evidence of, both in his countenance and in his reminder that he had never married. It had not been heartbreak over losing Anne de Bourgh that had been the cause of his sadness, of his never marrying – it had been losing *her*, losing his chance to marry Elizabeth.

She could hardly comprehend how any man could come to love her so, could come to admire her, much less the man who had once called her *tolerable.* Yet whatever it was, whatever attracted him to her – and she was required to admit now that the way he often looked at her could be seen as admiration, for someone who was not wilfully misleading herself – he had discovered it at some time after the Meryton Assembly and held true to it through all these years. And he intended to hold true to it for far longer, it seemed.

Elizabeth looked back and saw all of this now, and realised she could not have been more wretchedly blind, when it came to his attentions towards her. She had always been ready to invent some reason to explain the time he spent with her, to explain his manner towards her, because she had enjoyed his company so and wished to continue to see him. Over time, though, that enjoyment of his company had shifted, so gradually she had not noticed, into love. It could not be love of the same depth he felt for her – not when he had loved her for so long – but left unabated, it might well catch him up very quickly. He had loved her for longer, but he did not have such a partner to compare her against as she did him.

At this moment, she very nearly collided with Sir Benjamin, but whether this was due to his lack of skill in the dance or her own inattention, Elizabeth could not tell. They both blushed and stammered their apologies, and continued on until the dance ended, Sir Benjamin attempting – and generally failing – to make conversation with his very distracted partner before the next dance in the set began. Elizabeth was relieved when that moment finally came, and tried to turn her focus to the dance, but once again failed.

Her every intent at this time was still to refuse Mr. Darcy, and she thought of what he had said, when she had asked if they could continue on as friends if she did so. He had thought his wounds would be so great that it would pain him to see her, for a time. Elizabeth had known he was leaving to return to Derbyshire, had known she should no longer have his company for some time. There had been his house party at Pemberley to anticipate, though, and she realised there would be no house party at Pemberley – at least for her – if her answer was no. She might not see him for the remainder of the year, and whenever he *was* ready to be in her company again was entirely dependent on when he felt sufficiently healed. She might not see him again for months, if not years, and the thought of this, of how deeply she would miss him, brought tears to her eyes, turning the ballroom blurry for a moment.

Elizabeth blinked, and looked about her to see if anyone had noticed her distress, but it seemed none of her fellow dancers had. *You could have his company constantly, if you marry him*, she thought, *you could have his love and his friendship for the rest of your life.* She found herself far more tempted, now, at the thought of accepting his offer of a celibate marriage, and she considered what it would be like to live in such a marriage, spending her days with him, and even her evenings, up until they retired.

What happiness they would have, in the beginning! Heartbreak avoided, and such loving companionship as they would give each other. Only in the beginning, however. His resolve in promising to write celibacy into the marriage contract had helped her understand how thoroughly she could trust him. He would keep to his word, regardless of whether it was in the contract, and even if he came to regret his promise, if he came to wish to bed her, he would not do so. Their happiness would end, however: he would look to his frigid wife and regret that he had married her, and she would see his disappointment. Would she let him have what he wanted, then? Would the pain of his disappointment be worse than the marriage bed? She suspected it would be.

Elizabeth knew then that if she intended to marry him, she must intend that it be a complete marriage from the beginning. She tried to envision what it might be like to be with him, rather than Collins, but she was not able to conjure an act substantially different from what she had known. Mr. Darcy would be more respectful, surely, and more solicitous, and it could not be denied that he was a far more attractive partner. She still might not like it, but might she be able to bear it, if it pleased the man she loved? If it gave her the possibility, however slight, of having her own child?

The dance ended, then, ceasing her conjecture, and Sir Benjamin escorted her back to her mother and sisters, although Elizabeth did not remain with them. She informed them she was a little overheated from the dance and intended to go to the terrace, glad that as a widow, there could be no objections to her doing so by herself.

The night chill had now truly set in, but Elizabeth found herself refreshed by it, and formed the determination to stay here until she better understood herself. She was so unsure of the marriage bed, with Mr. Darcy. She felt the necessity of it, but did not want to learn what it was like to be with him on her wedding night. Once the vows were said, she would be locked into matrimony, into doing *that* every night he desired it for an even longer period of time than she had been required to do it before. Elizabeth had felt trapped in a marriage once before, and she was petrified at the thought of feeling it again, particularly because this time she knew her husband would see her unhappiness, would be deeply wounded by her regrets over her decision. Then, very simply, it came to her, in the words of Caroline Bingley, of all people.

Unless you wish to become his mistress, Caroline had said. There was nothing to prevent her lying with a man once; she was a widow, and while there was the potential for scandal, it was not nearly the same as it would have been if she was a maiden. If she did so, she would no longer need to conjecture on what it was like to be with him: she would *know*, but she would know before she had locked either of them into a marriage they might regret.

Elizabeth stood there for some time longer, silently contemplating her idea, and the more she thought of it, the more she felt it to be the best course for them to take. She did not know how Mr. Darcy would respond to such an indecorous proposal, but she hoped he would accept it. The risk, after all, was greatest for her – *he* would not be judged at all. Desirous now of finding him, she returned to the house.

Darcy did not leave the library after his conversation with Elizabeth. He did sit, overwhelmed by all that had happened, and there he passed his time in silent reflection.

He had lost his patience, that much was certain. It had brought him such joy, to see Elizabeth so entirely happy, to see her gleefully reeling in that white muslin gown. She had seemed almost reborn, in it, and he had felt himself reborn with her, had felt that even as they teazed each other over the last Netherfield ball, this was their second chance, the culmination of their starting anew with each other. And then with one comment, Elizabeth had unintentionally provided him with a most complete reminder of his past failings.

At least she had come after him – at least her feelings for him were clearly such that she felt badly over wounding him. Yet in truth, the blame should not be placed on Elizabeth. He had wounded himself – it had been *his* comment, at the Meryton Assembly, *his* arrogant dismissal of the woman he had rapidly come to admire, and she had merely teazed him with a reminder of it. It had been his doing, although it had taken years for him to feel the pain of it.

She *had* followed him, though, and she had called him the most kind and honourable man she knew. Such statements from her, in his moment of greatest vulnerability, could not but prompt his confession that he had loved her then, and loved her still. And she returned his love! In what moments of hope he could allow himself, he rejoiced in this.

There was an obstacle, though, one he had not foreseen, although he should have. Even if he had held out for longer, had held true to his patience, her history would not have changed. Her history would still have been there, waiting, to further grieve him over what she had suffered, and present a barrier to his happiness, and hers. Stupid fool, to think that the Elizabeth of his fantasies could exist, when she had been married to Collins! That she would act in such a manner! Why should that aspect of her marriage have been any better than the rest?

Poor Elizabeth! Poor, poor Elizabeth! He had meant what he had offered her, although he had offered it in desperation. He knew himself capable of a celibate marriage; he knew very well how he had spent the last several years. The temptation of the object of his desires living so near to him would make things more difficult, but he had no doubt in his ability to overcome this when in her presence, and to use those outlets he used presently for his lust, whenever it became unmanageable.

She had not believed him, however, and this had upset him, had made him respond in a way that had distressed her so. Yes, they would both be alone if she refused him, but she should not be blamed for it. If he had proposed to her as he should have done after her father's death, she might not have suffered the miseries of her marriage to Collins. She might not have become this poor wounded woman who could not yet trust him fully, and why should she? He should have waited much longer to earn that trust, and he had not. He was only grateful that she had been willing to wait to give him her answer, although he had lowered his hopes, upon her asking if she could still retain his friendship, if it was no. She had sounded as though she was sure it would be.

Darcy sighed, and looked around, realising it had become quite dark in the room. He rose and went to the cabinet to light the lamp there, then poured himself a brandy. After he returned to the chair, he hardly sipped it, however, his mind too full of everything she had said, and what his responses had been. It took him a little while to realise the library door had clicked open and someone had entered. Cursing the intrusion – and knowing he had no right to do so, for it was a public room, even if one barely used in this house – he rose to face the door, and started when he saw it was Elizabeth who had entered.

"I am glad you are still here," she said. "I wished to speak with you again."

Utterly confused, he stood there, watching her approach him. She would not be so cruel as to come to him now with a *no*, yet he did not think she could have had enough time in contemplation – particularly in the midst of a ball – to change her mind to a *yes*.

"What – what is it you wished to speak about?" he asked.

"I have a proposal to make to you, although I am not sure what you will think of it."

"Tell me, and if it is within my power, I will do it."

"I want to be your mistress," she said, and rushed to continue in a most flustered manner: "I mean – I don't mean – permanently. Just to – to lie with you once, before I give you my answer. Then I would know what it is like, with you, and if I find it is something I can bear – at least occasionally – then I will marry you."

Darcy gaped at her. Once he moved past his initial shock, he could see the sense in what she proposed, but the thought of proceeding in such a fashion was one that would take a little time to fully attune his mind to.

"Are you sure that is truly what you want?" he asked.

"I am. We can find a quiet morning, at Longbourn, when my mother and sisters have gone into Meryton, and steal upstairs to my bedchamber – "

"No," said he, firmly. "No. If we are to do this, I would wish to do it properly, not rushed in some stolen moment. I will have my house party at Pemberley – and I will ensure you are housed in a bedchamber near mine."

"I believe that would be a much better way to go about things," she said. "Thank you, for thinking of it."

They stood in silence for some time – there was hardly anything else that could be said, between two people who had just decided on such a plan. There was more, of course, that would need to be discussed in the future, but Darcy was only just beginning to comprehend what that might be.

Eventually, she said, "We should return to company."

"Yes, I suppose we should. Would you like to dance the supper set?"

"I fear you are too late. They were beginning the second dance when I came in here."

"Might I at least escort you in to supper, then?"

"Yes, I would very much like your company during supper," she said, smiling faintly.

Darcy realised then that he should kiss her, that their agreement should be sealed with a sign of his affection, with a promise of what was to come. They should not simply walk out and go to supper, he thought, and he reached out and took hold of her arm, to draw her nearer, and stepped closer himself.

He had thought his touch gentle, but she emitted a little gasp, and her countenance was not one of a woman who wished to be kissed.

"I know it was my proposal, but this is still a very new idea for me, to be with you," she said.

"Of course." He released her arm, but now felt he must do *something*, something that would not trouble her, that would instead give her hope that being with him would be more pleasant than what she had known – he would not have thought that even kissing was something she wished to avoid. He lifted his hand to brush a curl from her forehead, whispering, "You are so beautiful, Elizabeth. I wish I had told you so when I first recognised it."

This was received much better, with modestly lowered eyes and a quietly murmured thank you. He withdrew his hand and offered her his arm, and they left the library quietly, Darcy still considering what had happened. It gave him a better understanding of just what an undertaking he had agreed to: he would need to convince a woman who had known nothing of pleasure in being with a man that it could indeed be had. If he *could*, if he could love Elizabeth as he had always wished to love her, if he could rouse out some of the passion he hoped was still there, beneath her fear, it would be the most wonderful thing in the world. Yet if he failed, he would have to face the pain and fear of the woman he loved, and the guilt of knowing it to be his own doing.

He would have agreed to anything she had proposed, and although this idea of hers had shocked him at first, he understood why it was favourable to her. She would not commit herself beyond what she was comfortable in committing to, and Darcy thought it right to do whatever made the decision easier for Elizabeth. The burden it put upon him, though, felt tremendous. He had one night, now. One night, to decide his entire life's happiness.

CHAPTER 10

August 14, 1815

Even if Mr. Darcy had not declared himself at the Netherfield ball, Elizabeth suspected she would, by now, have come to understand her feelings for him, for in his absence, she missed him terribly. She was thankful for their arrangement, for the knowledge that there was still a chance for her to spend her life with him, for she suspected as well that without it, his absence might have worn down her resolve not to marry him. The thought of a far longer separation than the one she faced was unbearable, and Elizabeth doubted her ability to endure such a thing.

He had written to her, a somewhat stilted letter in which he had said much about his return to Pemberley, but had only once vaguely referenced their intended night together. Still, he had written of how much he missed her, and signed his letter, "With all my love, FITZWILLIAM DARCY," and this had been sufficient to make her heart race. It was a very strange thing, to be in love.

Elizabeth had immediately readied her writing things to respond to him, and had found herself struggling – as he must have – to determine how much of her affections to put into her letter. She did not wish to raise his hopes too high, when things were still undecided, and yet she did want him to have some reassurance of her love. In the end, her letter was very like his. She wrote of the progress on Mr. Wendell's field, and the new tenant she had found for Boyce's old farm, Mr. Triggs – a very cheerful and diligent young man. She wrote of driving out with Chip in the pony phaeton, and how although her skills were now sufficient to feel comfortable in driving anywhere, she missed her instructor deeply – for his presence, rather than his instruction. Still, it had not seemed quite enough, when she had reached the point of having nothing more to tell him, and so she had added the final lines, "I love you. I wish September could arrive more quickly."

This was mostly true. She *did* long to see him again, and she *did* long for some resolution in the matter of whether she would marry him. What she did not anticipate with eagerness was their attempted union. She had been glad of his saying they should wait until the house party at Pemberley, allowing him to visit her in her bedchamber, both because it did seem a better way to go about things, and because it meant she need not expose herself to the act so immediately. There was little she could do to prepare, but she did what she could, which was to think about it, to ready her mind. She had been unprepared in the library, when he had attempted to kiss her. It was logical, of course, that he should do so – she *had* just asked to become his mistress – but she had been thinking of her status as such as something belonging to the future, not the present. Startled by his advance, she had realised quite suddenly that he had consumed an indeterminate amount of brandy, and she was alone with him in a dimly lit room. He had understood – although it must have disappointed him – and his actions thereafter had been so very lovely, she thought of them often during her preparation.

This preparation could not be undertaken in the most logical place – her bedchamber – and so she took to lying beneath her favourite oak tree on Longbourn's grounds, and imagining. She thought of him brushing her hair back from her face, telling her she was beautiful, and then seeking to kiss her – a kiss she would endeavour to welcome, the next time he attempted it. She thought of what must come after the kiss, of his lying atop her, of his – his mounting her, and she planned for how she would handle any unpleasantness that might follow. She would think of how very much she missed him now, of how she loved to be around him – outside of that unpleasantness – and the love she would gain in being married to him. If she did all of this, she thought she should be able to bear the act quietly, without too much outward discomfort, for she had a strong sense that Mr. Darcy would not proceed if this discomfort was apparent to him. That, in itself, was a change that might make all the difference.

She was engaged in such thoughts beneath the tree when Mary approached, saying, "I am done with the accounts, I think, if you wish to check them."

Elizabeth sat up, and blushed, although it was not as though Mary should know she had been lying there, thinking of Mr. Darcy's presence atop her, and inside her. "Are you done already?" she asked. "You are much faster than I."

Although Mr. Darcy had invited all of Elizabeth's sisters to attend his house party, Mary had shown no interest, and had offered to help manage what she could for the estate while Elizabeth was gone. This Elizabeth was glad of, for otherwise she might have needed to rush to find a new steward, and in the course of teaching Mary her temporary duties, she had found her logical sister had quite a head for them.

Elizabeth rose and followed Mary back into the house and then the library, looked through Mary's entries in the estate's book, and then did her own calculations to check Mary's work.

"You have done it perfectly, Mary," she said, once she had finished. "You shall have to be careful, for you are far better at mathematics than I, and I shall be reluctant to give up your assistance, once I return."

"I would not mind if I kept helping with the books," said Mary. "It is nice to have responsibilities."

"I quite agree," Elizabeth said, "and I have enough that I should be happy to lend out some of them to you for as long as you wish to have them, particularly when you do so well with them."

Mary smiled at the praise, and said she wished to look over her work once more before her pianoforte practise. Elizabeth left her and went down to the storeroom. At first, she had taken care to warn Mrs. Hill every time she did this, but very quickly, Longbourn's servants had come to know that Mrs. Collins came down every morning to steal into the storeroom for an apple, and showed themselves clearly prepared for her entrance, so Elizabeth had left off her warnings. She had, as well, after some subtle prodding from Cook, taken to selecting the worst of the apples rather than the best, for as Cook noted, ponies were not overparticular about the quality of their apples.

Chip was assuredly not overparticular, for he whickered to her when she entered his stall, in anticipation of his treat, and ate each slice with relish. Elizabeth then scratched him behind his ears, amused as always by the disproportionate amount of enjoyment he seemed to get from this, and thinking very fondly of the man who had found him for her.

"D'ye wish to take him out today, ma'am?" Rodney asked her, peering into the stall. He always asked this, although Elizabeth went out in the pony phaeton nearly every day, save Sundays.

"Yes, just to Netherfield," she said, and went to wait outside the stable while the pony and his phaeton were prepared, and Longbourn's only hack saddled for her groom, Jacob.

The drive was a short one, enlivened only by Mr. Finchley, who was riding along the lane just before Netherfield. He reined his horse to a halt, and Elizabeth did the same for Chip.

"I am sorry to miss you," he said. "I was just going to call at Longbourn. Let me at least wish you good day, now."

"Good day to you, Mr. Finchley. I am sorry to miss you as well, but please do not let me detain you," Elizabeth said, knowing full well he was not calling for *her*. Starting the morning after the Netherfield ball, he had called consistently, and it was apparent that Kitty was his object. He was the last guest remaining at Netherfield, kept on cheerfully by Charles, who said he could not consider sending a man back to town in this heat. They all knew, of course, that Mr. Finchley might very well have found somewhere else to go but for the young lady at Longbourn, but none of them spoke of it.

Elizabeth left Chip to Jacob's care in the drive, and entered the house only to learn that her sister had taken little Charles outside. In the present heat, there were few places that could be comfortable, and Elizabeth made her way to the path through Netherfield's gardens that was most heavily shaded by trees; there she found Jane, seated upon a blanket in the shade, with her son sprawled out beside her on the blanket, sleeping peacefully.

"It gets so hot in the nursery, during the day," Jane said, moving to make room for her younger sister on the blanket. "He could not take his nap there, poor little dear. I think we shall have to move the nursery to another room before next summer, unless we do choose to purchase before then."

"He seems rather content there," Elizabeth said. The Bingleys had been speaking of purchasing an estate ever since their marriage, but had never committed to doing so, and so she gave this portion of Jane's statement little notice.

"Yes, he is," Jane said, gazing fondly at her son. "Oh – I have some news I think you will like: Caroline will not travel with us to Pemberley."

"Well, that should make for a more pleasant journey. To Derbyshire with Caroline in the carriage was not something I was particularly anticipating."

Jane allowed the slightest little giggle to escape her. She had long since come to understand that Caroline did not like her, but Jane generally seemed to attempt at least politeness towards her sister-in-law; Elizabeth thought this due to a desire to promote at least the appearance of familial harmony, rather than any wish to win Miss Bingley over to the role of affectionate sister.

"May I presume she found company she preferred over ours? Or somewhere more fashionable to go?"

"Yes, both – she intends to go to Brighton with the Hursts. I understand Mr. Althorpe is to be there as well."

"I hope with all my heart she receives an offer from him," Elizabeth said, dryly.

Jane seemed to understand her perfectly, but did not respond beyond a smile. They sat quietly, for a time, Elizabeth considering the thing she had been wanting to ask her sister – and aware there could be no better time than in their present privacy – but needing to summon the will to ask it.

"Jane – I am going to ask something – something I suspect shall be exceedingly embarrassing for the both of us," Elizabeth said. "Yet I am going to ask it anyway. You need not tell me in any detail – indeed, I think I would rather you did not tell me in any detail, or I shall not be able to look at my brother in the same way – but will you tell me: what has the marriage bed been like, for you?"

Jane turned entirely pink, but did reply: "I never spoke of this to you, because I knew it did not align with your own experience, but I have always found the marriage bed to be very wonderful."

"Wonderful? Truly?"

"Yes. When a man loves a woman – when a man attends her well, a woman *can* feel every bit as much pleasure as a man from the act – at least, that is what I have found," Jane said.

Elizabeth stared at her sister: this was not what her mother and her accoucheurs had led her to believe at all, but Jane would never lie to her on any topic, much less this one.

"Why do you wish to know, Lizzy?"

"Mr. Darcy – I am going to be his mistress, just – "

Elizabeth was prevented from saying anything more by Jane, who, speaking low so to avoid waking her son, but in an entirely furious tone, asked: "How *could* he? He told Charles very specifically that his intent was marriage, and instead he does this! Lizzy, please do not let him take advantage of you in such a way – you deserve far more than what he has offered."

"No, Jane, no, please do not blame him. It was I who proposed it – I was not ready for more. *His* intent was always to marry me, but mine has been to never marry again."

"Oh, Lizzy – could love not persuade you to do so?"

"You knew I was in love with him before I did, I think," Elizabeth said. "If I had better heeded our conversation, I would not have been so shocked by my own feelings."

"I was not sure, but there was something in your manner when you spoke of him, and you seemed determined to continue to spend time with him," Jane said. "As I already told you, I was in support of the match, so long as his intentions were honourable, but I realised you could not speak to his intentions, so I asked Charles to question him instead."

"You knew he loved me, then, and you said nothing?" Elizabeth asked, shocked and as angry at her sister as she could ever be towards Jane.

"Charles and I both agreed that we should not interfere," said Jane. "Nothing good comes of interference in matters of love. I did try to warn you, but in truth I am glad the two of you have come to this point on your own, as you should have. I only wish the outcome was more favourable."

"It is my fault that it was not. I did not explain myself well, about being his mistress," Elizabeth said. "I think I am ready to trust him in most of what a marriage entails, but Jane, I hated the marriage bed so very much – I did not know if I could bring myself to do it again. I asked to be his mistress – just once – so I could see what it is like, to be with him."

"It will be better, Lizzy – surely it will be better. You might even find you like it very much."

"Let us not go that far," Elizabeth said. "I would be content if it was only mildly displeasing – like sitting through Mr. Yawley's sermons."

"Lizzy! You did not just compare the marriage bed to Mr. Yawley's sermons!" Jane cried, with a nervous glance toward her son, who continued to sleep soundly.

"I believe I did." Elizabeth giggled. "Oh, poor Jane, to have such a scandalous sister. I promise I shall be very discreet about it."

"Will it happen at the house party, at Pemberley?" Jane asked, then realisation dawned on her countenance. "Lizzy, is that the *reason* for Mr. Darcy's holding a house party? Just so he can spend a night with you?"

"That is not the reason – he had planned it before we came to this arrangement. Although I suppose he intended his courtship of me to continue when I came to Pemberley, so perhaps I was the purpose for the house party, more generally. He did not intend to confess his affections so soon as he did."

"Did he do so at the ball? I noticed he disappeared for most of the evening, and both of you were absent from the supper set. And I found a handkerchief embroidered with his initials in my dressing-room."

"It did all happen during the ball. I was crying, and he gave me his handkerchief to me – that was dreadfully careless of me, and I am very glad it was you who found it. Do you – do you still have it?" Elizabeth asked, thinking she would like to keep it if Jane did, as a little talisman of her love, a reminder of him.

"No, I told Charles it had been found after the ball, although not where it had been found. He gave it to his valet, to give to Mr. Darcy's valet."

"Oh – thank you for returning it so discreetly," Elizabeth said. "Did anyone else notice our absence?"

"No, I have not heard it spoken of – I believe they were all thinking more of their own partners and the white soup than of where the two of you had gone to, and by then we had other rumours, for the gossips. It was said that not everyone kept to their own beds during the house party."

"Do you know whom the rumours referred to?" asked Elizabeth.

"I do not, and I do not wish to, but I do hope you will be very careful when you are at Pemberley," said Jane. "Perhaps we should plan to arrive there early, before the others. I should hate for poor Mr. Darcy to encounter someone else in his hallways, seeking to do the same thing he does."

"Yes, I do think that would make matters easier, and put us at less risk. And I see your opinion of Mr. Darcy has changed rather rapidly. When I first mentioned my being his mistress, I believe you would have run him through, were both he and a sword readily at hand, yet now he is *poor Mr. Darcy.*"

"My opinion of Mr. Darcy will always be influenced by how he treats you," said Jane, "but it must be a difficult position for him to be placed in. I dearly hope all works out well between the two of you – more for your own happiness, but also for his."

On her return to Longbourn, Elizabeth once again passed Mr. Finchley, who seemed very distracted, and barely managed to nod to her. Elizabeth did not mind, for her own thoughts were occupied with what Jane had said, with this notion that the marriage bed could actually be pleasurable. She tried to envision how that could be so, and did not attend to her driving as well as she should have, but Chip knew his way home quite well by now, and took her there regardless.

She entered Longbourn to find the house in an uproar.

"Headstrong, foolish girl!" Mrs. Bennet was exclaiming. "Do you intend to spend the rest of your life under this roof, living off of us?

Elizabeth looked at the object of her mother's wrath, weeping piteously on the sofa in the parlour, and took a deep breath. "It is *my* roof, and Kitty may live under it for as long as she wishes. Others will not be so fortunate, however, if she continues to be harangued in this manner."

"Oh, yes, I suppose you are back to be all high-and-mighty about how you own this house, now," Mrs. Bennet said.

"I did what I had to in order to give us a home, and I suffered for it, and now, yes, I shall utilise the outcome to my benefit, and my sister's."

"Oh yes, your *suffering*. You brought your suffering on yourself, Miss Lizzy, for not being as dutiful a wife as you ought to have been."

Elizabeth had no desire to continue this old row when her thoughts had been so optimistically turned during the drive home and poor Kitty looked to be in great need of comforting. Elizabeth had a good suspicion of what had happened, that Mr. Finchley had offered marriage and been refused, and she wondered at the reason for this refusal even as she wished to make clear that Kitty would never be required to marry.

"Perhaps I did, but perhaps you ought to be more respectful of my status here, if you do not want me to lease a cottage for you in Northumberland."

This did not prompt Mrs. Bennet to be any more respectful, but she did at least vacate the room after one last glare at both of her daughters. Elizabeth crossed the parlour and sat beside Kitty on the sofa, putting her arm around her sister's shoulders.

"I'm sorry, Lizzy. I did not want to be the cause of any further argument between you and mama."

"She and I shall never get along any better, I do not think. I am not sure if I can ever forgive her for the way she acted while Mr. Collins was alive, and I do not think she can ever forgive me for taking her place as mistress of the house."

"It does wear on her, I think, to not have the position and the responsibilities she once did," Kitty said, "particularly since you are both widows, now."

Elizabeth recalled her conversation with Mary, about having responsibilities. Perhaps being given some responsibilities back would make Mrs. Bennet easier; perhaps Elizabeth could extend an olive branch and ask her mother to mind the household accounts as Mary would mind the estate, in her absence.

"I do not wish to talk about her, though, I wish to talk about you," Elizabeth said. "I passed Mr. Finchley on the road. May I presume that he offered for you, and you refused him?"

Kitty replied that this was true.

"May I ask why? I meant what I said – you shall always have a home here. So do not think I am attempting to be rid of you. I only wish to know where your heart lies."

"Oh, Lizzy, thank you for that. Mr. Finchley is nice, it is true, but he is so very dull. Even if he was not, I would have refused him, though. I do not ever intend to marry."

"Kitty!" Elizabeth exclaimed. "I do not want you to feel pressured to leave, but I would much rather see you happily married, if you find a man you love."

"Marriage is not always happy, Lizzy. You know that better than anyone."

Following such a reminder of her own days of misery, Kitty's comment was most painful, although Elizabeth knew it had not been intended to wound. She attempted to rally herself, and encourage her sister: "Jane's marriage is very happy. You should look to her and Charles, and even Charlotte and Mr. Gilmore."

"I hope you do not expect me to marry some old man like Charlotte did," Kitty said, looking rather disgusted. "Maria says she is more nursemaid than wife to him."

"Perhaps she is, but he treats her very well, and Charlotte is happy with her situation," Elizabeth said. "I do not expect that of you, though, Kitty. I merely meant that you should look to marriages where the wife made her own choice as your example, rather than my situation."

"I know my situation would not be the same as yours, but it just seems too much of a risk to lock myself into matrimony. You were fortunate, that Mr. Collins died – oh, don't look at me like that, Lizzy, and don't try to protest! – you were, and I am not ashamed to say it. But I would not wish to be in a marriage where my husband's death was my only chance at escaping my unhappiness."

"I understand – I understand you completely. Do you wish to come to Pemberley with us, and get away from mama, for a time?"

"No, I think not. Then poor Mary shall have to remain home alone with her," Kitty said. "And I am sure there will be more single gentlemen at Pemberley, and I am not ready for another courtship so soon."

"I wish you would reconsider, but I will not press you. I think if you were courted by the right man, by a man you could love, it would make all the difference," Elizabeth said. "Even I am contemplating marriage again."

"With Mr. Darcy?"

"Yes, with Mr. Darcy."

"I do think he is very good to you," Kitty said. "But Lizzy, aren't you afraid?"

"I *am* afraid, Kitty," Elizabeth said, although she found that after her conversation with Jane, she was not so afraid as she had been. "I am afraid of being with him, but I am also afraid that if I do not marry him, I will lose my chance at being as happy as I think I might be, to be the wife of such a man."

CHAPTER 11

September 13, 1815

They were late. Darcy had expected Elizabeth and the Bingleys sometime before the noon hour, and now it was questionable whether they would even arrive in time for dinner. Any number of comparatively innocent problems could befall travellers of such a distance, and so he told himself not to worry, yet worry he did.

His spirits had already been agitated enough without the addition of worry. Both in person and in their correspondence, he and Elizabeth had discussed a number of useful things: that it would be him that came to her in the night, rather than her trying to find the master's bedchamber in an unfamiliar house; that she and the Bingleys would arrive a few days before the rest of the house party, so he did not encounter any guests in the hallway; that only Mrs. Reynolds would be informed that Mrs. Collins was Pemberley's prospective mistress, although not what this was still contingent upon. Yet there had been so many things he did not think to speak of with her, and many of them were far more critical. They had not even settled on which particular night they were to make their attempt – he had thought they would be able to find a little time in private after her arrival, and speak of which night would be preferable to her.

Darcy strode through Pemberley's hallways; his was a temper that bore agitation better when in motion, particularly when he could find some purpose for this motion. His footsteps echoing, and startling at least one servant with the rapidity of his pace, he walked, and contemplated when that most important event was to occur. It would not be that night. He had already decided upon this. In this courtship he had attempted to conduct with all the patience in his capacity, he would not find himself rushed, giving his attentions to a woman exhausted by travel.

It would be tomorrow night, then, if not later. Having this take place at Pemberley had given Darcy some additional time to prepare, although there were limited options for preparing for such a thing. He was not an inexperienced man, but his experience had come from that ill-kept secret among gentlemen, the fabric shops where more than superfine and kerseymere could be bought, and the women of such establishments were not focused on teaching a gentleman in how to pleasure a lady. He had never kept a mistress. Elizabeth, the woman he loved painfully, would be his first mistress, if she could be called such a thing. He did not think of her as such: Elizabeth was everything.

He had considered returning to the establishment he had gone to in his younger days – those days in which he had wanted *any* woman, and not a particular one – and requesting a woman, someone who could help him learn such arts, but to do so would have made him feel inconstant to Elizabeth. So he had gained his knowledge through books, as best he could, books sold in the unsavoury little shops on Holywell Street, read during the carriage ride back to Pemberley and ever since. It was not unusual for the master of Pemberley to hide himself away in the library or his private sitting-room for much of his day, so this prompted no particular notice from his servants, although they all would have been wholly scandalised if they had known what he was reading. They would have been still more scandalised, to know the state of arousal some portions of these books put him in. To read of such things, to see such illustrations, and then consider doing them with *her*, was to know an almost overwhelming desire. Yet this desire rarely needed to be alleviated in the old manner. No sooner had he felt the extent of his passions than he had considered how the complete exposing of them was very likely to intimidate his partner. No sooner had he considered how glorious a successful union could be than a vision of failure was rising strongly within his mind, and desire was supplanted by a cold, leaden terror within his belly.

Thus vacillating between desire and fear, he had completed this lewd education he had embarked upon, and only then had he approached his plans for that night, thinking carefully, rationally, of how he should touch her, how they should *be* together. In the time he had spent thinking, he had attempted to avoid being too discouraged by his failure to achieve something so simple as a kiss at Netherfield, but it was difficult to do so completely. With such a beginning, he feared things would progress too slowly, and they would reach the point of their union late in the night, when they would both be exhausted and he would be more prone to make a mistake, to fail to read her reactions as carefully as he knew he needed to. He intended, therefore, to focus his efforts entirely on pleasing her, and to ask for an additional night if it grew too late. Darcy was hopeful she would allow him this, so long as everything she experienced was pleasing to *her*.

His own pleasure could wait, and his arousal could be alleviated in fantasy, once he returned to his own bedchamber.

That bedchamber was in this wing, but on the storey below his present location, the hallway in which the single females were to be housed. In determining the rooms for the house party, Elizabeth's apartment had been assigned first, and all else had followed. He had chosen one of the larger chambers for her, a space decorated in a style he thought she should prefer, and possessing a fine view of the grounds. And it would be easy enough for him to reach her here, but without being so blatant as to house her in the same hallway as him.

Darcy opened the door and stepped inside, glancing about the room to view all of the little improvements Mrs. Reynolds had suggested to make the room more comfortable for the young widow. Everything that had been promised was in place, although Darcy still racked his mind for anything else that could be done to make the room more inviting for Elizabeth. He could think of nothing more, however. The room was ready, and the best of his present maids, Rachel, had been assigned to look after Mrs. Collins particularly during her stay. Darcy wondered again what – if anything – his staff suspected regarding his romantic intentions. Mrs. Reynolds, being privy to the secret, would not share it, but any of those who had accompanied him to Hertfordshire and had their suspicions might have hinted to Rachel about the importance of her charge.

Darcy made to close the door, intending to return to the entrance-hall in the hopes that a carriage would be visible in the drive. He stopped himself just before he did so, though, glancing about one last time. In this room, his future would be decided; in this room, he would bring all of his preparations to bear, and could only hope they would be successful.

However, he had prepared for failure as well, for what he would do if it did go badly, if she disliked their union. This had been easily decided upon: he would offer her the celibate marriage again, and he would plead his case as thoroughly as he could. In this, as in everything, he would have to be careful. His every temptation would be to do so immediately. But if she was upset – which she almost certainly would be, in such a situation – he would have to require himself to leave her, to find an opportunity to speak to her the next day, when she could be more receptive to his arguments. He hoped and prayed it would not come to this, but at least he would be prepared if it did. If he lost her again, it would be his undoing.

To his great relief, the Bingley carriage arrived shortly after the dinner hour, with tales of a broken carriage wheel just before Belper that had taken most of the day to see repaired. He had them all shown to their rooms, and ordered as much of what had been intended for dinner as could be repurposed brought up for them to sup, and as he had been too tense to eat much at dinner, he ate almost as voraciously as the rest of them. Before and during the meal, he had noticed a certain reserve on Elizabeth's part towards him, and he hoped it was nothing more than nervousness; he wondered if she thought he intended to come to her and attempt their union that night.

In the drawing-room, she handed over *Waverley* to him in an almost perfunctory manner, saying only that she had enjoyed it and hoped he would, as well. There was no repeat of her teasing over lending him a book, and when he promised she should finally have her chance to see Pemberley's library, she said she would like that very much, but with what sounded like tension underlying her tone. He had only ever heard her speak like that once before, in the phaeton, when their path had been about to intersect that of Mr. Boyce.

The travellers all retired early, speaking of their exhaustion. When Elizabeth would hardly look at Darcy as he bade her good-night, he determined he should go to her, if only to say he did not intend that this be the night, and speak of the other things he wished to discuss with her in private. He sat silently in his own chambers, waiting to hear Rachel go down the service staircase nearby, and waited for some time after that, to ensure Rachel had not been sent on an errand, rather than being dismissed.

There was nothing but silence, however, and he left his own chamber, the light from his candle the only illumination visible in the hallway. Up the stairs, and relieved to find no-one in the hallway there, either. He had a right to be in any part of the house he wished, at any time, but for one of the servants to see him here would require him to speak to that servant in the morning about being discreet. He did not want to have that sort of talk with any of his servants; he had already been required to send his valet to town on an errand, to ensure Mason was not waiting up for the bell to change him.

Knocking ever-so-softly on her door, he found it opened almost immediately, and himself admitted to the bedchamber, where every candle was still burning.

"I was not sure if it would be tonight," Elizabeth said, looking as though she feared he was going to eat her alive, and not in the manner he had read about in the books. She wore a nightgown and dressing gown, with her hair long, plaited behind her. The sight of her in such undress stoked his ardour – it could not be helped – but not so much that he would ruin everything. He must return to his patience, now. He must return to it, and hold firm.

"I do not think it should be," he said. "You must be tired – I expect you would rather rest tonight. I did not wish for you to wait up for me, though."

"Thank you, yes – I would like to rest tonight." She relaxed, visibly, and seemed willing to look him in the eye now. "I think tomorrow would be best. I do not want to leave things undecided for *too* long."

"Then I shall return again tomorrow. Before then, I did wish to speak with you of something, and to see if there was anything you wished to speak with me about." He motioned to the chaise beside the fireplace. "Will you come and sit with me?"

He sat first, to allow her to choose her own distance from him, and found she sat nearer than he had hoped, but not so near as to touch him with any part of her person.

"You and I have not spoke about what may – perhaps – become the most important thing," he said. "If you find things displeasing, I do not intend they go so far as to create the possibility of a child resulting from our union, but I would still like to plan for it."

"I do not think a child likely," she said. "Not – not because I do not believe things will go so far – I do intend to bear it, if it is at all possible. But because it will be one night, and in all the nights of my marriage, I have never conceived a child."

"I will not take pleasure in that which you merely bear, Elizabeth, and I wish to speak on that more, but first I must say this. If there is – by any chance – a child, will you give me your word that you would marry me, then? I would not touch you again if you did not desire it, but the child would be heir to Pemberley and Longbourn. I could not see him or her born a bastard."

"Of course. I would not desire that for my child, either. I give you my word."

"Thank you." Darcy did not think she looked at all convinced that there *could* be a child, but at least she had made the promise. He wanted to persuade her into marriage, not entrap her, but if there *was* a child, that child's future life would be of the utmost importance. "Elizabeth, now I do wish to return to what you said, about intending to bear it. There is something I would like to ask of you, although I fear it may pain you, and it is that you tell me of what it is particularly that you did not like about the act, so I may try to rectify it tomorrow."

She looked horrified, although whether this was over his having asked, or her having to recite it, he could not tell. Perhaps both. After some time, and looking across the room, rather than at him, she did finally begin, however, in a quavering voice:

"I did not like his weight on top of me – he was a heavy man, and grew heavier throughout the course of our marriage. The sweat, and the smell of him – " He longed to take up her hand, to give her some comfort, but he feared he would only startle her. " – the whole act felt horrid to my every sense. And it was painful, not just the first time, as I had been told it would be, but every night. Not so bad as the first time, but there was always discomfort. That is why I spoke of bearing it. When I saw a physician, he prescribed the use of sweet oil. I have brought it with me."

"Sweet oil?"

"Yes – to make the – the chafing less."

"Oh, Elizabeth." She caught the sympathy in his tone, and returned her gaze to his. He had made her cry, and could only hope that asking her to confess all of this could assist him tomorrow. Darcy felt the pain of having put her in such a state, and hesitantly reached out his hand and laid it on her shoulder, encouraging her into his embrace. She yielded easily, but this first time of holding Elizabeth in his arms was not what he had thought it would be, with her sobbing against his chest as the end result of his own query. Still, he *was* holding her, and she showed no reluctance towards this intimacy, which Darcy thought should indicate at least some little progress, although his greater concern was in comforting her.

In time, she pulled away from him, and said, "I want for this to work. I want for this to work so badly – I hope you know that."

"Of course," he said, drawing his arms away from her, and retreating to the distance she had established before.

"I am glad you came here tonight," Elizabeth said. "I know it may not seem as though I am, but I am glad we spoke of these things now, rather than before – before we attempted the act."

"If you are glad, then I am as well." He rose, taking up his candle, and she accompanied him to the door. When they arrived there, he thought he should use this time alone with her to make some further progress before tomorrow night, but he should go about it better than he had at Netherfield, and he asked, "Elizabeth, may I kiss you?"

"Yes, you may," she said, softly.

He was required to hold the candle well away from them, and therefore had only one free hand with which to caress her cheek, and brush over her lips with his thumb. She inhaled sharply when he did this, and closed her eyes, so he could see those long, lovely lashes against her skin before he leaned closer and touched his mouth to hers.

Finally, to be kissing those lips he had desired for so long! But patience, patience, patience. He kissed her delicately, carefully, and knew he had been successful when he felt her respond, hesitantly, but respond nonetheless. Then he pulled back from her, and saw a pleasing blush upon her cheeks, and a look of wonderment in her eyes, when finally she opened them.

"That – that was beautiful," she whispered.

"Then we will do it as many times as you wish tomorrow. Good-night, dearest, loveliest Elizabeth."

He reached out to touch her cheek once more, and then let himself out of her bedchamber.

CHAPTER 12

September 14, 1815

When Elizabeth awoke, sunlight was already streaming into her bedchamber, but she had no regrets over having slept so late; she *had* been exhausted from her travels, far more than she had expected she would be. It had been a most agitating journey. All that time in the carriage beside the turnpike road, while they waited first for their outrider to go ahead to the next inn, while they waited for that inn to send someone for the repair, and then while the repair itself was done, Elizabeth had grown increasingly tense that they should reach Pemberley late in the evening.

They had, with Elizabeth trying to avoid checking her watch every five minutes, and not entirely succeeding. Charles must have thought it was just a general desire to be done with the journey, or to see Pemberley, but Jane had looked at Elizabeth with concern when they arrived in the drive so late.

Elizabeth had wished for time alone, to prepare her mind for what was to take place, and she had wished to do what she could to make her person agreeable to him, for having known repulsion in her own bedchamber, she would have been horrified to be the cause of it for another. Instead of the long, leisurely bath she had desired, however, she had been required to sup still dusty from the road. And all of the tension she had carried throughout the day had seemed to catch up with her after Rachel had helped her change, and Elizabeth had desired nothing more than to pull back the covers of the very fine bed and go to sleep. It had all seemed a very inauspicious beginning.

Yet Mr. Darcy had known this, and shown himself to be fully attuned to her wants and needs. She should have known he would be, for he had been the one who had wished to go about things properly. Elizabeth was once again glad of this.

She rose to have a better look around her bedchamber, which she found to have been furnished in tasteful elegance and scattered with items meant to see to her comfort. She had seen – and smelled – the vases of roses the night before, but now she saw them to be magnificent, perfect Pemberley roses, and she wished to see the garden in which such specimens were grown.

There was a neat little secretaire, and a japanned cabinet, upon which had been placed a decanter of wine, which she had partaken of perhaps a little too liberally the night before, when she had thought relations with Mr. Darcy a possibility. There were landscape watercolours – perhaps of Pemberley's grounds – on the walls beside the fireplace, and there was the chaise, where she and Mr. Darcy had sat.

Elizabeth recalled the mortification of what they had discussed there; she had not been able to look at him, while relating such things, and had nearly been undone by the sympathy in his eyes when finally she looked at him again. She felt a rush of nervousness – to be loved so deeply by such a man, and to know tonight would decide whether she could marry him!

Yet she had greater cause for hope, now. When he had kissed her, it had been so unlike her previous experiences that she had gone to bed wondering if everything else could be unlike her previous experiences. She prayed it could be.

Elizabeth and Jane never having seen Pemberley's grounds, and the day being fine, it was decided that after a brief tour of the house, the party would drive out to view them. The equipage Mr. Darcy kept at Pemberley for such purposes was a practical-looking curricle, although Elizabeth expected it possessed every feature that a man passionate about driving should care for, and would not be noticeable to her inexpert eyes.

Once they set out, she was too taken with the delights of the grounds to care at all about her conveyance. Elizabeth admired all she saw; every detail of both house and grounds spoke of the finest natural taste, one that aligned very much with her own. How wonderful it would be, to walk these grounds or ride with Mr. Darcy in this curricle, to have him periodically gain her attention to point out some particular feature of the landscape, to stop for a delightful nuncheon in the shade. Elizabeth was reminded that by the next morning, she would know whether this was to be her life, she would know whether she was to lose his company, and she felt dread briefly clutch at her stomach. She glanced about her with more vigour, then, seeking to give herself over to enjoyment of the day, although she did endeavour to sit nearer to him for the rest of the drive. This, she found, made the drive more enjoyable rather than less, to feel his presence in a more physical manner. It reminded her of the way he had held her last night, how soothing and comforting it had been to be enveloped in his arms.

If Mr. Darcy had noticed this change in her positioning, he said nothing of it, but Elizabeth came to believe he had when he next sought to gain her attention, for he did so by placing his hand upon her knee. It was the very lightest of touches, his fingertips gone before Elizabeth comprehended he had done it. She remembered doing the same to him – with a much firmer touch – when she had been so startled by Mr. Boyce's appearance, and blushed thoroughly in remembrance. Still, she found herself glad when he did it again later, and his hand lingered for a little longer, for something far more pleasant than dread briefly overcame her stomach.

The drive had taken much of the morning, but they still had ample time for a walk in the rose garden before they would need to return inside and change for dinner. The two couples set out together, but during the walk, Jane seemed to discover a particular zeal for roses. This zeal required her to lead Charles at a rapid clip through the garden, commenting on every new favourite she saw, until the Bingleys had reached the opposite wall and she was pointing to something beyond it, leading Charles through the gate.

Elizabeth very nearly laughed at her sister's apparent plot to leave her and Mr. Darcy alone in the rose garden, for even if they had not discussed all they needed to last night, they would have had ample time to do so during the drive. Then he turned toward her, and she understood Jane might not have left them alone for conversation.

"I have always liked this garden, but never so well as I do now, to see you within it," he murmured.

"It is beautiful," Elizabeth said. Part of her felt a certain eagerness to reach that night, not in anticipation of the act, but in finally knowing the outcome. Yet part of her wanted to remain in this moment forever, with the scent of roses all around them and the birds chirping in the sunlight and every possibility still before her that she could be mistress of this place, that she could be married to the master.

"It is very beautiful," he said, with a look that indicated he meant her, more than the roses. Then, slowly, he leaned forward to kiss her, and Elizabeth realised she had wanted him to kiss her, had wanted this expression of his love.

This kiss was no deeper than what they had shared the night before, but made all the better for Elizabeth's knowing from the beginning that she should enjoy it. With both of his hands free, now, he placed them both lightly on her cheeks; one of Elizabeth's held her parasol, but she mimicked him with the other, and once she released her hand, he did the same with his, ending the kiss.

They were silent, in that moment, looking very intently into each other's eyes, and Elizabeth felt a little of that quivering sensation in her stomach again, a little of that racing heart she had felt when she read his words of love. Never had she felt more optimism towards their night together than she did now, and she found herself exceedingly grateful towards Jane, right up until her sister returned:

"Mr. Darcy! I hope you do not mind – I asked your undergardener for a few clippings," Jane called out, entering through the gate with a handful of flowers, Charles a few steps behind her.

Elizabeth and Mr. Darcy rapidly turned back toward the path and resumed walking, and he told Jane he did not mind at all, promising she should have whatever flowers she preferred from any of his gardens. Following this, the party returned to the house and separated, to meet again in the drawing-room before dinner. Elizabeth went upstairs and rang the bell, found Rachel prompt in answering, and asked if it would be possible to have a bath drawn for her in her dressing-room.

"Oh, but they are just fetching the water for Mr. Darcy's bath," Rachel said. "So it may be a little while, but we shall have the water up for yours as soon as possible, ma'am."

Rachel spoke as though she would be disappointing Mrs. Collins, but in truth Elizabeth was glad to hear what the maid had said. That Mr. Darcy would bathe either meant he had listened carefully to her account of what she had disliked, or his hygiene was such that he would have done so anyway, and either was a positive sign.

She was surprised when not a quarter-hour later, a succession of footmen came into the dressing-room that adjoined her bedchamber, carrying buckets of steaming water. Rachel followed them, and said, "Mr. Darcy said his guest was to have her bath filled first."

"That was very kind of him," Elizabeth said.

The bath was filled, and Rachel ensured Elizabeth had all she needed, informing her charge before she left that bottles of lavender water, rose water, and orange flower water had been left on the dressing cabinet for Elizabeth's use if she wished them, as well as the soap for her bath. When Rachel had exited, Elizabeth removed her shift and climbed into the bath, sinking down gratefully into the warm water and staying there until it began to grow cold. After climbing out and drying herself, she considered the various waters on the dressing cabinet and chose rose, for it seemed most in harmony with this place. She splashed it lightly upon her person, donned her shift, and went to ring for Rachel, feeling much better prepared for that night.

To be ready, and then to sit through dinner, through cards in the drawing-room and a small supper to close the evening, was to have the dread, slowly but strongly, return to Elizabeth's stomach. Jane's nervous glances toward her sister were kindly meant, but only increased Elizabeth's agitation, and by the time she had returned to her room and been changed by Rachel, she was so nervous she was nearly shaking. Once again, she resorted to taking a glass of wine, in pursuit of some measure of equanimity. She tried to remind herself of Mr. Darcy's kisses, of his calling her beautiful, but it was far older memories that imposed themselves upon her.

She started, when his knock on the door finally came, and opened the door to find a man who looked even more tense than she, so tense he very nearly looked ill, and now she felt the deepest sympathy for him, saying, once he had closed the door: "Mr. Darcy, I fear I have put you in an impossible situation. If things do not go well tonight, we should try again tomorrow. We should try again as long as I can bear it."

He nodded, and seemed to visibly relax, motioning toward the chaise. "Perhaps we should talk a little, first."

She followed him there, and tried to sit a little closer than she had the night before. He *was* handsome – it was not the most important quality of his, in her estimation, but she was struck with it now, as she looked at him.

"Do you mind?" he asked, motioning about his cravat, and when Elizabeth said she did not, removing it. It struck her as equal parts sweet and absurd, that he should ask to remove one garment that must have been most restricting, when she wore nothing but her nightgown. Once he had unwound the fabric from his throat and draped it over the back of the chaise, however, they suffered for a topic on which to speak.

"How is Chip? Does he miss me?" he asked, finally.

Elizabeth laughed. "I cannot say that he does."

"No, I suppose he would not. He has a very handsome mistress, who spoils him, and it is natural his attachment should be strongest to her."

"His attachment is to anyone who will scratch him behind his ears or feed him apples, and you have not been around to do either of those things."

"Give him my apologies. Tell him I was required to return to my home and prepare it for the most important of visitors."

"It is a very beautiful home," Elizabeth said. "I have so enjoyed all I have seen today."

"I am glad you did. It is very important to me that you approve of it."

It seemed to hang unspoken between them, that same thing Elizabeth had thought earlier, which was that this night would determine whether she would continue to enjoy all Pemberley had to offer for the remainder of her life. Still, sitting here – away from the bed – and talking in the way they usually did had relaxed her, and she was glad he had suggested it.

Elizabeth looked at him, and although she did not desire all the rest that would come that night, she did wish for him to kiss her again, and he seemed to sense this. Allowed more time than he had been in the garden, he caressed both of her cheeks with his hands, he ran a thumb over her lips, even more slowly than he had last night, he drew closer to her, and shortly after Elizabeth closed her eyes, she felt his lips touch hers. This kiss continued on for much longer, but as it continued to be wonderful, Elizabeth found herself parting her lips, found him very gradually deepening the kiss. He tasted of brandy. It was a pleasant taste. Indeed, every sensation she could feel now was exceedingly pleasant.

He drew back and looked carefully at her, as though to ascertain she had not yet been discomfited, and then spent some time in caressing her neck, eventually reaching her braided hair.

"May I?" he asked, and she nodded, feeling him pull the plait toward him so he could untie it. He let the braid out slowly, and Elizabeth was surprised at how very delightful it felt, to have a man's hands in her hair. Oh, if marital relations were nothing but this, these genteel little acts with a handsome man!

One of his hands had returned to her neck, and he wanted to kiss her again, a kiss Elizabeth very much desired returning. When he had finished with her mouth, however, Elizabeth found he had not at all finished with kissing her, for her neck, her throat, and then her collarbone were to follow. She should have grown accustomed to the feel of his lips upon her skin, but every kiss seemed to further erode her poise, to loosen whatever lingering tension remained within her. He went still lower, and she gasped, realising she felt not only that trembling in her stomach, but also the strangest sensation between her legs.

Somehow, one of his hands found hers, and he asked, "Elizabeth, are you well?"

"I am very, very well," she said, quite breathless, and unable to catch her breath entirely, for he resumed kissing her décolletage, and cupped one of her breasts in his hand. Her nightgown was of fine muslin, and when his thumb grazed her nipple, she felt it acutely. She gasped again, and found the sensation between her legs had become an ache, gradually building as he transferred his attentions to her other breast.

How long things continued in this manner, Elizabeth did not know, but she revelled in the sensations, as the ache between her legs grew to throbbing. He ran his hand down her stomach, over her mound, resting his fingers on the place that was throbbing, and rather than recoiling at the touch, Elizabeth shifted her hips to meet it. What had become of her? To desire his touch in such a place, to feel its lack, when he withdrew his hand – how had this happened? Elizabeth did not know, but she thought she had only desire, and not fear, in her head.

"Lie back," he whispered, encouraging her with his hands to recline against the chaise, and now the fear returned so rapidly it overwhelmed her. *He will pull your nightgown up, lay himself upon you, and enter you, right here on the chaise*, she thought, and all of her plans, all of her preparation, were nothing against such panic. All she managed to do in reaction was to draw her legs close together and say, "I'm not – I'm not ready – please – "

"Elizabeth." He gently laid his hand upon her cheek. "I have waited for a very long time to be with you, and I do not intend to rush this, nor to require you to do anything you do not wish to do. When the time comes for our union, I want it to be your choice."

She nodded sheepishly, noting, now that she was thinking more rationally, that he had yet to remove anything beyond his cravat, and that someone with so much self-command as he possessed should be able to wait until he was in a greater state of undress and they had moved to the bed, at the very least. "I am sorry – I overreacted."

"Do not be sorry," said he, now caressing her cheek. "I think it is a very brave thing you are doing, Elizabeth."

"I do not believe most people would say so; it should not be an act of bravery, to lie with a man who loves you, and whom you love in return, particularly when he has already offered you marriage."

"I meant everything you are doing – yes, lying with a man again, after disliking it so, but also merely to contemplate marrying again. I have been thinking, since we spoke at Netherfield, and I understand better what I have asked you to give up. I hope you will allow me to tell you how much I appreciate your willingness to even consider it, and I promise you that I will endeavour to make the sacrifice as minimal as possible. Elizabeth, you must know how very much I abhor the thought of you suffering at any man's hands, and I could not bear it if you did so under my own. If you dislike *anything* that I do – now, or in the future – please speak. You need only speak, and I will stop."

Tearfully, she nodded. *You must trust him*, she told herself. *He is not his predecessor. He loves you so very much, and he has only ever acted out of that love.* Feeling the emotion of these thoughts, she leaned forward until her lips met his, for an exceedingly long kiss. In kissing him, she thought perhaps he was in as much need of reassurance as she was; her sudden fear must have startled him even more than it had startled her, although he had been so very solicitous. Knowing she must be the one to allow things to progress, Elizabeth eventually ended the kiss and leaned back against the chaise, giving him a look she hoped communicated her trust in him.

"I just want to touch you," he murmured. "Just with my hands, for now. May I?"

"Yes," she whispered, and her trust proved to be most thoroughly warranted, for one of his hands again found hers and clasped it, while the other came to rest lightly on her ankle. Although Elizabeth had told him he could touch her, he seemed to be watching her carefully, to ensure she was not discomfited, and when he could see she was not, he began stroking her calf, languidly caressing her skin, which resulted in the most wonderful sensations. Elizabeth felt herself returning to the state she had been in before, felt that curious ache building again between her legs, and his hand trailed up to her thigh, pushing her nightgown up along her legs, going ever closer to the ache, but slowly, painstakingly slowly, so that the ache only grew and grew.

Then one of his fingers touched her where she had most been longing to be touched, and it felt so good as to be completely overwhelming. Her hips writhed, and she felt the hand that had been holding hers grasp it ever more tightly. Elizabeth's eyes had for some time been closed, as she had lost herself to the sensations of his touch, but she opened them now and found he was gazing at her, waiting for her to acquiesce to his continuing. She nodded, and his finger once again slipped within her slit, stroking her there, and she was once again required to close her eyes, for the sensation was almost unbearable, yet she did not want him to stop.

Then he slipped the finger inside her, leaving his thumb to continue with its prior ministrations, and Elizabeth realised that all that had come before this had led her to become incredibly wet between her legs. She observed this very nearly like a natural philosopher, the curious part of her brain registering it before his slickened thumb increased its pace, and she felt him slide a second finger inside her. Then there was no room for the curious part of her brain, for all her mind was capable of registering was pleasure: impossible, unprecedented, incredible pleasure.

Elizabeth could feel it was all building to something, the sensations becoming more and more incredible, but she did not know what, until suddenly it felt as though something had broken loose inside of her, and every fibre of her body was tingling in a most exquisite manner, and this was followed by a series of convulsions that shook her entire being. She would have been worried, if it had not been the most wonderful set of sensations she had ever experienced.

"Elizabeth, Elizabeth, dearest Elizabeth." He had withdrawn his hand, the one that had been pleasuring her, although the other continued to grasp hers tightly. She opened her eyes and found he was gazing at her with some uncertainty. Once he could see she was well, he was kissing her again, and she returned the kiss ardently, without any hesitation. He released her hand, but only so he could wrap his arms about her, drawing her close to him, murmuring her name again.

What had happened had seemed to draw all rational thought from her mind, and left her clinging limply to him for a little while. When she felt more recovered, she drew back a little and said: "Well Mr. Darcy, you have found a way to render me entirely speechless."

"Are you still to call me Mr. Darcy, even now?"

"Why should I not? It is a name with which I have every possible pleasant association."

"I hope it shall always continue to be so," he said, taking up the hand he had held so carefully during those most delicate intimacies, and kissing it several times.

This all reminded Elizabeth that there was still more to go, more he was likely impatient to reach, and more she felt herself better ready for; she had never felt so thoroughly relaxed in her life as she did at present. It had been wonderful of him to pleasure her in such a way – Elizabeth had not entirely believed her sister, but Jane had been right, that a woman could feel as much pleasure as a man – oh, so very much pleasure! – but now it must be his turn to take his pleasure. Mr. Darcy was an incredibly patient man, however, and she understood it must be her to suggest they proceed.

"Should we – ?" she looked in the direction of the bed.

"Perhaps we should wait until tomorrow night," he said, entirely stunning her. That he could be so selfless as to pleasure her in such a way and then wait for his own release seemed impossible – even for him – and she began to wonder what else might be the cause.

"Is it – do you not find me desirable?" she asked, hesitantly, fearing that perhaps he was not aroused by such a reluctant partner. Then she laid her hand on his knee, more heavily than he had done to her earlier that day, seeking to show him she was not so reluctant, now.

"Good God, Elizabeth, you must not ever think that," he said, hastily removing her hand and standing. He walked stiffly away from the chaise, his shoulders shaking as he took a long, ragged breath, and then he turned back toward her. "There is hardly a moment when I am in your presence that I do not find you exceedingly desirable."

His eyes were darkly ardent, and far from the only sign that arousal was not the cause of his reluctance. He had allowed his self-command to slip, and in his expression, even more than his words, Elizabeth understood the full extent of his desire for her: it was every bit as strong as his love. She opened her mouth, but could not manage to speak, and she watched him breathe deeply again, seeming to summon some power over himself, for he returned to the chaise and seated himself beside her, taking up her hand.

"Elizabeth, you have granted me additional nights, and I am inclined to use them – to make good on my promise not to rush this. This is too important to rush."

Elizabeth thought she could feel her heart swell. "That is entirely too good of you, but I do not wish to stop. Everything has been so different, tonight. I *feel* so very different. I want to know – I want to know if the act itself is different. I want to wake up in the morning and know whether I am to be your wife in the way I want to be. Now that I know what I do, I could not bear to spend another day without knowing everything."

"Are you sure?" he asked, squeezing her hand.

"Yes, I am. And it is not just for myself that I wish to continue – there are your needs, to consider."

"My needs are not important on this night."

"They are to me," she whispered, and only in saying it did she fully understand it. She had begun the night fearing the possibility of its being uncomfortable for her, but now that he had done this – this amazing thing – for her, she was aware of a desire to reciprocate, a desire to give him what he so clearly wanted and yet had been willing to sacrifice, and a willingness to bear at least a little discomfort to do so.

"Elizabeth, it is *you*, who is wonderful," he said. "If you do wish to continue, then we shall, for now, but you must tell me if you want to stop. I would be loath to damage such a beginning."

She replied that she would tell him if she wished to stop, and he asked her if she was ready to move to the bed.

"I am, but I think you are not." She touched the cuff of his coat.

"Yes, of course," he said, laughing softly. "Give me a few minutes. I understand if you would need to – to relieve yourself – while you wait."

Elizabeth did need to do so, she realised, and was glad at his indication that he understood this was necessary. She did not know how long they had been going about the act – if it could even be called *the* act, when it seemed there were so many things that might be involved – but it was certainly far longer than her prior experiences. She had always thought it a good thing, a merciful thing, that marital relations had not lasted very long, but on this night – this long, beautiful night – she was glad things had gone so slowly.

Standing on legs that proved to be rather shaky, Elizabeth went through the door to the dressing-room rather than using the chamber pot in the nightstand, for she was not nearly ready for that sort of intimacy. When she returned, she saw he had draped his coat and waistcoat over the back of the chaise, and was removing his shoes. There was a fastidiousness to his actions that seemed wholly incongruous with the man who had touched her in such ways, earlier, a man who had looked at her with such a darkly desirous countenance. He was, she thought, a man with such a veneer of reserve to him, a veneer so strong she had not seen beneath it, in her earlier acquaintance with him; she had not understood that beneath it all he was a man of the deepest passions. A man who felt those deep passions for her, and yet loved her enough – and possessed the strength – to suppress those passions, to treat her with such patience as he had shown tonight.

She went to the bed to wait for him, and before she climbed in, found herself facing a decision she had not anticipated. Before, she had always worn her nightgown, not liking to leave any more of herself bare to her husband than necessary, and then he had pushed it up far enough to allow himself access to what he wanted. Elizabeth shook her head – she should not be recalling such memories now – and decided in that moment that she would remove it. She had liked being touched by Mr. Darcy thus far, and she had found it very – very arousing – when he touched her bare skin. So she pulled it over her head, dropping it on the floor, and then she climbed into bed.

There, she laid back against the pillows to wait, and felt a rush of embarrassment when it seemed he was to climb into bed without his trousers, but still wearing his shirt. What must he think of her, to have disrobed herself so?

But he said, "My God, look at you," and did so, his countenance a mixture of adoration and desire, the latter returned to something near its former intensity. Elizabeth felt her heart pounding and tried now to remember all of her preparation, tried not to be intimidated at being so evidently wanted. The bed was large – larger than any at Longbourn – and he crawled across it, Elizabeth bracing herself, for surely he was to mount her now. Surely it would be easier, for his earlier ministrations had made her so very wet between her legs that she had not even given the sweet oil a thought until now, but Elizabeth could not be entirely optimistic about that which had been so unpleasant so many times.

He did not mount her, though. Instead he came up beside her and appreciated her with his hands as he had done with his eyes, grazing his fingertips along the curves of her breasts, her belly, her hips. Elizabeth found herself very glad she had removed her nightgown, and felt the throbbing between her legs grow anew. It grew more substantial yet when he placed one hand on the bed beside her, to steady himself when he leaned over her and applied his mouth to her breast. She moaned at the feel of his tongue circling her nipple, and could not help but notice that he remained balanced above her – he had yet to put his weight upon her at all.

"I think you should – I am ready for – " she said, as best she could, when she found the throbbing had reached the point where it seemed his entering her might actually be a good thing, might lessen the ache, and at this moment Elizabeth thought this could truly work, that she might even *enjoy* the bedchamber, with him.

"Are you sure, Elizabeth? We can still stop, if you wish it."

"I am sure."

He drew back, so he was kneeling before her, and removed his shirt, placing it beside him on the bed. Elizabeth appreciated this first look at him very much, the muscular arms, the taut definition that comprised his chest and stomach. Then she had her first sight of his rod, large, and very, very ready, and all of her newfound optimism dissipated. Her breathing quickened, but from tension, and not desire.

He touched her hand, and it was only then that she realised she had been clutching it in a fist. "Relax, Elizabeth. Rise up, and come here to me."

She did, so that she was kneeling as well, facing him, and she waited, for this was all most irregular to her. He leaned in to kiss her, on the mouth, this time, although stroking her breasts with his hands as he did so, and Elizabeth, hesitantly at first, reached out to make her own explorations, finding his skin hot and firm beneath her fingertips. She relaxed, again, and when the kiss ended, she thought to attend him with her mouth as he had her, planting a hesitant kiss upon his neck, which prompted him to whisper her name. Elizabeth kissed him there a second time, and as she did this, she was reminded of scent, something that had previously not been anything she needed to be reminded of, for it had imposed itself upon her. Yet even her deepest inhalations, with her lips pressed against Mr. Darcy's neck, brought her only hints of soap, of bay rum, of man. She found this mixture of scents rather pleasant, but her attention was diverted from them when he laid his hand upon her thigh, reminding her of the throbbing between her legs.

"Elizabeth, if you are ready, you may put me inside you – at your own pace," he said, softly.

"I am ready, but – here? While we are seated?"

"Yes, here – like this." He put his hands beneath her thighs, and pulled her forward, onto his lap, so she could feel the firmness of his rod between them. It seemed a very strange way to go about things, but she understood better what he meant, now, and shifted her feet so they were on either side of his hips, enabling her some little leverage to rise up. He helped her, sliding his hands beneath her bottom and supporting her there as she took his rod up in her hand and found it hotter than the rest of him, and twitching at her first touch, which startled her. He groaned painfully as this happened, and although he had told her to go at her own pace, Elizabeth did not wish to prolong things more than was needed – she had no idea how long he had been in such a state, and marvelled at his patience.

Still, she had not been expecting to have the responsibility for this part – although she understood why he had given it over to her, and she loved him for it – and it was with some hesitation that she aligned him with her entrance, and put the tip of him in. To her surprise, she found this to be more pleasurable than not, and braced herself, lowering her hips down slowly, finding her wetness even more of an aid than she had expected. It was not enough to prevent her reaching a point where she felt discomfort, for she did, and was required to stop for a moment. She shifted a little, to change the angle of his entry, found this helped, and continued on, listening to him as he murmured to her to relax. She watched him, as well, and found his face increasingly overcome with what seemed ecstasy as she progressed, until finally he closed his eyes and moaned deep in his throat, slipping his hands from her bottom as it came to rest upon his thighs.

Elizabeth had taken the whole of him in, and rather than feeling any pain, she felt full, pleasantly full; more than this, she realised: she felt complete, and most intimately connected to the man she loved, with his chest pressed against hers, his body between her thighs, and that deeper connection that had so affected him that only now did he open his eyes and look at her.

"Are you well, Elizabeth? Is there any pain at all?"

"No – none at all," she said, finding her only discomfort now was that her knees were bent in a slightly awkward fashion, and she shifted her feet until she felt more comfortable. This brought him just the slightest bit deeper inside her, but still it did not hurt, and for a moment she felt entirely overcome with a pure, simple sort of happiness, for she felt almost certain she would be able to have her heart's desire.

Then he kissed her again, and Elizabeth found that although she had thought this a strange manner of coupling, she liked it. It maintained this wonderful closeness to him, without his being on top of her, letting her look him in the eyes and put her arms around him, and him to do the same to her. Holding her close, his bare skin against hers both soothing and arousing, he kissed her once again, and then began to move inside her, rocking up and down from his kneeling position on the bed.

Elizabeth had been prepared to judge this portion of the night on whether there was any pain, and as there was not, liked those first few movements only because they seemed to give him an immense amount of pleasure. Then he put his hands on her bottom and rocked her hips in time with his motion, creating a sensation so exquisite, she cried, "Oh!"

He stopped immediately. "Have I hurt you?"

"No, the opposite. That felt – that felt – I can hardly describe how it felt, but I would like very much for you to do it again if you can." Elizabeth could not tell if her blush was specific, to say this to him, or if she was just becoming overheated from the overall act, but her face felt tremendously hot.

"Like this?" he asked, and did it again.

"Oh! Oh yes, like that, please, yes, like that," she gasped.

He proceeded to do precisely that for some time, gradually increasing his pace, groaning low in his throat with each movement, several times murmuring her name with a sensual sort of reverence. Elizabeth realised she was moaning herself, almost in unison with him, and that this seemed to further enhance his reactions. Once again, she had become a creature she did not recognise, to take such enjoyment from this as to begin to move her hips of her own volition, enhancing his efforts and creating the most exquisite sensations deep within her. She kissed him, then, kissed him with desperate passion as they moved together, kissed him in both love and gratitude, for making her feel better than she had ever understood she could feel, for being the man that he was.

That wondrous thing that had happened to her before happened again, and this time it seemed to come from even deeper inside her, and with such an intensity she cried out. It seemed to go on for longer, as well, with her gasping and quaking against his chest, feeling her insides pulse around him as he moved inside her once, twice more, closed his eyes, and with a tremendous groan, loosed his seed inside her.

He held her close, after that, and Elizabeth laid her head on his shoulder and wept.

Eventually, she became aware of him stroking her neck, her shoulder. "Are you well, Elizabeth?"

"That was the most wonderful experience of my life," she whispered. "I am sorry if I worried you – I am just a little overcome."

"It was the most wonderful experience of my life as well," he said, and resumed stroking her shoulder.

"I once thought you inconsiderate. I could not have been more wrong," she said. "I love you. I love you so very much."

"But will you marry me?"

"Yes, oh yes, I certainly will."

"Thank God," he said. "Oh, thank God! I love you, Elizabeth, and there is nothing I desire more in this world than to see you are pleased, and happy, and safe, and I promise I will endeavour to do this every day – and every night that you wish it."

He kissed her, then, with an ardour even beyond that of what had come before, kissed her until she was breathless, and Elizabeth knew the happiness of having made the man she loved so incredibly happy.

Eventually, he broke the kiss, and it was to say, "Elizabeth, I loathe the thought of ending this moment, but I find my legs are tingling, and not in a pleasant way."

"Oh, I am so sorry!" she said, and somewhat clumsily made to get off of him, feeling the absence of their connection as she did so, and immediately missing that which she had presumed she would dislike, before all that had just passed. "I am glad you did, but I wonder at how you managed to do this. You must be terribly strong."

"There are some advantages to riding horses so much as I do." He rose from his kneeling position and seated himself more naturally on the bed, wiping himself clean of the remnants of his seed with his discarded shirt.

"I told you not to attempt to make a horse-rider out of me, but I suppose I must be pleased you are such yourself."

"I am glad that you are – pleased, that is," he said. He had finished cleaning himself with the shirt, and now hesitantly placed it between her thighs, looking her in the eyes, and, when she did not protest, delicately swabbing the remnants of their coupling from her legs.

Somehow, this act felt every bit as intimate as anything else they had done that night, and yet there was something about it Elizabeth disliked, as though he was removing the evidence of their union, a union she now found most important. She understood why he did it – it would not do for the maids to find her sheets stained and stiffened with his seed – but now she longed for a day when such actions would not be necessary, when the maids would find the evidence of the natural actions of a married couple, a couple who could remain together through the night, as she and Mr. Darcy could not, presently. She was his mistress, for now – a strange sort of temporary mistress – and she longed deeply to become his wife.

"I know you will need to go back to your apartment," she said, when these thoughts had thoroughly imposed themselves upon her, "but will you stay with me for a little while?"

"Of course. Do you wish to lie together? Not in that way – but just to be together, before I must leave?"

Elizabeth desired this very much, but in her present sated, exhausted state, she could only nod languidly. Once he had laid back against the pillows, she crawled up beside him and laid her head upon his shoulder, experiencing the lingering effects of all that had happened that night, a looseness in her limbs, a feeling of the deepest satisfaction, fulfilment, and love. They laid there together quietly, him stroking her arm with the lightest of touches, a sensation that seemed a delicate echo of all that had come before. Elizabeth wondered how the same act could be so very different with two different men. Mr. Darcy had been right, that marriage could be different with a man who loved her: everything could be different with a man who loved her. She smiled, and found her eyes so tired, she thought she would just close them for a moment, to rest them.

When she awoke, it was to a darkened bedchamber, and the bedcovers pulled up around her naked form. When with *him*, Elizabeth had come to enjoy her nakedness, had enjoyed his reaction to it and his skin against hers, but now it seemed lonely and discomfiting to be in such a state. Rising from the bed, she found her nightgown had been neatly folded and laid upon the nightstand, and put it on.

She went to the window, feeling the autumn chill through the glass and staring out over what little of Pemberley's grounds she could see in the moonlight. Between her thighs there was a mild soreness, but it was not an unpleasant soreness; it was a most physical reminder that Mr. Darcy had been there. He had been there and he had touched her, loved her, and roused something deep within her.

And then he had left her. It was impossible to avoid a momentary feeling of panic, of worry, even of betrayal, at this thought. She had lain with him and then he had left her, and some deep-seated female instinct within her felt all of these emotions in rapid succession. A moment's reflection recalled her to her own situation: it had been Elizabeth who had proposed this night; *he* had always wished to marry her, and had even offered her a celibate marriage; *he* had been overjoyed at her saying she would marry him, and a man who had been in love with her for all these years would never forsake her in the morning's light, particularly after a night in which he had undoubtedly achieved his own satisfaction.

That panic quelled, she felt that certain hollow exhaustion she knew all too well enveloping her person. She returned to the bed, lying down quietly and tracing her fingertips over linen of the finest quality, recalling in passionate detail the loveliest moments she had experienced in this bed, and yet inevitably missing her partner in these experiences. For the first time in her life, Elizabeth found herself saddened by the empty pillow before her, and it was some time before she returned to sleep.

CHAPTER 13

September 15, 1815

Darcy woke late, later, perhaps, than he had ever done, so late he had some concern over everyone in the house wondering what had prompted his absence. After having achieved his every desire last night, he had felt so relieved and so sated that sleep had seemed to wish to seize him and drag him down into its depths, particularly after Elizabeth had fallen asleep upon his shoulder. It had been the greatest temptation to remain in the room with her, to sleep with her in that manner, and he had been required to summon a great deal of self-command in order to slip out from beneath her, to cover her and dress himself.

To his great relief, he had not encountered anyone in the hallway, for he did not know how he would have explained his dishevelled appearance, that he was carrying his thoroughly soiled shirt, with his cravat wrapped around his neck and tucked into his waistcoat as a poor substitute. Aching with exhaustion, he did not think he had remained awake for a full minute, once he had finally climbed into his own bed, and in that time, he could only think that he had succeeded, that she had agreed to marry him, and in such a manner as to make him have no concerns in this morning's light that she would change her mind.

The morning sun had heated the room, and Darcy threw off his bedcovers, but made no further move to rise. Although he should have begun his already-late day, he could not bring himself to do so: there were far too many things he wished to recollect in privacy, so many memories of that wonderful, wonderful night.

It was not gentlemanly to speak of marital relations with one's wife, but genteel behaviour diminished with enough drink, and Darcy had heard rather numerous tales of frigid wives, both at White's and around dining tables, once the ladies had departed. Before last night, he had not been entirely sure whether all of Elizabeth's reluctance was due to Collins's ineptitude or indifference, or whether there was some natural frigidity to her. It had seemed very unlike Elizabeth's personality to be so, however, and he had hoped for a better response from her, once presented with a more loving partner. Now, he could not help but wonder if most of those frigid wives were indeed the fault of their husbands.

How wonderfully she had responded to him! He had read so much, but feared his lack of actual practise would expose him as incompetent and awkward, but both the things he had planned to do and those he had found himself desiring to do, in the sensations of the moment, had all evoked such beautiful reactions from her. How delightful it had been, to bring her such pleasure, and when he had slipped his finger inside her and felt how tremendously wet she was, he had thought then that all could come right of their union. He had relished watching her response to being touched in such a place, and proud that her pleasure was his doing. Ever since he had come to understand his former character, he had been vigilant against pride, but surely it was honourable to take some pride in eliciting such reactions from his love. Perhaps this would now become his outlet, for his natural pride; there was something very satisfying to the male ego – to his male ego, at least – in seeing Elizabeth so affected by his attentions.

It had not all gone perfectly, of course – he could still recall that moment when her fear, always lurking there below the surface, had emerged, and he had thought everything ruined. He had been terribly glad she had taken the pressure off of him, in promising additional nights if things did not go well, and never more glad than in that moment. Those additional attempts were not necessary, though, for she – his bravest, loveliest Elizabeth! – had trusted him, had laid back on the chaise and allowed all of the wonderful things that had followed, had wished to continue even when he had offered to stop and end on such a pleasant note.

On the whole, it had been far better than he had hoped for, and he thought now that the real Elizabeth might, in time, come to more closely resemble the Elizabeth of his fantasies, the young, passionate woman who desired him, and was confident in her desires. She had gone from touching him so hesitantly – yet oh, how very stimulating even that had been – to moving with him as he had moved within her. This had been most unexpected. He had gone into their coupling planning that if she was at all discomfited, they should stop, and if she was not, that he would seek his own release as quickly as possible, so as not to prolong the experience for her. He had been as surprised by her finding pleasure in it as it seemed she had been, and after that he had summoned the willpower to hold out for as long as he could, so he could continue pleasing her. In this, their position had aided him – their motions were less vigorous than he had known in his limited prior experience – but his partner had not. To be there, inside *Elizabeth*, to have her naked form pressed against him and see her truly enjoy his cock had brought him very nearly over the edge several times.

He had held out, however, and that had caused both the most wondrous and the most worrying thing that had happened last night, that she had been so pleased as to cry out in her climax. At that moment, he had lost control of his own body, although thankfully it no longer mattered. Hearing her cry out, knowing it had been him to make her do so, feeling her convulsing around his cock, had immediately driven him to his own most exquisite release. And yet it was very possible she had been overheard, although he had placed the Bingleys in another wing. Nothing was to be done of it now, however; it had happened, and if anyone did suspect what Mr. Darcy and Mrs. Collins had been about in the night, they would soon enough think it merely anticipating their vows, which could not be considered a particularly scandalous act with a widow fully out of mourning.

Mrs. Collins – how very glad he would be to have that name become *Mrs. Darcy*. He was saddened, then, to think of how it might have been Mrs. Darcy much sooner, if he had managed matters better. How much was he to blame, for all she had suffered as Mrs. Collins, for failing to give her the choice he had wished to? He meditated on this in guilt for some time, before requiring himself to stop. Today was a day for the happiest of thoughts. He could not change the past, but he could have every influence over Elizabeth's future happiness, and it was time to rise from bed and get about it.

Mrs. Bingley and Elizabeth were still in the breakfast room when Darcy – dressed by one of his footmen, Henry, who had seemed entirely perplexed at his master's hour of rising, but had of course not commented upon it – walked in. Darcy had the sense immediately that he had interrupted a tête-à-tête between the sisters, and he had strong presumptions as to what the topic had been, particularly since it appeared the footman who should have been in attendance had already been dismissed. Perhaps, then, at least one of the Bingleys would have known what he was about in the night regardless of whether Elizabeth had been overheard.

Elizabeth looked up at him, her eyes so filled with tender adoration that he knew now a pleasing sensation in his chest, the opposite of the pain he had felt there so many times before. He smiled to her, and wanted very badly to kiss her, but was required to merely greet them both and take up his food from the sideboard.

When he had seated himself, he said, "I apologise for my late arrival. I had – " Elizabeth was looking at him now through lowered lashes, an expression of great amusement upon her face, and this made it very difficult to continue " – I had a matter to attend to."

"Do not worry yourself over it, Mr. Darcy," Elizabeth said, her voice thick with what was surely suppressed laughter.

"I had wondered if you would wish to see more of the house today, although I would understand if you prefer to be out of doors, for it looks to be another fine day."

"I would very much like to see more of the house," Elizabeth said.

"Oh, I fear I must make my regrets – Charles and I were intending to go for a long ride this morning. He had gone down to the stables to see if a suitable mount could be found for me. Lizzy, I hope you do not mind?"

"No, of course not. You should enjoy your ride."

Darcy was fairly certain that at least some of this must have been decided upon prior to his entrance, but if there was a conspiracy between the two sisters that Mr. Darcy show Mrs. Collins the house without anyone's accompaniment, Darcy was perfectly pleased by it. His purpose had been that Elizabeth see it more thoroughly, particularly the master's and mistress's apartments, and they discuss how much of their married life was to be spent here, versus Longbourn, and this would be much more easily accomplished if it was only the two of them.

He ate hastily, and was very nearly done when Charles entered, greeting his friend and saying that the horses were arranged. The Bingleys took their leave, therefore, and once the door had closed behind them, Darcy gazed at his future bride, not sure if he was to have the tender Elizabeth of his entrance, or the one who had teased him with her eyes shortly thereafter. He did not mind which, for he loved them both.

"I missed you, when I woke," she said, softly; the tender Elizabeth, then.

"It was very difficult for me to leave you," he said, "but soon enough, we may stay together."

"How soon would you wish to be married?"

"As soon as you wish. If you desired me to have my carriage readied to go into Chester and procure a licence, I would ring the bell for it now."

She laughed. "Not quite that soon, perhaps – it is not that I do not wish to be married to you right away, but I would like for my sisters to have a chance to be bridesmaids in a happier time. Perhaps we could marry by licence once they are able to join us? I presume we must be married from here, else your guests will think you an abominable host."

"I suppose we must, so long as you do not mind it – " she replied that she did not – "I find that a more prudent timeframe, as well. It will give us more time to prepare, and I want to be very careful with the marriage contract. Elizabeth, there is something I want to promise you of now, although I will wish you to review the contract and tell me if there is anything within that concerns or displeases you. However, I want you to know that Longbourn shall remain in your name alone – it will be yours to run as you see fit, and the profits yours to do with as you please."

Tears welled in her eyes, and as he had not sat near enough to her to take up her hand, he moved to do so.

"Mr. Darcy – I – thank you. I would not have thought to ask that of you, but I love that you have offered it. I do have one condition, though, or rather, two."

"Name them, please, so I may grant them."

"My first condition is that you continue to assist me, as you have been, and my second is that Chip and my phaeton be brought here to Pemberley, where I may enjoy the use of them more often. And then you may drive us about, when we return to visit Longbourn – I had thought two or three times a year?"

"Elizabeth, are you certain? I had assumed you would wish to spend more of our time at Longbourn, or at the very least divide it between the two estates." This was far more than he had hoped for; Pemberley had been his home for his entire life, a much-beloved home, but he had resigned himself that much less time must be spent here if he married her. On the balance, it would have been an easy sacrifice, and yet now it seemed one he would not have to make.

"I am sure. Longbourn has many memories for me – some good, and some bad. Here, though, everything is fresh and beautiful. I want to start a new life here with you. Indeed, I feel as though it has already begun, and it has been so wonderful."

This time it was she who kissed him, who laid those delicate, slender fingers upon his cheeks and leaned in close, pressing those soft lips against his. She still smelled of roses, stirring every pleasant memory of the night before. It was a sweet, lingering little kiss, which he was glad of, for a passionate one might have undone him. Rather than slaking his desire for her, he had found that having been with her the night before had made him eager to repeat the act as soon as it might be done, and he had resolved that they not do so until after they were wed, and even then, only so often as she desired it.

"If you change your mind, after having seen the whole of the house and your chambers, you must tell me," he said, when they separated.

"I will not change my mind – I have other reasons for my decision. The house at Longbourn may be returned to my mother's management, which will please her very much, and so long as she does not exceed the income I give her by *too* much, I shall not need to come begging to you for pin money."

"You will never need to beg for anything; ask for it and it will be yours. You must never hesitate to tell me of anything that might be done or procured for your pleasure."

"Chip and I shall enter into competition, to see who may be more spoiled."

"I will be very cross if you do not win."

"Then show me how I may be spoiled – show me your Pemberley."

Darcy wished for her to see the apartment that would be theirs, and then the library, but he did show her the principal rooms on their route thither. He found the hallway door to the mistress's bedchamber locked – the room had been closed after his mother's death, although it was cleaned periodically. He had briefly considered having it aired before Elizabeth arrived, but had feared such presumptiveness would have been risking his luck. How strange it was to remember now that until last night, everything had been dangerously uncertain.

He led her down the hall to the master's bedchamber, instead, to see the apartment from that end. Perhaps this was better, anyway, he thought – the mistress's bedchamber and dressing-room were terribly outdated, and he did not think she would prefer the style. Better to let her see his own taste, first, and then promise her that those rooms should be redone under her direction.

Elizabeth was pleased by his taste, he was glad to see, expressing her admiration of the décor, and the view from the windows. She trailed her hand across the bedpost as she was making her way about the room, and then looked over to him, her cheeks suffused with the loveliest shade of pink. So she, too, was thinking of what would occur in their marriage bed, of the many nights of happiness they had before them.

Darcy led her through to his dressing-room – such thoughts were dangerous, particularly when he was alone with her in his own bedchamber – and then to the private sitting-room that adjoined the two apartments. There, he found the door to the mistress's dressing-room also locked, and said, "I am sorry, you must think me ridiculous, to not even have access to rooms within my own house, and so near to my own, but they have been closed up for some years. Let me go and find Mrs. Reynolds: she will have the key. Are you comfortable waiting here?"

"Yes, very comfortable. I like this room very much – I think we will pass many happy hours here."

"I think we will, as well."

The proper thing to do would be to go to his dressing-room, ring for a servant, and have that servant go and fetch Mrs. Reynolds, but Darcy knew the rhythms of his house well; Mrs. Reynolds should be in the housekeeper's room at this hour, and if she was not there, he could ring the bell from his own study down the hall and have a servant arrive much more quickly to find her. So rather than keep Elizabeth waiting for longer, he went to fetch the key himself, finding Mrs. Reynolds in her room. She apologised, for she had known Mrs. Collins to be visiting the house as its prospective mistress, but Darcy bade her not to worry over it; it was one detail to mind amongst all those Mrs. Reynolds needed to attend to, in preparing for the house party, and she was not in the habit of needing to prepare for house parties. She had several questions she wished to ask him, regarding the arrangements for the next few weeks, and this required him to summon a great deal of patience in order to avoid giving her short answers, for he did not like to keep Elizabeth waiting.

It was as he was walking back to the apartment that he was reminded of the bookshelf in the sitting-room. He kept copies of some favourite volumes there, to have them nearer at hand than the library, but of late he had also been storing his Holywell Street books there. His stomach sank, and he increased his pace; he would have run, but for fear of encountering a servant and prompting worry. If Elizabeth saw them, she must surely think him depraved, to own them, so depraved, perhaps, that she would worry he had not shown her the full extent of his inclinations last night, that he would ask her to do some of the more outlandish things from the books. She had been a little uncertain, at first, over the manner in which he had asked her to go about their coupling, although he hoped she understood his reasons for it, that they had been for her. He hoped she had been distracted by something else in the room, or perhaps one of the more usual books on the shelf.

He entered the sitting-room and found things were even worse than he had feared, for she was seated upon the chaise, holding a piece of paper crumpled up within her hand, and sobbing miserably. Darcy suspected the cause of this; when he came closer, he saw the opened first volume of *Sir Charles Grandison* and had his suspicion confirmed. All those years ago, he had not disposed of the final draft of his letter to her, before copying it out fair; he had not been able to bring himself to do so, even after reading of her marriage, and so he had tucked it away in a favourite book and brought it here for safekeeping. For some time, he had forgotten of its presence there, and now he had the most painful reminder of it.

"I was looking through your books – there was a paper inside – I did not mean to pry." Elizabeth had noticed him, and in addition to looking terribly upset, she looked guilty, as well.

"It was not prying to look through books you would share soon. It is I who should apologise that it was there for you to find. I should have told you of my intentions during that time, I think, but it should not have come about in this manner."

"I wish you had sent it. Everything might have been different."

"I did send it. What you hold is the prior draft. I sent it under cover to your mother, and asked that it be given over to you. I suspect it was misdirected in the post, and she never received it."

"That is why you mentioned *in person*, when you spoke of your condolences," she said, and after he confirmed this, she asked, "Was there anything remarkable about your letter? Would it have been evident that it was from you, from Lady Catherine's nephew?"

"It would not have been identifiable as coming from her nephew, particularly – my aunt chose to revert to the Fitzwilliam seal after the death of her husband, but I have always used the Darcy seal," Darcy said, worried about where this line of questioning led. "The letter was franked, however. I wished to spare your family the expense at such a time, and solicited the assistance of a neighbour of mine."

"Oh, your intent was very honourable, but how I wish you had not done so! I believe that would have been sufficient to rouse his curiosity," Elizabeth said, in a wavering voice. "I am certain Collins destroyed it. He took on management of the post at Longbourn almost immediately, and he would have been very curious about my mother's receiving a franked letter."

In all the time he had thought over his letter, Darcy had not considered this possibility. That a man could act in such a manner, could intercept a letter addressed to another, was so deceitful he could hardly conceive of it. Yet it had been Elizabeth's first thought, and if a man could act so deceitfully, it did make sense to him. If Elizabeth had broken her engagement with Collins, it would have been that man who was embarrassed in his new neighbourhood, and she could never choose another if she did not know she had a choice.

"Do you think that the most likely scenario?" he asked.

"Yes, if it had been misdirected in the post, I believe it would have come to us eventually. I hardly know whether it would have been better or worse, for my mother to receive such a letter when I was nearer to my wedding, or worse, already married."

He had been so overwrought by all of this, he had not even managed to offer her his handkerchief, and he gave it over to her now. The doing of a simple, gentlemanly act, and that she was still willing to accept it from him, soothed him a little. There were still so many difficult things he would need to speak of, however.

"If you *had* received it, would you have chosen me?"

"I – I am not sure. I hope that I would have, but my opinion of you at that time was so completely different, and so completely wrong. If I would have chosen you, it would not have been for very honourable reasons, but rather because you had the more attractive face and figure, you had promised separate bedrooms, and I understood Pemberley to be a very large house, one in which we might have seen less of each other. I hope I might have seen it was better to marry an intelligent man I thought arrogant, rather than a foolish, pompous one. And your letter did show much more sympathy for my situation than I had – than I had received elsewhere, although you *should* have done more to speak of your love. This reads more like a business proposal than a confession of your heart."

"I did write of my affections," said he, defensively.

"The depth of love you have shown me should not be described as mere *affections*."

"I do not think I understood the full depth of my love until after I knew I had lost you. But in truth, I did not believe my love to be the most valuable thing I had to offer you, at that time. You had just lost your father, and Charles had just cut me down most thoroughly," Darcy said, reminded now that there was another thing from the past they needed to discuss. "I believe I thought my income and an establishment for your family more desirable than the love of a man such as me."

"Oh, Fitzwilliam, you must not think that. Your love is the most valuable thing I have ever known," she said, laying her hand over his. "And I do think if I had chosen you, I would have seen you for yourself soon enough. We could have been happy together so much sooner."

"For that, we have only me to blame. I was a coward, Elizabeth, and I would not go and ask you in person. You must have seen that my skill in conversation is not so good as that of others – I do not always express myself so well as I would like to, and I thought it would be better to write to you. In so doing, I left everything to chance – my happiness, and more critically, your own."

"You cannot blame yourself, my love. If you *had* come to Longbourn and declared yourself in person after I was betrothed to another, I cannot say that I would have reacted well, that I would have listened to your proposal with every proper consideration. I hope, again, that I would have, but what if I had refused you? Would you have returned to my presence and courted me in the manner that you did?"

"I do not know that I could have. Like you, I hope that I could, but such a rejection from you would have been difficult to put behind me."

"Then I think we must put it behind us, now – both of us. You loved me then, and you wished to provide me with a marriage that I would have, in time, been very happy in. That is all I wish to remember, and soon enough I will be in that marriage. We must not let the past ruin our future together."

She leaned forward to embrace him, the deepest comfort at a time when his thoughts were still swirling about all of the possible paths the past could have taken, rather than the one it had. But Darcy pulled away from her before he could lose himself in such comforts, before he lost his resolve.

"Elizabeth," he said, noting her confusion at how quickly he had separated himself from her, "before we finish speaking of the past, there is something else I believe we should speak of. You have never asked me about my role in separating Charles from your sister."

"Your role in *what*?" she asked, looking both confused and concerned. "I do not know what you are speaking of."

"The breach between Charles and I – I had presumed one of the Bingleys informed you of what prompted it," Darcy said, with a feeling of the deepest dread in his stomach.

"No, Jane only said you had done something you should not have done."

"Your sister is an even more excellent creature than I had realised, then," he said. "I must tell you now, however, for I would not wish this to be a secret between us, even if – even if it changes your opinion of me. After the first ball at Netherfield, all those years ago, I acted with Caroline Bingley to convince Charles to stay in town. At the time, I thought your sister indifferent to Charles – I saw no outward evidence of any affections on her side – and feared my friend would find himself in a match where both fortune and affections were unequal. Caroline and I endeavoured to convince Charles of this lack of affection, and to keep him separated from your sister. When he learned of it, he said a great many things to me that I needed to hear, and fortunately determined to make his own decisions as regarded your sister, for anyone who observes them now can see how much she loves him. I was wrong, and I interfered where I should not have interfered."

She gaped at him, and in that moment, Darcy feared that even after having gotten through what had seemed the difficult part – having gotten through last night – he was still going to lose her. That fear seized him in waves of cold panic, and he attempted to speak, to explain himself further:

"You see, your opinion of me back then was not completely wrong, Elizabeth. I was the man who tried to separate Charles from your sister. I was the man who spoke so rudely of you at the Meryton Assembly. I was that man, and I abhor him, now. I abhor him, and I am ashamed of him," Darcy said. "I did not know whether you had received my letter, but I thought it possible you had, and your opinion of me was so low that you did not even intend to respond. When I knew you were lost to me, it broke my heart, but I endeavoured to become a better man, to become a man who would have been worthy of you, because it was all I could do. Now I fear I have not done enough, or perhaps there is nothing I could have done to recover my character in your eyes from such an action. I know how close you are to your sister, I know how horrible my actions have been, and that I have made matters far worse for revealing this to you after you have lain with me – "

Elizabeth laid her hand on his cheek. "Shh, my love. My silence is surprise, and nothing else. I believe a part of me *wants* to feel anger, but I find I cannot – all I feel is love. I tried to make Jane tell me what you had done, and she refused to do so, for she thought you should not be judged now for your actions then. You are right that she is an excellent creature – she is the most excellent creature that ever lived! If *she* can forgive you, though, it is not my place to hold a grudge, particularly when you are so sincere in your remorse. You have done *everything* you should have, to improve your character, and I believe I love you more for it than I would have if your character had always been as it is now."

"Oh, Elizabeth, I know my wounds are of my own making, but no-one could ever heal them as you have just done."

"I am glad," she said. "The last few years have not been good for either of us, I think, but now I am so hopeful. Think only of the past as its remembrance gives you pleasure, and be hopeful with me. I believe we have such a beautiful future ahead of us."

"My darling Elizabeth, if you will still give me that future, I promise you it will be beautiful."

"There now, that is better, and of course I will," she said. "I am glad to see you be so sure of this."

"If I did not fully believe I could give you a beautiful future, I would not have asked you to marry me," he said. "You must know that I intend to spend the rest of my life endeavouring to make you happy."

"What of your own happiness? I promise I shall make my own endeavours, to see to it."

"I am sure you shall, but Elizabeth, you must understand the tremendous happiness it will bring me to finally see you as my wife, when for so long I thought you lost to me. Your happiness will be my happiness."

Elizabeth smiled tenderly, leaned forward, and touched her lips to his. It was an hopeful kiss to match her hopeful words, meant to provide comfort, and between the kiss and her words, Darcy did feel himself comforted, felt himself gradually soothed out of the panic of potentially losing her. He was forgiven; he was still loved; he was the most fortunate man in the world.

Slowly, so gradually he hardly noticed at first, the kiss became much more ardent. This was all Elizabeth's doing, although Darcy responded in turn, unsure of what had prompted such ardour from her. When finally they separated, she was breathing heavily, and she said, "Even last night, I believe you changed, for me. Those *other* books on the shelves, with the illustrations – you studied them and decided on the manner of coupling you thought would be best for me, did you not?"

Her cheeks were pink, again, and his mortification was complete. "I did, and I hope you do not think I expect you to do anything beyond what we did last night. I do not routinely read such materials – they were meant for my own education, to be – to be better prepared."

"That you would do such extensive reading, that you would take such care in your preparation, speaks of just what a wonderful man you are, and I would be remiss if I did not say that it was for the better of everything that you were so – *prepared*," she said. "You chose exceptionally well, and once we have been together for longer, I think I would like to attempt some of the other things – the – the easier ones, at least."

"If you wish to, then we shall," he said, and could not manage any more, for he found the prospect of this tremendously arousing.

"You must think me a mercurial creature, to nearly refuse to marry you over the act, and then to speak as I have. I did not understand it could be so very different, particularly given – given my past experiences. I had been told such conflicting things on whether a woman could feel any pleasure from the act."

"I think you a complex creature, rather than a mercurial one," said he. "I believe pleasure for a man is far more straightforward than it is for a woman."

"*You* seemed to have no difficulty with these complexities. Such sensations you aroused – "

She did not complete her thought, but her eyes brightened, and her countenance turned quite pink, seemingly in remembrance.

"As you are now well aware, I did a great deal of reading to learn how I might arouse them," he said, feeling his own face grow warm. "I am only glad we chose your proposal, instead of mine."

"Oh, to think of us in a celibate marriage now seems most absurd! Perhaps in time you would have wooed me, though. I am only glad you wished to do it here, at Pemberley. You were right that we should not rush, and I suppose now that it gave you time to read your books."

"Indeed it did," he said, feeling his face grow hotter still.

"Oh, you wonderful man." Once again, she laid her hands on his cheeks and kissed him, although this kiss was passionate from the very beginning. Darcy was pleased, tremendously pleased, that she had meant what she said about leaving the past in the past, that he had been forgiven for all of his previous mistakes, that last night had seemed to give her confidence, to awaken in her the desires he had always thought likely to be a part of her nature. Elizabeth pulled away from him with a breathless little gasp, and a provocative look upon her countenance.

"Mr. Darcy?"

"Yes, my love?"

"I do hope you intend to use the additional nights I granted you. Will you come to me again, tonight?"

Darcy's earlier resolve that they not do the act again until their wedding night dissipated almost immediately. No resolve could have withstood the imploring look of such a woman.

"Yes, I shall visit you, if you wish it," he said. "You asked to be my mistress, once, but I think we shall find from now on that I am your – your – whatever is the male equivalent of a mistress."

She laughed. "I believe most people would say master, if you had meant the other sort of mistress."

"No, no. That is most certainly not it. I will not ever be your master."

"So we will have one mistress here, and no master?"

Darcy chuckled; it was going to be a delight to have the companionship of such a witty and well-read wife. "Yes, Queen Elizabeth – I shall be your courtier. Request my presence, and I am yours – at least for a few more nights. Once the single females begin to arrive, I should much prefer I not be caught slinking around in their hallway during the night."

"We must set our wedding date before then, so we may bear the separation."

"It is not much of a separation," he said. "We will still see each other during the day, aside from my trip to Chester."

"I want *all* of your company, now, but I suppose I shall have to be content with what I am allowed, before we are married," she said, archly.

He gazed at her – his future bride – with her confident, happy eyes, and thought back to the startled young woman in the library at Netherfield. How she had changed, and how it delighted him! She reminded him more now of the spirited, passionate young woman he had known before her marriage than she ever had before, and he hoped to continue in his endeavours to restore what she had lost. She could never be exactly that woman again, however, for despite her intention to move beyond it, her past would always be there, lurking, and he must always remember that past. Painstakingly, he had earned the trust of that woman in Netherfield's library, and he must always do his utmost to be worthy of that trust.

"May I ask something else of you?" she said.

"Of course."

"Since I may not be in your presence so much as I wish to, may I keep this handkerchief? It may sound silly, but I would like for something I may keep to remind me that this is all real, when I am not in your presence."

Darcy found her request entirely charming, but asked her if she would prefer a fresh one, for there seemed something inauspicious about her keepsake having been stained with her own tears. She said she would, and he went to retrieve it, quietly picking the letter up off of the floor before he did, for she had said nothing about keeping *that*. Once he reached his dressing-room, he realised he had much more to offer her, now that he had access to his mother's rooms. He searched his dressing cabinet, first finding the key he sought, and then the handkerchief. It was one of his favourites, "FLD" carefully embroidered by Georgiana's hands, but he did not at all mind relinquishing it to Elizabeth, for he still had several others Georgiana had done.

He returned to her and gave over the handkerchief, was very prettily thanked for it, and asked her if she was ready to see her chambers. She replied that she was, and rose to follow him as he went to unlock the door to the mistress's dressing-room. As soon as they entered, Darcy found himself wishing that he *had* ordered the rooms cleaned, even if fate should have been tempted in the process. The décor of the rooms could never have been said to align with his own taste, nor, he expected, his betrothed's, but presently, there was a haze of dust in the air, stirred by their entry, and a certain mustiness to the room. Darcy rushed to the nearest window to open the shutters and then the window itself, and reminded himself that there was little to be done about it; he would never have wished to update these rooms when that action should only be done by their new mistress. That woman, the young widow who presently emitted a shockingly loud sneeze, made for a moment as though she was going to dab at her nose with his handkerchief, then caught herself.

Darcy smiled in fond amusement, and said, "I do have others, my love, if you require of that one."

"No, this one is special to me. I shall not spoil it, and I hope you do not intend to have it back."

"You are going to make a rather undemanding wife, if all you ask for is a handkerchief," he said, "but I did intend to give you something else, at least for now. Eventually, all of it will be for your particular use, although you may wish to have the pieces set anew. As you may notice, my mother had a tendency towards the grandiose."

Elizabeth said nothing, but followed after him as he produced the second key and unlocked the cabinet here, a massive affair marked with the most intricate floral marquetry. It had a fall front, swinging open to reveal a series of long, flat drawers, and Darcy pulled open the first, revealing a portion of the Darcy family jewels.

"I thought you might wish to choose a piece – or several, if you like – to keep for now."

"I would like that very much," she said, softly, and began to peruse the selections within the first drawer.

She went through each drawer carefully, gazing over the pieces and occasionally picking up something to examine it more closely. Darcy passed the time by watching her thoughtful progress and thinking of coming to her room again that night. He wondered if he should do the same things he had last night, in the hopes of repeating his success, or attempt something new. He had a desire to try using his tongue between her legs, for if she had reacted so considerably to such attentions from his hand, he thought a more substantial – and therefore delightful – reaction possible. Darcy enjoyed the thought of this, of bringing Elizabeth to such a beautiful state again, but decided against introducing anything new on just their second night together. She would approach tonight knowing how wonderful it could be – that alone should make it quite different – and he would dedicate himself to reinforcing that knowledge, to continuing to build her trust.

With this decided, Darcy returned his full focus to his betrothed's perusal of the jewellery before her, and if she noticed his breathing had become a touch heavier, she said nothing of it. When finally she made her selection, it was one of the simplest pieces available to her, his grandmother's poesy ring, a band of carved gold with a little ruby flower. It was the choice of the lady who had worn white muslin to the Netherfield ball, and a choice he wholly agreed with: Elizabeth needed no adornments, only things that should complement her natural beauty. This, as well as her wit, was what he had failed to notice about her at first; he had been so accustomed to the trim and flounce and feathers of the ton that he had very nearly lost his capacity to judge a woman for herself, and only learned it again in his admiration of Elizabeth.

Darcy agreed with her choice so well he worried the ring would not fit, and they would need to wait for his trip to Chester to have it sized, but when she slipped it on the ring finger of her right hand, it appeared perfect.

"I would like for this to be my wedding ring, if you do not mind," she said.

"I do not mind at all – I think it perfect for that purpose."

"Until then, I shall wear it here as the reminder I sought. You had better be careful, though, for you shall turn me into a demanding wife – I asked for a handkerchief, and received both what I asked for, and this beautiful piece."

"I hope Chip understands you are winning, in your competition, for I doubt anyone shall give him jewellery."

Her laughter echoed throughout the room, momentarily brightening the heavy old décor, and Darcy said, "should you like to see your bedchamber? I am afraid it will be more of the same."

She nodded, and he opened the door there to another haze of dust, then set about opening the shutters and windows, telling her as he did so that she could begin her redecoration even before their marriage – he would procure some catalogues, when he went to Chester. He was about to begin telling her of what warehouses he preferred in town, when he recalled her uncle Gardiner was in trade there, but could not recall precisely what trade – a detail he now intended to learn – and said merely that she should have whatever she wished from town, as well.

"I am not overly worried about the state of my chambers, my love, and nor should you be, for I like the décor of *yours* very much. So once you are done being my courtier, I shall come to visit you."

"If that is how you wish to arrange things, you are welcome there on *any* night, even if you do not desire marital relations."

"Then you may depend on seeing me there very regularly," she said, then continued softly, "I wish you had not been required to leave, last night. I do think we went about this in the best manner for me, but if I had known, when you proposed, how very wonderful everything could be with you, I would have had no qualms about marrying you. We could have stayed together, on our first night."

"Soon enough, we shall have a whole night together, and then so many more after that," he murmured, and reached out to caress her cheek. "Would you like to see the library, now?"

"I *should* be eager to see the library, as you know I have very high expectations of it, but I am enjoying our privacy here."

"I expect Charles and Jane are still out riding, and they are not likely to go there, anyway. No one else shall disturb us there."

"Oh, then it is settled – let us go," said she, "although I believe I have already seen the most interesting books in the house."

Elizabeth had set her expectations high, in her imagining of what the Pemberley library should be like. She found it even more magnificent in reality than it had been in her imagination, however, and could have spent hours there even if she had not spent them in the manner she had on this day, which was delightedly perusing the shelves whilst holding her future husband's hand, and periodically stopping to share a kiss with him. How lovely it had been, to speak of books with him and discover they had even more favourites in common than they had realised, and how delightful it had been to find new volumes she had a great desire to read. Once, she had recalled a different time, a different man, and a different library, but rather than paining her, that memory had merely served to provide a contrast, enhancing her current happiness.

Elizabeth carried a few of her selections with her as she climbed the stairs. It was nearing time to change for dinner, but she had required herself to leave the library early enough to speak again with Jane, for this would be her only opportunity to do so for the remainder of the day – the gentlemen had not sequestered themselves in the dining-room last night, with only two ladies to await them in the drawing-room.

It would be her drawing-room soon enough, she thought giddily. This wonderful house would soon be her home. Its wonderful master would soon be her husband. Such a thought reminded her of what he had said earlier: *I will not ever be your master*. They had been speaking in a teasing manner, then; she had sought to distract him from his earlier guilt, and she had allowed this statement to pass lightly over her. Yet during her time in the library she had come to dwell on it, and she understood he had truly meant it. If she had possessed any remaining doubts about marrying again, she would have used that statement as a talisman, running her mind over it again and again to soothe those doubts away.

She had no doubts, however, only anticipation, and she knocked lightly on the door to the Bingleys's bedchamber, hoping her sister was inside. Jane was, but the door was opened by Charles, who gave Elizabeth a particular look and said, "I suppose I am to make myself scarce again. You have not come here to speak with *me*, I think. Will half-an-hour be sufficient? I do still need to change for dinner."

"That is very good of you, Charles," said Jane. "I believe that should be sufficient."

After he left, Elizabeth had a thought, and felt her face grow very warm. "Jane, he does not *know*, does he? About last night?"

"Oh no, of course not, Lizzy! He is aware there is a serious courtship, but no more. Although you are fortunate I ensured he was very sleepy last night. A little port and – well, never mind that – he was asleep and did not hear you."

Elizabeth's face grew hotter still. "*You* heard me, then."

"Do not worry over it, Lizzy. We are the only other guests here, and the servants's quarters are so far away, I do not think they would have heard anything. For my own part I was glad – I could not sleep, I was so nervous for you. I knew I certainly did not need to worry for you after that."

"So at breakfast, when I told you it had gone very well, you already knew just how well," Elizabeth said, still mortified, despite Jane's reassurance.

"I did," said Jane, smilingly. "Here, come and sit with me, and we shall find something else to speak of, if this embarrasses you so."

Elizabeth followed her sister to a very handsome settee – it seemed every room in the house was decorated in a manner preferable to that of the mistress's bedchamber, but Elizabeth liked the thought of having a space she was expected to make all her own. There, they were seated.

"I do have something else I wish to speak of," Elizabeth said, "and it is that you are *too* good, Jane – you are entirely too good. When we spoke of what Mr. Darcy had done, to cause his breach with Charles, I never could have thought you were the party most injured by his actions."

Jane coloured at her sister's praise, and said, "It is not so much goodness as you make it out to be. I was hardly injured by Mr. Darcy's actions – Charles did offer for me, and we were married."

"True, but at least a little anger over his motives would be entirely understandable. There cannot be anyone else in the world with so little vindictiveness as to avoid telling me what Mr. Darcy had done."

"He apologised very sincerely to me, when we first met again, and I did mean what I said, about not judging him for his past actions," Jane said. "Although I believe *you* formed as much of my motivation as he did. I know you, Lizzy – you would have been far angrier on my behalf than I was, towards Mr. Darcy."

"You are very right. If you had told me then, when I did not know my own heart, I am not sure my affections would have survived my anger, and I might have ruined everything. He told me this morning, though, and now I understand him so much better. And with you as such a model, I could hardly punish him for something you had already forgiven him for."

"I am glad, then," said Jane, smilingly. "You deserved to be in love, Lizzy. I wanted that for you, so badly."

"And now I have it – I truly have it. Jane, I did not think it possible to feel such joy!" Elizabeth exclaimed. "We are going to share the news of our betrothal before dinner. Mr. Darcy intends to bring the servants up, so they do not hear of it through the footmen. You will have to do your best to appear surprised."

"Oh, Charles will presume I knew already, but he will not mind," Jane said, embracing her sister. "Lizzy, I am so happy for you. I think you and Mr. Darcy shall do so well together."

"We will," said Elizabeth. "We have a beautiful future ahead of us."

CHAPTER 14

September 26, 1815

Perhaps it was for the best that Darcy had been required to leave off visiting Elizabeth's room at night, for as his house had filled with guests he found himself harried during the day, and exhausted when finally he went to bed. Unlike the Netherfield house party, he did genuinely like *all* of his guests, but the sheer number of them meant he was constantly endeavouring to spread his conversation amongst them and direct their entertainment. They wanted to shoot and had to be supplied with guns and dogs; they wanted to fish and needed rods and tackle; they wanted to ride and required suitable mounts; they wanted to drive out in their carriages and asked for recommendations on local sights; they sought books in the library and could not understand the very logical way in which the shelves had been arranged. Most of the work involved in preparing each of these things was done by his servants, but Darcy was beginning to feel as though he spent much of his mornings directing those servants, and the remainder engaged in that sort of light conversation he had always struggled with.

He was thankful Elizabeth was helping as she could. There was only so much she could do, without being his wife, but for the last two days she had organised morning entertainments for the majority of the ladies, taking it upon herself to arrange things with Mrs. Reynolds. The houseguests had all been surprised, to arrive and learn they were invited to attend a wedding during their stay, but they had all been gracious towards Elizabeth and indicated goodwill regarding the match. Some had been less enthusiastic in their goodwill than others – namely the single ladies and their mothers. However, as the arrival of those single ladies had meant the other rooms down Elizabeth's hallway were to be filled, ending Darcy's nocturnal visits, the betrothed couple had felt an equal lack of enthusiasm towards them.

In time, however, all of the parties had come to accept their lot, and fast friendships seemed to be growing between Elizabeth and at least some of the ladies. They were taking tea in the rose garden at present, and the last of the gentlemen had gone out, a shooting party, but one Darcy had declined to participate in. For however long he could, he would enjoy his present peace and solitude.

Against his every inclination, he did not retire to his study, nor even the library, but went to the saloon, where he would be more visible if anyone should need him. He did at least have the comfort of picking up the book he had taken to keeping there, and he read quietly for some time until Parker came in to tell him the Brandon post-chaise was in the drive. Darcy's relations, the Earl and Countess of Brandon, would not be attending the house party – their daughter-in-law's approaching confinement would prevent most of the family from leaving town for some time – so this could only be his cousin Edward, Colonel Fitzwilliam. Usually, Darcy would greet his cousin in an entirely happy manner, but today he felt a touch of nervousness – he had written the colonel of his impending nuptials, and so was likely about to learn the entire Fitzwilliam family's reaction to the news. This reaction would do nothing to change his plans, but still, he would much prefer harmony within his extended family, if possible.

He strode out to the drive, and found Edward just alighting the carriage.

"Darcy, how do you do?" he asked.

"I am well," Darcy said, with a puzzled look towards his cousin. He would have thought the topic of his marriage to be the first thing Edward would have commented upon. "And how are you? How was your journey?"

"Good, but it ought to have been, as short as this portion was. I stopped in Birmingham for a few days to see how one of my men, Lieutenant Patterson, is getting on. Lost his leg at Waterloo, but he does as well as can be expected. And he has a very pretty sister, which rendered the visit far more pleasant than I had thought it would be."

"You did not receive my letter before you set out, then?" Darcy asked.

Edward shook his head. "Have you cancelled the house party? Am I appearing uninvited?"

"No, no, not at all, but there was some news within that I should share with you – good news, so pray do not worry. Come inside to my study, and I will tell you."

The news itself could have been given there in the drive, or anywhere in the house, but Darcy wanted Edward's honest reaction – and his honest assessment of how his family should take it – and that could only be had with a guarantee of privacy. They walked thither quietly, and after they entered, Edward helped himself to a brandy, glanced at his cousin, and poured out a second glass.

"So what is this news of yours?" he asked, handing over the glass and then flopping down into one of the seats before the desk.

"I am betrothed – "

"By God, the rumours were true! And to think I said they were nonsense!"

"There were rumours?" asked Darcy.

"Yes, that you were dangling after some widow in Hertfordshire," Edward replied. "I said it was impossible, that my cousin was not the sort to dangle after any woman. Yet it appears you have. Who is she, Darcy?"

"She is a widow: Elizabeth Collins, née Bennet."

"Some said she is an heiress – is she?"

"Yes, she is the heiress of Longbourn, a small estate."

"Darcy, is all well with Pemberley? You do not *need* to marry, do you? There have been some who claimed you were holding out for a woman of large fortune, but I never believed it."

"Pemberley is as successful as it has ever been. There is no *need* for me to marry, and the primary benefit of her being an heiress, so far as I am concerned, is that it ought to ease our way in the ton," Darcy said. "The truth is, I have been in love with her for nearly four years. If I would have gone about my proposal better back then, she might not have been a widow."

Edward's eyes widened, and he took a heavy sip of brandy. "So you have been nursing a broken heart all this time – that does explain a few things. What sort of woman is she, that she has managed to capture your heart so thoroughly?"

"Handsome, and spirited," Darcy said. "I would have said impertinent, at the beginning of our acquaintance, but she has – she has changed, over the years."

"That is a shame. You would have benefited from an impertinent wife," Edward said. "You have been much too used to getting your way. I suppose if she is spirited, though, she will still contradict you from time to time, when you need it most."

"I hope that she will," said Darcy, meaning it fully. "I shall have to write to your parents, of the news – I had thought you would receive my letter and inform them. How do you think they will take it? I should tell you – as I will them – that while she is a gentleman's daughter, her family has connections to trade."

"Oh, they shall take it well, I think. If you had been as mercenary as some of the men at White's thought you were, you would have chosen an heiress of better connections, but everyone else shall say you finally married, and she was an heiress, as they expected. As for my mother and father particularly, I believe they will be glad you married at all, for they were beginning to despair of you. Even aunt Catherine thinks you have mourned poor Anne for far longer than you should have."

"Has everyone been speaking of my marital status?"

"Not to put too fine a point on it, Darcy, but yes, they have, for Pemberley's future, as well as your own."

Darcy had knowingly and willingly tied himself to a woman who might not be able to bear his children, and so there might be very little change in Pemberley's future as a result of his marriage – Georgiana's child might still inherit the estate. He did not share this with Edward, however. "Well, they need speak of it no longer. I have procured a licence, and we are to be married on the fourth of October, in Lambton."

"Oh! Well I must say that when I set out, I had no notion I was to be attending your *wedding*. I am very much looking forward to making her acquaintance, for I have a great deal of curiosity about this lady."

Edward's curiosity was made to wait until dinner, for he had gone up to his room to change when Elizabeth and the ladies came in from the rose garden. The entire party seemed in good spirits, their footsteps echoing through the entrance-hall amidst a fair amount of giggling. Darcy rose from the seat he had resumed in the saloon to view a number of muslin-clad backs ascending the stairs. No-one had noticed him in the saloon, and Elizabeth was amidst them, laughing over something.

It was very strange, Darcy thought, to be living together in this manner, with her in the house as a guest amongst the others, knowing that soon they would be man and wife. He missed the early days of her residence here, when he had enjoyed so much more of her time, both before and after they retired for bed. Even after they married, it would be this way whenever they entertained, but at least then they would spend the night together.

Sighing, Darcy left the saloon – not to go up the stairs, although it was nearing time to change, but instead to walk to the housekeeper's room, to check with Mrs. Reynolds on whether all was set for dinner. In addition to the house guests, he had also invited a number of people from the neighbourhood to dine tonight. It was far from the largest dinner Pemberley had ever hosted, but it would be the largest ever held by its current master. Tonight was to be most of his neighbours's introduction to the future Mrs. Darcy, and he wanted it to be a success.

He was assured by Mrs. Reynolds that all was well, and then ascended the stairs to his bedchamber, passing through to the dressing-room. He had just rung the bell when the door leading to the sitting-room swung open, entirely startling him.

It was Elizabeth, and she furtively swept across the dressing-room, stepping readily into his embrace and kissing him ardently.

"I have hardly seen you today," she whispered. "I missed you."

"My darling Elizabeth, I have missed you as well," he murmured, holding her tight. "Oh, how I wish you had come in before I rang the bell. Mason will be here soon."

"That is likely for the best – it would never do for both of us to be late for dinner."

"Very true," he chuckled. "While you are here, I should tell you that my cousin Edward arrived earlier. He is very eager to make your acquaintance."

"And I his, but I am not interested in your cousin at present."

She kissed him again – those delightfully soft lips so wonderful against his – until all of the agitations of earlier in the day were forgotten. They kissed until Mason's steps could be heard on the servants's staircase, and then she broke away from him and fled back toward the sitting-room door, pausing in the doorway to look back at him.

"Elizabeth, do you intend to make a habit of this? I do love your presence, but it seems rather risky."

"Well Mr. Darcy," she said, with an arch look, "I want my rooms redecorated as soon as possible, and how am I to plan the décor if I do not visit them? If you happen to be in your own chambers at the same time, I suppose it cannot be helped."

Chuckling again as she closed the door, Darcy required himself to think on her humour, rather than the sensation of holding her in his arms, of kissing her, for at that moment Mason entered, and Darcy did not need any lingering evidence of her presence in the room.

Edward was already in the yellow drawing-room when Darcy, who had thankfully been able to don his trousers without the need for any embarrassing explanations, entered. He went to stand beside his cousin and introduce Edward to those he had not already met, and they were thus when Elizabeth entered. Darcy knew himself to be particularly biassed, but he thought she looked glorious that evening. She wore a pale yellow dress and the pearls he had bought for her in Chester, meant to bridge the time it would take before the first of the family jewels could be reset. Several of the women in the party did not like to come to dinner without adorning their persons so that they were entirely dripping in jewels, but Elizabeth had kept quite staunchly to the pearls, despite access to any number of pieces that could have outdone anything that had been seen at the dinner table thus far.

"Well," Edward murmured beside him, "I must presume that is her, and if I am correct, I think her entirely worth dangling after."

"That is her," Darcy said. This was not the first time admiration for his future wife had been expressed to him by another gentleman of the house party. At first, he had felt some perturbation over such statements, but after a great deal of reflection in the hours he once again spent alone at night, he had arrived at the opinion that it was not such an horrid thing to have a woman who was betrothed to him admired by so many, particularly when she very clearly had no romantic interest in any but him. If there was anything he should dislike about it, it was that others could come to admire her more quickly than he had, and it was this that still caused him the occasional pang of regret.

Elizabeth noticed them standing there and came over, curtseying substantially after Darcy made the introduction, and receiving not only a bow but a kiss of her hand in return. Darcy's cousin was not a man who had ever been accused of scrimping on his gallantry towards women, and again, Darcy might have been far more perturbed were it not for a certain impish glance Elizabeth directed towards him, after the kiss was completed. It was momentary – Edward would not have noticed it – but a man could be sustained for a very long time on such glances from the woman he loved.

Such sustenance was necessary, for in the remaining time before dinner he was required to introduce Elizabeth and others in the house party to those within the neighbourhood, a harrying process because he needed not only to make the introductions, but to do so in a way that ensured everyone understood what this did for precedence within the line.

He considered, once the line had formed and they were going in, that at least Elizabeth was not yet taking up the place at the opposite end of the table that she would hold as his wife, and so her seat was among those nearest him. Edward's was, as well, and they all passed the time talking agreeably of Derbyshire and Hertfordshire, of travelling and staying at home, of new books and music. It was evident that Edward admired Elizabeth, but his manners were always everything they ought to have been.

Up and down the table, his guests seemed to be enjoying themselves. Darcy had never doubted Cook's ability to put several removes of the highest quality before his guests, nor his butler's ability to ensure it was all accompanied with fine wine and port. As the pace of consumption slowed on the last remove, he realised with some satisfaction that it had been a success. A success he would endeavour to repeat again, but only once he was married.

Elizabeth had not taken the mistress's seat at dinner, but she was recognised as the arbiter of the ladies's departure from the room, and when she delicately discarded her napkin and said she should go through, she was readily followed out. This had once been his favourite part of the evening – a respite from the matchmaking mamas and mercenary young ladies he had often been required to dine with – but now Darcy could not enjoy a description of the day's shooting and fishing in the same way he had before. He listened with impatience, and required himself to leave the room at a normal pace when Parker finally announced that tea was ready in the drawing-room.

There, he required himself to continue with his duties, to circulate amongst his guests and have a little conversation with each of them, although he found this wearying. At least he now had the reassurance of being able to glance across the room and see Elizabeth, to see her doing the same and giving him a smile. Between them, they saw to the tea, the setup of card-tables, and the encouragement of several young ladies to go to the adjacent music-room and exhibit for them. This portion of the night, too, was a success, and no one from the neighbourhood seemed inclined to call for their carriages, nor anyone from the house to retire upstairs, for a great many hours.

Eventually, however, they began to take their leave, and as those who remained were entrenched in their own entertainments – particularly the loo-table – Darcy took the opportunity to seek out Elizabeth. She was saying good-night to Miss Pelham and praising the young lady for her performance on the harp, and he realised she looked even more exhausted than he felt. She smiled to him, momentarily enlivening her countenance, and indicated they should sit together in a quiet corner of the drawing-room.

"Are you well, Elizabeth? You should go up if you are tired – I shall manage those that remain," he said.

"Oh, I am well enough, although I do think I will go up soon."

"I must thank you for your assistance with all of the guests, particularly in arranging entertainments for the ladies."

"You need not thank me – it will be my role soon enough."

"Yes, but your efforts have been great at a time when I would not have blamed you for claiming to be indisposed and keeping to your room."

"Indisposed?" she asked, with a puzzled look upon her countenance. "Oh! – I did not realise you knew about that little secret."

"You must remember that I had a younger sister in my care for many years," Darcy said. He still would not have guessed at the potential need for Elizabeth to claim she was indisposed and needed to rest in her room, but they had chosen to delay their wedding because she was to have her courses this week. After she had shared this, in a tone of some embarrassment, they had agreed they did not wish to have the event disrupt their wedding night, and so they had set a date for a week later than they would have preferred.

"Yet another reason, I suppose, to be very glad to be marrying a man so understanding of the intricacies of the female body," she murmured, giving him a rather sultry gaze.

He returned her gaze, and knew in that moment an almost overwhelming desire. For so long, he had been patient; he had desired only the *chance* to win her hand and heart. Now that he had them, however, Darcy felt the erosion of such patience, particularly when faced with a future wife who no longer seemed tired at all. Indeed, she looked as though she would have welcomed a visit from him that night.

Such a thing was impossible, however. Even if she was not yet *indisposed*, the risk was now too high. Darcy consoled himself with the thought that in little more than a week's time they would be wed, and that would be the end of this celibacy he now found so intolerable. They sat for a while longer, talking of the day's events and what was planned for the morrow, until exhaustion once again encroached on her countenance, and he encouraged her to go up; he could manage the remaining guests.

The ladies all took Elizabeth's departure as a cue to go up or call for their own carriages – to the chagrin of at least one husband – so that rather rapidly the room cleared of all but those either playing at loo, or watching them. Darcy, upon returning from the entrance-hall after seeing off the last couple, would have gone over to watch the game, but he found Edward approaching him, and encouraging him to sit somewhat away from the rest of the group.

"You are done playing?" Darcy asked.

"If there is nothing else I have learned in my military career, it is when to bring my time at the card-table to an end," Edward said.

"I believe I know a few dozen men in town who could benefit from such knowledge."

"Ah, yes, but I did not come over to speak of gambling," Edward said. "I came to tell you that I like Mrs. Collins. I like her very much – so much I might have given myself leave to like her better if she was not betrothed to you. You may be assured of a favourable report back to my parents."

"Thank you for that."

"I believe I see how it is with you now, Darcy. You have spent your adult life being pursued by women – if only they had known that in truth you wanted to be doing the pursuing."

Darcy chuckled. "I believe there is at least some truth to what you say. However, it does not give enough credit to Mrs. Collins. She was – and still is – unlike any woman I have ever met."

"I entirely agree with you, and I see a little better now why you pined after her for so many years," Edward said. "You are smitten, Darcy, entirely smitten."

"I will fully admit that I am," Darcy said. "And now I intend to watch this card game before you attempt to tease me any further."

They did so for some time, until Darcy felt he had done his duty well enough as host, and those men who wanted to continue on at the card table could be left to it without any guilt on his part. He went into his dressing-room, lit the candles there, and was about to ring the bell for Mason when curiosity bade him to wait. He went through the door to the sitting-room, and then the mistress's dressing-room and bedchamber, looking to see if Elizabeth was truly beginning her redecoration, or if it had been a ruse to see him.

She had made no apparent alteration to the bedchamber aside from opening the secretaire and removing a very pretty silver writing set Darcy vaguely recalled from his youth. It seemed the ink stored within had still been good, for as he drew closer to the secretaire, he found a sheet of paper lying there, with fresh writing in a feminine hand:

Elizabeth Darcy
Elizabeth Darcy
Elizabeth Darcy

In the first line, her Christian name showed the confidence of having written it for most of her life, but the attempt at her soon-to-be surname had been made with some awkwardness. The awkwardness improved in the second line, and her third attempt – the one that must have satisfied her – looked quite natural. Nay, it looked *happy*, the y ending with something very near a flourish.

Darcy was charmed by this attempt of hers to practise her future name, charmed by the name itself and her apparent eagerness to bear it, and felt himself momentarily seized with the impulse to take up the pen himself and write *I love you* beneath it. Fearing this might embarrass her, however, he refrained, and merely kissed the tips of his fingers and touched them to the writing. Edward had called him smitten, and any man who should do such a thing deserved the label, he thought, but his affections had gone on for too long and were too deep to be only *smitten.* This woman: Elizabeth Bennet; Elizabeth Collins; soon-to-be Elizabeth Darcy; had entirely claimed his heart, and he was most ardently in love with her.

CHAPTER 15

October 4, 1815

"Oh, Lizzy, I do not think you have ever looked lovelier!" exclaimed Jane, and Elizabeth, examining herself in the looking-glass, thought Jane was very likely right.

She had chosen her dress with more than usual care, a cheery shade of yellow, and a sharp contrast to her last wedding dress. Rachel had arranged her hair to perfection, as well, but she thought the true cause of Jane's compliment was the happiness that formed Elizabeth's countenance.

Rachel had been dismissed, already, and Mrs. Bennet rose from where she had been seated, on the chaise. Mrs. Bennet's choice had been a source of mortification for Elizabeth, for she could not look at that piece of furniture in her present bedchamber without thinking of Mr. Darcy's hand between her legs, pleasuring her. Now, Elizabeth realised she would never again sleep in this room, and the thought made her feel a little wistful; she would always leave it decorated as it was, she decided, and occasionally she might come in and sit for a little while, to better reminisce about that night, a night that would always remain treasured in her memories.

"Well, I shall say this for you, Lizzy," Mrs. Bennet said, halting her daughter's mind, which had threatened to drift into joyful recollection, "you have managed to marry exceedingly well, twice over. All those years I thought you were not listening to my advice on how you must get an husband, but clearly you were, my dear daughter. You would do well to follow after your sister, Kitty and Mary. Twelve thousand a year! But you had better give him an heir, Lizzy."

Elizabeth had a response for this that would have utterly shocked her mother, but she chose not to provide it, and gave Mrs. Bennet a perfunctory embrace. Her mother departed the room, and Elizabeth hugged Mary, next, "Thank you for looking after Longbourn for me, Mary. I know you shall do wonderfully. I hope the new steward will do well in his duties, but if he does not, write to me and we shall find another. I do not want it to be too much of a burden upon you."

"I shall, Lizzy. You look very pretty – I am very happy for you," Mary said, and departed the room as well.

Elizabeth embraced Kitty next, and told her: "Kitty, do not ever listen to mama, about getting an husband, and if she does harass you over it, write to me, and I will demand she stop. You have a home at Longbourn for life, if you wish it, although I am going to set more money aside, now, for portions for you and Mary. Do not let anything but the deepest love compel you to marry, but if you do find that love, I want your word that you shall."

"I will promise you that," said Kitty, brushing a tear from her face, and then saying, nearly in a whisper, "Lizzy, are you still afraid?"

"No, Kitty, I am not afraid, now – I am just immeasurably happy."

"I hope you will always stay that way," Kitty said, and then slipped from the room.

"Will you help hold her to her promise, Jane?" Elizabeth asked, now that the two of them were alone. "Mary may prefer to remain unwed, but Kitty was, I think, formed to be in love, and I cannot bear that she avoids it because of what she witnessed during those years. I shall not be around to watch over them so much as I was – that is one of my regrets, in leaving Hertfordshire. That, and being parted from you."

"Oh, Lizzy, I cannot promise you that so well as I would like, but at least I may do away with one of your regrets," said Jane. "Charles and I have decided we should give up the lease at Netherfield, and find an estate to purchase. We intend to begin our search in Derbyshire – he knows I would struggle to live too far away from you, and now that he and Mr. Darcy have reconciled so thoroughly, he is eager to live near the both of you, too."

"Jane, you have completed my happiness!" cried Elizabeth, embracing her sister tightly. "There could be no better news, in addition to the events yet to come today."

Jane returned the embrace, and said, "It shall mean leaving Mary and Kitty to live with mama without either of us near, but perhaps we can have them both to visit, often."

"Yes, we must do so."

Releasing her sister, Jane asked, "Do you need a moment to yourself, Lizzy?"

Elizabeth smiled and touched the pearls at her throat, thinking with every fondness of the man who had given them to her. "No, I am very eager to become Mrs. Darcy. Let us go."

She and Jane went down to the entrance-hall together. Outside in the drive, they found the carriage with the Bennet ladies already departing, leaving only a very fine landau, beside which Charles Bingley was standing, awaiting his wife and the woman he was to give away, in Lambton's parish church.

Elizabeth and her betrothed had been required to choose between that church and the private chapel at Pemberley. Mr. Darcy, ever a reserved man, might have chosen the chapel were it not for his role in the neighbourhood, but he had thought it right, and Elizabeth had agreed with him, that they should be married where they could be seen by the villagers and his tenants and servants, as well as his houseguests. Elizabeth had been very pleased by how the news of the approaching wedding had been received by most of the latter, and so far as she was concerned, the guest list could only have been improved with the inclusion of Charlotte Gilmore, whose husband was not well enough to travel; her aunt and uncle Gardiner, who could not leave his business on such short notice; and more of Mr. Darcy's family. Elizabeth had been assured that the absence of the latter was due more to timing and distance than anything else, and had these assurances reinforced by two letters from her future aunts: a somewhat imperious missive from Lady Catherine de Bourgh, and a warmer message welcoming her to the family from the Countess of Brandon. Nothing could yet be expected from Georgiana, but Mr. Darcy had told Elizabeth that his sister was well aware of his longstanding love for her, and would be absolutely thrilled with the news.

Charles handed them both into the carriage, and they made the drive there in peaceful silence, until they raised the village and people could be seen lining the street. Nothing like this had happened in Elizabeth's first marriage, and she thought back to when she and Mr. Darcy had talked about his responsibility for his servants and tenants, and she had likened his role to that of a father. If he was the father, then she was to be the mother, and most of them had not yet seen her. Elizabeth smiled, and waved to that sea of curious faces, hesitantly, at first, until a few of them waved back. *When next I pass you all*, she thought, *it will be as Mrs. Darcy, with Mr. Darcy beside me, and you shall see I love him even more than you do.*

Elizabeth was right in her prediction, and her second ride through Lambton's streets had found her gazing lovingly at her new husband. If she had been received curiously before, she had found a much more enthusiastic reception once seated beside him. That quiet man had been cheered as the horses had trotted down the street, and although he had seemed embarrassed by the attention, Elizabeth had revelled in it, in understanding how well-loved he was by those dependent upon his estate. She had revelled, as well, in his kisses, once they had raised Pemberley's grounds; kisses that might have turned into far more, had they not been in an open carriage, with the rest of the wedding party following behind them.

The wedding breakfast had gone wonderfully, and had, Elizabeth thought, been well-hosted. Her husband was easier in the company of his friends and neighbours than he had been amongst strangers, but he still occasionally seemed to have regrets about the quantity of people he had invited into his house and was required to play host to, although he performed the part well. This was something she would help him with in the future, though; with a wife as hostess, he would no longer need to carry the burden alone.

And perhaps he had merely been impatient, for Elizabeth had at times felt a goodly degree of impatience welling up within her. This time she was not a virgin bride, awaiting the night with trepidation, nor was she a widow who recalled the act with disgust. She was a woman exceedingly desirous of her husband's touch, the touch she knew and longed for, and at times the breakfast had seemed interminable.

It was all over now, however, and the long-awaited night had finally arrived. Elizabeth – *Elizabeth Darcy* – took one last look about the dressing-room of her new apartment, and smiled. Rachel had changed her already and departed, and Elizabeth had but one thing to remove, an article she had once thought she would never again wear: a wedding band. It was lovely, and she adored both that it had a history within his family, and the simple inscription within the band, "My precious love," for that was how her husband made her feel, as though she was most precious to him. Her greater pleasure in it on this day, however, was for what it symbolised, the vows they had taken together in the parish church.

Elizabeth opened the door to the sitting-room to pass through to the master's chambers, filled with the most delightful anticipation. She had been wet between her legs for some time already, in thinking of finally being able to see her husband in the night, as his wife. For too long, she had been sustained by nothing more than stolen kisses and provocative looks, although she suspected the latter had done more harm than good, for such looks from him had put her in a very aroused state, one that could not be mitigated. Elizabeth shook her head over how completely she had changed, to go from repulsion to the strongest desire when she thought of the act.

She strode through the master's dressing-room and then the open door to his bedchamber, where she was greeted with the scent of roses and glimpsed several vases filled with them. Then she could observe no more, for she saw her husband and he rushed to meet her, taking her up in a fervent embrace. Elizabeth was reminded that he had wanted this for years; he had pined for her, and now, finally, he had his heart's desire. She had hers, as well, but it had only been since she had come to Pemberley that she had understood all it encompassed, to love and to be loved by this man: heart, mind, soul – and body.

They spent some time in merely kissing, far more passionately than they had in the landau, although in time Elizabeth ran her hands down his back, enjoying the feel of his body. He took this as his cue to do the same for her, pulling her closer, so that she could feel his growing arousal. She had enjoyed the slower pace of their previous couplings, all those pleasurable moments slowly growing to something bigger, but she suspected this night might go more quickly; they had both had a very long time for their need to build.

Eventually, they broke the kiss, although Elizabeth did not move her hands, nor did he.

"I cannot believe we may do this every night, now, that we are free to be together whenever we wish," he said. "I did enjoy our little rendezvous in my dressing-room, but I needed more. I want so much more of your presence than I have been allowed."

"Oh, you have it – you shall have it every night – for I am just as needful of your presence." She slid her hands from him, so she could remove her nightgown. It felt brazen to do so, to stand there before him in her nakedness, but as he stood there gazing at her in appreciation for some time before removing his own nightshirt, it further bolstered her confidence.

Once she had moved beyond thinking she would always detest the act, Elizabeth had felt herself inexperienced, compared to him. This was a strange thing, because she rather suspected herself to have participated in the act more than him, but then, that was the crux of it – only with him had she felt herself a full participant. Her confidence had grown every time she was with him, but she still felt herself to know so little, and she intended to steal into the sitting-room and read his books. She had a sense that there was more she could be doing to pleasure him – although simply finding his release inside her did seem to give him a very great amount of pleasure.

"You looked so beautiful this morning when you came into the church, I could hardly breathe when I first saw you," he said, brushing a curl back from her forehead in a manner that reminded her strongly of when he had first done it, back in Netherfield's library.

"And you looked exceedingly handsome," said she. "You are always so, but it is much enhanced when you smile."

"I believe it will be enhanced frequently in the future, then. And I must tell you I find you even more handsome, at present. Let other ladies have their trim and fripperies – my wife is at her best when she wears nothing. Absolutely nothing."

Elizabeth felt herself blushing profusely, felt it overspread her entire body with a delightful warmth. Once again it was him who moved first to please her, lowering his head to kiss her neck and her throat in the way he often did, but to experience it standing very nearly made her knees buckle. She tried to touch him, to caress his skin in ways she thought he would like, but it was so very difficult to focus when he kissed her in this way. When she could bear no more, she took him by the hand and led him over to the bed, for there was one thing she had planned, to bring him more pleasure, and this could be the beginning of it.

The master of Pemberley's bed was a large, high, quite magnificent affair, and it was something just to pull down the covers and climb up into it, to lay down on very fine sheets and put her head back against the pillow. Elizabeth gazed at him, and took a deep breath. She trusted him. She trusted him completely.

"Tonight I want you to do it in the usual way," she said. "I presume it is more pleasurable for the man, in that way."

"Elizabeth, are you certain? I fully enjoy the way we have been going about things," he said, looking rather concerned.

"I am sure, Mr. Darcy. You are always so focused on pleasing me. Tonight I want you to do what feels best for you."

"Still you call me Mr. Darcy, even on our wedding night."

"I had been hoping you would call me Mrs. Darcy, in return. I am very enamoured with that name."

"Very well, *Mrs. Darcy.* If you truly wish it – " Elizabeth replied that she did " – we may do it in that way. But if I am to do what I wish, may I also try something else that is new to us?"

"If you would like to," Elizabeth said, not entirely certain what she had gotten herself into. The biggest change in their prior couplings had been her increasing confidence; in essentials, they had all been fairly similar.

He nodded and climbed into bed, coming to kneel at her feet. Elizabeth relaxed a little when he laid his hands on her ankles and slid her legs farther apart, for this was not so very different from what she had known before. Then he leaned over and lightly kissed the inside of her knee, and she gasped, at how very much this increased her arousal.

He looked up at her. "Elizabeth, I have not done this before: you will know, now, how I have learned of it. If you find you do not like it, you need only say so."

She nodded her acquiescence, and he continued, kissing her knee again and then very slowly kissing his way up her thigh. Elizabeth laid her hands on his head very lightly, so as not to require him to continue – surely he would not continue with this *too* much farther – but enough so he could better sense the pleasure he was giving her, for her fingers twitched of their own accord at each of his kisses. She was gasping, as well, gasping in rough, uneven breaths, and he seemed much encouraged by this.

Elizabeth had thought he intended this to ensure she was well and truly ready for him to lie upon her, and she was – oh, she most certainly was! Then he kissed the very inside of her thigh, and transferred his attentions to her – her bud, with a first, delicate lick, and the sensation was almost unbearably wonderful.

"Fitzwilliam!" she exclaimed.

He halted his attentions immediately, then, and looked up at her. "I am sorry, my love. I should not have attempted something like this so soon."

"No – it was entirely more pleasurable than I was expecting. It is I that am sorry – I have disturbed your progress."

"So you did find it pleasurable?"

"Yes, almost more than I could bear."

"Would you wish me to continue?" he asked, and when she nodded, he leaned over again, kissing her inner thigh before he once again slid his tongue over that most sensitive place. He licked her again and again there, and Elizabeth struggled to contain her reactions, for she had thought she understood how very incredible it was possible to feel, and he was now redefining it. She mewled, at each movement of his tongue, and when he slipped it into that deeper place inside of her, she had to grasp the bedsheets, to keep her hands from flailing about his head. His attentions were delicate, but relentless, and she rapidly found herself on the precipice of a most prodigious climax, then tumbling rapidly over, crying out and shivering in ecstasy.

He looked up at her, watching the echoes of her pleasure, which continued on for a very long time as she laid there, breathless and spent, although *she* had not done anything. When finally she recovered, Elizabeth felt the mortification of how very wanton her reaction had been, and covered her mouth with her hand. "I was very loud, was I not?"

"Not *too* loud," said he. "Although now that we are married, I would be perfectly happy to let the whole house resound with how happy *Mrs. Darcy* is."

Elizabeth giggled. Her body had surprised her so often over the last fortnight or so, and it seemed it had once again managed to do so. She had noticed in her intimacies with him that he seemed to have a certain satisfaction in bringing her to a climax – as well he should – and his countenance showed this now.

"At least I now know an effective method of prompting you to call me by my Christian name," said he, rising from the bed and going over to the cabinet.

"*That* is not required for me to do so," said she. "I have grown very used to calling you Mr. Darcy, though. You will have known your formal name since you ceased being young Master Darcy, but I have known three in my life, and the most recent is by far my favourite."

"Yes, I know you are quite enamoured with it, as am I." He returned to the bed with two glasses of brandy, handing one to her. "I have been calling you Elizabeth for some time, for I did not like to call you by – by your former name. So perhaps tonight you may be Mrs. Darcy, and I may be Fitzwilliam."

"Perhaps, Fitzwilliam," she said, then continuing in a tone of embarrassment: "Was the taste so very bad, that you must eliminate it with brandy? That – what you did – was an incredible thing, but do not feel you must do it again, if it was so unpleasant for you. This night was supposed to be for *your* pleasure."

"Eliz – Mrs. Darcy, please do not think that. Were I presented with – with such a taste on my dinner table, I will admit that I would not have preferred it, but when it came to me with such reactions as you have shown, I found it more pleasant than not, and I fully intend to do it again." He sipped his brandy. "My pleasure will come, eventually, and as for the brandy, I thought it might help ensure you were relaxed."

"Oh, I assure you, the brandy was not necessary for that." Elizabeth blushed and sipped at her brandy anyway, and found it far stronger than she had expected, so that a great deal of coughing must follow. After this, she sipped even more carefully, and did find it not only increased her present relaxation, but also seemed to begin her arousal anew.

He – Mr. Darcy – Fitzwilliam – her husband – this man she loved with all her heart, whatever was to be his identity now, took the glass from her when she had drunk it all, and said, "Elizabeth, do you still wish to couple in the traditional way?"

"Yes," she whispered. "I want you to lie upon me."

"Do you need a little time, first?"

Elizabeth shook her head. "I do not need any time."

On this night when everything thus far had been so novel, she felt it quite possible that she should enjoy that which she had not before, so long as it was with this man. She spread her legs farther apart, so he could have better access to her, but he murmured to her to wait and took up a spare pillow from the bed, indicating it should be placed below her bottom, and then assisting her in positioning it there. Elizabeth would not have thought to do this, but she sensed immediately how it should make things more comfortable for her, and found herself grateful for his books, and his dedication in reading them.

Elizabeth shifted her hips upon the pillow, and he kneeled between her legs, placing his hands on either side of her and kissing a path up her belly. Her bosom was to follow, and he took the tip of one breast and then the other up in his mouth, doing the most delightful things with his tongue. Elizabeth's breasts had been particularly sensitive, of late, and the sensation was so good it was nearly dizzying. It took a great deal of effort to conjure speech, and say: "You have – you have waited long enough for your pleasure, Fitzwilliam, and I am very, very ready for you."

He nodded, and slid his hands farther up the bed, alongside her shoulders, so that he was hovering over her, and then he slowly lowered himself down on her. She was struck, once again, with the observation that he was very strong, and this aroused her further, that such a strong and virile man could love her in such a gentlemanlike manner.

His weight was not entirely enjoyable, but it was not unpleasant, and it became better when he lowered his mouth to hers and kissed her thoroughly. It would be fine, she thought, his tender gaze meeting her eyes, his taut, muscular chest upon hers, his hand down between them, taking his rod and guiding it toward her entrance. He had always let her take him in, giving her complete control over the pace of this, and as he began to enter her, he whispered to her that she should tell him if he was going too fast. He did not, however; he went more slowly than she had in their last few couplings, so she had ample time to adjust to the feel of him filling her.

He did not speak, to ask her if she was ready, but he looked her in the eyes with a questioning gaze, and Elizabeth nodded. Then, only then, did he begin to thrust inside her, slowly. It was not bad – the pillow undoubtedly helped – but neither was it particularly good, and she did not think it likely she would climax again that night from this, although he periodically kissed her, and gave her those attentions he could in such a position, even sliding his hand between them and using his fingers on her bud in an attempt to please her.

Elizabeth felt certain, though, that she would never enjoy this as much as their previous couplings. She thought it would still be worthwhile if he liked it better, and for herself, at least she had proven the past was truly in the past. With this in mind, she ran her hands down his back, then lower, to see if she might find more to like about this manner of doing things.

He continued on for only a little while longer, seeming to experiment with his pace, before he stopped altogether, and said, "My love, it was good of you to wish to try this, but I find I do not prefer it. May I try something else, instead?"

Elizabeth nodded, relieved. The change he made was simple – he raised himself up on his arms again, so that most of his weight was no longer upon her. Lowering his head to kiss her tenderly, he began to move again. In the greater range of motion he had been granted, Elizabeth felt him experimenting with the angle at which he entered her, until finally he found one that gave her a more intense sensation, prompting her to gasp.

"There?" he asked.

"Oh yes – yes – there."

Once he had found this angle, he kept to it, thrusting slowly in and out of her, and as Elizabeth's hips were now free to move, she began to match his rhythm, and this further enhanced her sensations. Although it was different than their previous times, with him above her, it was once again pleasing to her, particularly when he would lower his lips to hers and kiss her in that reverent way of his.

"Mrs. Darcy," he murmured in her ear after one such kiss, and his timing was perfect, for it was this that finished her, quietly this time, only the slightest little sigh emerging from her lips as she trembled from the intensity. When it was done, she had the feeling that she might just sink into the very fine bed and melt away, particularly after he closed his eyes, moaned very deep in his throat, and climaxed himself. This seemed to weaken him almost as much as it had her, for he lowered himself back down upon her and gave her a long, languid kiss, before he withdrew from her and came to rest on his side next to her, running his hand lightly over her breasts and belly. Elizabeth lifted her hips and silently removed the pillow, pushing it over the edge of the bed.

"I am sorry I suggested something that was displeasing to you," she said, quietly, turning her head to face him.

"Do not ever be sorry for proposing we try something, my love. But do you understand why I did not enjoy it? I did not enjoy it because I could see you were not enjoying it. If you are to be sorry over something, let it be that you did not ask me to try something else yourself."

"It was not bad – I did not *dislike* it."

"Neither did you enjoy it," he said. "Elizabeth, to see a beautiful woman – to see the beautiful woman that I love – react in the way you usually do is the most arousing thing possible. I enjoy all that our coupling brings, but the feeling that is most delightful to me is when I – when I feel you move with me, when I feel your reaction."

"I understand, but Fitzwilliam, I do not know if I can explain to you how very different everything is with you. If I had thought, when you proposed to me, that marital relations were to be as they were when you were laying upon me tonight, if that had been all I ever knew of the act, I would have agreed to marry you without any hesitation."

He gazed at her as though he better understood her past, now, and it saddened him. It saddened her, as well, and she felt somehow more naked, as though there was some other layer she had divested, something more intimate than mere clothes.

"That is not enough for me, Elizabeth. It will never be enough, now that I know what pleasure you can have from the act."

"I am sorry. I wanted to return some of the pleasure you have given me, but I know so little – "

"Elizabeth: *no*. I will not allow you to believe yourself lacking in any way, or that our time together has somehow not been pleasurable for me, for I assure you, it has been – you cannot know how very much it has been, to know the woman I have longed for all these years in this way," he said, in a raspy voice. "You must understand – every moment I am with you, every moment I thought I would never have, brings me pleasure. More than pleasure – it brings me joy."

His words prompted a very strong bout of weeping from her, and she found herself being pulled into his arms, her hair gently stroked as she cried. She was glad neither of them needed to leave this room, that she could lose control of her present emotions, and he could hold her close, murmuring to her that they were together, now, and all would be well.

"I am sorry," she said, once she had calmed. "I have been so emotional, of late."

"You must stop apologising, my love. I have been quite emotional today, myself."

Elizabeth had thought she would wait a little longer to tell him, so she could be certain, but she found she could not bear to keep her secret any longer, not when she was lying here so intimately with him, and they had been speaking so openly.

"Yes, but I believe there is something particular enhancing my emotions beyond even what they would have been, and I hope you are prepared, for this is likely to continue for some time," she said, gazing at him. "You were right, to consider what should happen if a child resulted from our union."

"You believe that it did?" Now it was her husband, who looked completely overwhelmed.

"I never had my courses last week," she said. "And there are – there are other symptoms. Among other things, it takes very little to turn me into a tearful, emotional creature."

"Oh, Elizabeth," he said, in a tone of deepest emotion, drawing her still closer to him. Elizabeth burst back into tears in spite of herself, and he continued, gently, "Are you happy, at the prospect of having a child so soon?"

"I am," she sobbed. "I know it may not sound as though I am, but these are tears of the greatest happiness. I have wanted a child so badly, and to know I am to have one with *you*, to know it was not my fault, before – 'tis all more happiness than I deserve."

"I cannot agree with you there. I believe you deserve every happiness."

Elizabeth chuckled softly, wiped at her eyes, and asked hesitantly, "How do you feel, about the prospect of a child?"

"Immeasurably happy – both for myself, and for you. I did not think it was possible to be happier on this day, but this is indeed the one thing that could make me so."

"I am glad I knew before we married. I knew I was not condemning you to a lifetime without children."

"You would never have been condemning me to any life, in marrying me. It does make me even happier than I had been, to know that you carry our child, but even if there had never been the chance of a child, I would still have been so very happy with you. You must know you are the only woman I have ever loved, Elizabeth. I would rather be in a childless marriage with you than have children with any other woman," he said. "I only wish I could have spared you your first marriage, so you never would have had to doubt in your ability to conceive a child."

Elizabeth sniffled. "Oh, my love, please do not dwell on those regrets – not tonight. We are together, now. We are together and we are going to have a baby."

He kissed her then, kissed her deeply but sweetly, and said, "You are right, my handsome wife. I shall speak no more of the past tonight."

"Good. Think of the future – think of our beautiful future. Think of how we may finally stay together, tonight."

"And every night," he murmured, laying back against the pillows.

Feeling exceedingly content, Elizabeth laid her head down on his shoulder and felt him wrap his arm around her.

"I did not ask if you minded it when I did this," she said, realising she might not have liked it so very much herself, if their positions had been reversed.

"I do not mind at all. I like it, just to lie here with you – to feel the presence of my lover. However, I shall reserve the right to limit you to an hour's worth of this, if we sleep in this way and I find my shoulder numb in the morning."

Elizabeth laughed, then, and was surprised when it turned into a sudden, violent yawn, prompting him to do the same. She smiled, and said, "I find myself torn; now that we *can* linger together and talk. I wish to, but I am so very tired."

"I feel the same, but perhaps we should sleep. It has been a long, emotional day, and we have a lifetime to spend together now," said he. "And I believe I am going to have the most delightful dreams, of my wife and my child."

"I think I may have good dreams, too," she said, nestling in even closer to him.

Elizabeth did fall asleep with her head upon his shoulder, but when she awoke, she found they had separated. If she had been dreaming, she could not recall what she had dreamed of, although she could feel that restlessness she often did in the middle of the night. But he was there before her in the bed, and she watched him – he seemed to sleep so deeply – and felt herself gradually growing calmer.

Everything was different here, so different as to reassure her: the nakedness of her person, made warm by the presence of the man beneath the covers with her; the remnants of their coupling between her legs; the handsome bed surrounding her. None of these, however, was as reassuring as the countenance before her.

I am Mrs. Darcy, and will be forevermore. Elizabeth smiled, closed her eyes, and returned to sleep much more quickly than she usually did.

CHAPTER 16

December 12, 1815

Darcy found himself glad he had chosen to make the journey from London to Longbourn by carriage, rather than on horseback, as he had contemplated. The distance was not far, but might have been a far more uncomfortable one, for he found himself periodically thinking about reuniting with his wife, and becoming very aroused at the thought.

They had intended to have this trip done far sooner, but Elizabeth had been reluctant to leave her new home. It had only been when they determined that they should go before Christmas, lest they be travelling when weather might delay their journey, that they had come south together. A fortnight in London had made the journey seem worthwhile: Elizabeth had become acquainted with the house there; introduced him to her aunt and uncle Gardiner, whom Darcy had found to be very fine company; had an appointment with an accoucheur; and taken her part of the needed meetings with his men of business. Darcy's business had taken longer to conclude, however, and they had eventually decided she should go on to Longbourn before him.

It was the most practical solution, and he had always thought himself a practical man, but that had been before he had married and experienced all the joys of having the company of a wife, both day and night. His connubial happiness had yet to decrease – if anything, it had increased, as they lived together and came to know each other even better. He could not have found a wife more perfectly fitted for him in every way, and was every day intensely glad she had finally been able to marry him.

Yet there was always an undercurrent of fear, for him, that came with this happiness, and this was that it could be taken away. She was carrying their child, a child they had both very much wanted and been so happy to learn of, but he could never entirely forget that this child could take her from him; it had been him who had wished for her to see the accoucheur, and would wish her to be attended by that physician when the time came, for anything that minimised the risks must be done, regardless of the cost.

He feared, as well, that he would push her too far – or, more likely, that she would push herself too far – in their marital relations. She would always carry the past with her, everything she had endured in the bedchamber of the house he now approached, and he thought that curious, spontaneous nature of hers would always war with it; he feared someday she would suggest something that, once done, frightened or disgusted her, and he would realise it too late, when damage was already done. Damage between the two of them could be repaired, now that there was so much fundamental trust between them, but he loathed the thought of hurting her, of damaging that trust and having to rebuild it.

He felt, though, that he was coming to understand the crux of what she disliked. After having to submit to the will of another through the whole of her first marriage, she could never enjoy anything that required her to be submissive. He could, on occasion, find it quite enjoyable himself, to watch her straddling him, riding him, and taking her pleasure from it, and the first time she had put her mouth on his cock, it had been unbearably good, so good he had needed to summon all of his resolve, to lie there flat on the bed, to keep his hips absolutely still, to keep his hands from her head, so she felt in no way forced to continue, letting her know only through the sounds he made – sounds he had not known himself to be capable of making – how incredibly good it had felt.

Darcy had never desired a submissive wife – he had fallen in love with Elizabeth, after all – and so gaining this understanding had lessened some of his fears. Edward had been right, that Darcy was too used to getting his own way, but his love and respect for Elizabeth made him naturally wish to solicit her thoughts. Every time he did so, he could see her trust in him growing still more, as he proved he would never require her to submit to his will, and beyond this, that he truly valued her opinions.

The carriage entered Longbourn's drive, ending Darcy's reflections and returning his mind to the eager anticipation of seeing his wife again, and it seemed ages before the horses halted and his footman was opening the door and drawing down the stairs. Darcy entered the house and was greeted effusively by Mrs. Bennet, and in a more subdued manner by the two remaining Miss Bennets, who informed him that Lizzy was in her library. This struck him as entirely too informal for his wife, although he supposed he was to be considered family now; Mary and Catherine were his sisters, and Mrs. Bennet his mother, which seemed particularly absurd. Elizabeth was still Elizabeth to him, and always would be, and he called her Mrs. Darcy in company, and periodically when they were alone, because she still seemed to enjoy it. She, for her part, still called him Mr. Darcy most often – it had surely reached the point where she was teasing him over it at least some of the time – and might only occasionally venture forth a Fitzwilliam. Darcy made pleasantries with the three women who had now become part of his family as best he could, and then left them to go see his wife.

He knocked on the library door and was invited to enter, and that first sight of her there, seated behind the desk and looking over the estate's book, was so like his fantasy that his breath caught in his throat. She looked up at him with those eyes – oh, how he adored those eyes, especially when they were directed towards him with such a loving expression! – and rose from her chair. He went to her there behind the desk, and kissed her very thoroughly.

"How have you been, my love?" he asked.

"Well enough. Preparing everything for my extended absence has taken more effort than I thought it would, but the new steward does seem to be very competent."

"Does he? I am glad of it. I am sure it will make both of us easier at mind to have someone you may trust in the role." He spoke to her, but could not help but be distracted by the presence of the desk, just beside them, and perhaps he glanced to it one too many times, for she said:

"Is something the matter? Something with your business in town? You seem very distracted."

"It is nothing. I used to – I used to fantasise about loving you, here."

"Loving me?"

"Loving you atop that desk, as your husband."

"Oh." Her eyes widened. "Well, you are my husband now. There is no reason why we may not embark upon your fantasy."

His cock hardened further, the result of both her words and the manner in which they were said. "Are you not unwell?"

"No, I have been feeling better for an hour or so. I *had* been hoping you would arrive later in the day, when I was well enough to fully enjoy being your wife. I have missed you so very much. You must tell me what to do, though – what it was you desired, in your fantasy." She closed the book before her, and did indeed move to place it on the bookshelf. As she did this, Darcy checked to ensure the door was closed and drew the curtains – never a consideration, in his fantasy, but the easiest way to scandalise the household, if someone should pass by and see them.

When they had reunited beside the desk and Elizabeth was looking at him expectantly, Darcy said, "We must spend some time in kissing."

"Well, thus far your fantasy aligns with what mine might have been, if I had one," she said, and then was twining her hands behind his neck and kissing him passionately for some time, until he put his hands upon her hips and lifted her very slowly up onto the desk. There was something intensely, almost painfully attractive about her in this moment, sitting there before him and breathing heavily, those lovely eyes dark with desire, and he resumed kissing her with even more fervour than before.

Darcy had spent a goodly amount of his separation from his wife recalling everything he loved about her, including her lips and her kisses, and he might have enjoyed these things for far longer, if it had not been several days since he had been inside her. In time, he broke the kiss, and upon his doing this, she asked: "What now?"

"You lie back on the desk, and I pleasure you."

"Mr. Darcy, are you quite certain this is *your* fantasy?"

"I would not complain if it aligned with yours," he said, waiting until she had done as he instructed to begin lifting her skirts up, until all of her that could be exposed was exposed to him. He would miss their complete nakedness in this encounter, and yet there was a certain frisson to going about this more quickly, and with more need than their usual pace, that he thought would make up for it.

Darcy spent a little time in enjoyment of the silk stockings upon her legs before moving to the bare skin of her thighs, and then to her centre. He had come to know her much better here, and could draw out her climax or speed it up, and as he was not sure how much longer he could wait himself, he brought her to it quickly, enjoying the look of her bosom heaving beneath her stays, of her eyes closed and her head thrown back, all so very much like what he had envisioned. As he enjoyed this sight, he unbuttoned the fall of his trousers, and freed his cock.

She did not have to tell him aloud that she was ready for him any longer; she was quite effective at doing this with her eyes, and once she had opened them she did so, and he contemplated what came next, what was to be that moment where he entered her and thrust in and out and achieved every long-desired sensation.

He dragged her hips closer to him, as he had done in his fantasies. He felt her tense, as he did so, and although neither of them spoke, he could feel the knowledge pass between them, that she had disliked this, and he understood.

Slowly, he leant over her, without putting any of his weight on her, and put his hands beneath her back, helping her to rise. He held her there where she sat, on the edge of the desk, and kissed her tenderly.

"I am sorry – I fear I have ruined your fantasy," she murmured.

"You have ruined nothing, dearest Elizabeth – I assure you, it is far better to have a real wife than a fantasy wife," he said, and then thought he would attempt humour to draw her out of the guilty mood that appeared to be forming on her countenance. "The desk was far too short, anyway."

She smiled, and her expression lightened. "I do still want you to have your chance to – to finish. Might we try the chair?"

"I think I would like that very much," he said, seating himself there and holding out his arms to her. "Come to me, my love, and help me make a new fantasy."

After the Darcys had spent a while clinging together in exhausted, blissful satisfaction on the chair in the library, they had spent an hour looking over the estate's current book together, seeing that all was right within and finding that Mary and the new steward, Mr. Moseby, had done well in Elizabeth's absence. When this was done, finding there was still time before dinner, Elizabeth desired to begin the process of going through her possessions, to determine what was to be donated or discarded, and what was to be sent on to Pemberley. Darcy had the choice of either going with her or going to sit with the rest of the family in the parlour, and he chose to go with her. He did wish to get to know his new sisters, but his patience for Mrs. Bennet was rather thin. Darcy thought himself very aligned with his wife, in this – indeed, she seemed to have even less patience for Mrs. Bennet, and Mrs. Bennet her, despite the very generous thing Elizabeth had done, in returning the Longbourn household to her mother's management.

Elizabeth led him up to a dusty attic, and he helped her open the first in a row of her trunks, then had little to do except seat himself on one of the other dusty trunks and watch his wife take out a great quantity of black dresses.

"I hardly know whether to keep these or not," said she. "It feels odd to keep black dresses for the chance they are needed. Perhaps I am being superstitious, though."

"You would have ample room to store them at Pemberley, although I fully understand your superstition. Indeed, I think I would rather you did not keep them."

"It is decided, then. I shall look to the future with the hope of not wearing black for a very long time, and these will go to the poor, although I suppose I should hold back a few of the better ones as perquisites for the maids."

This decision meant the first trunk was completed rather quickly, with only various gloves, stockings, and bonnets set aside to make the trip to Pemberley. When he helped her with the second, his nose was met with a certain musty foulness that was recognisable even above the other smells in the attic.

"Oh, they must have mixed up the trunks." Even in the dim light, he could see Elizabeth's countenance turn grim. "These belonged to Collins. I should go through them and get rid of them – I should have done it after his death, but I just ordered everything packed away and sent up here."

"Why do you not let me go through them? I would gladly spare you the task, and I will be better able to sort through a gentleman's things anyway."

"I hate to have you do that."

"I would much rather I do it than you have to. Let me help you open the next of your trunks, and then I will set about it."

It was only when Darcy began taking the first items out of the trunk that he felt how very morbid his present task was, to be a second husband going through the belongings of the first. These feelings were easily set aside, however, when he reminded himself that he did this for Elizabeth.

Mr. Collins had been a stout man in Darcy's brief acquaintance with him, and his increase in weight after he had married told in his clothes. They were the source of the smell from within the trunk, and of lesser quality broadcloth and poorer tailoring than Darcy thought Collins should have been able to afford. Even the shirts were thus, although better-made, and Darcy presumed Elizabeth had sewn them. He considered setting them aside to see if the male servants of the house would wish to have them, decided against it – he would make it up to them in his vails – and put everything with the dresses designated for the poor.

Rather glad to be through the clothes, he removed two pairs of shoes and one of boots, and did set these aside for the staff, for if any of them were a proper fit, it would have been a shame for them to be bypassed for this gift. Next books, seemingly remnant from Collins's clerical days, Fordyce and Hannah More the only names Darcy recognised, and he set them aside to go down to the library. Below the books was a rather nice-looking square of mahogany, which turned out to be a gentleman's dressing box, of much better quality than anything else that had been in the trunk thus far, and Darcy wondered if it had belonged to Mr. Bennet. He should have asked her about this, and whether it should be kept, but he was curious about the contents, and began removing and inspecting the various items, none very surprising.

The smaller items were kept in a little leather tray, and when he had removed them all, he removed the tray as well, to see what laid below, immediately feeling a clutch of the most dreadful feeling in his stomach.

Elizabeth had been right about Collins's interference: it was his letter. The seal to the covering letter to Mrs. Bennet looked to have been sliced under with a knife, for it was still intact, and might have been heated and stuck back to the letter with little difficulty, if Mr. Collins had intended to give over the letter, rather than hiding it away here. When Darcy unfolded the covering letter, he found his letter to Elizabeth in the same condition.

He knew now, without any doubt, what had happened to his letter, and he was contemplating whether to tell Elizabeth of his discovery when he noticed what appeared to be another letter below it. This he should not have read – this was surely some other private correspondence – but Darcy found himself so filled with rage towards the dead man that he unfolded it anyway, and found it was, in fact, for him:

"Mr. Darcy,

"I think it my duty, on behalf of myself, and my most noble former patroness, the Right Honourable Lady Catherine de Bourgh, to firmly remind you of your engagement to Miss de Bourgh. I find, moreover, that beyond your unfaithfulness to Miss de Bourgh, who might have been the most accomplished young woman in the country, had her constitution been stronger, I must protest at your paying addresses to my betrothed.

"Miss Elizabeth Bennet is engaged to marry me, and your attempting to give her another proposal must only be confusing to a mind presently suffering under the feebleness of grief."

The letter stopped, there, presumably when Mr. Collins had realised that to complete it, to send it, would not only expose himself as having opened a letter for another, but also undoubtedly bring Darcy to Longbourn as soon as he had received it, with a pair of duelling pistols in his carriage. For if Darcy had known Collins had intercepted the letter, he would have ordered his carriage readied immediately, with intentions to call the man out.

"That dressing box belonged to my father," Elizabeth said, suddenly standing over him. "I would like to keep it."

Darcy stood, bringing the letters with him and taking care not to disturb any of the bottles and instruments he had scattered about him on the floor.

"You should know of what was inside," he said, gently, and handed her the letter that had been intended for her.

Elizabeth's eyes filled with tears, she shook her head, and handed it back to him. "I am not ready to see that. Not in this house. Will you keep it for me, until we return to Pemberley? I know of the contents already."

"Of course," he said, and reached out to embrace her, holding her there for a very long time.

Elizabeth remained subdued through dinner and the drawing-room after, and they both suffered through conversation that generally consisted of Mrs. Bennet's recitations of all she intended to do to the house. Elizabeth sighed a few times during this, but made no attempt to check her mother, and Darcy thought to suggest to her later that they employ some of his men of business to ensure Mrs. Bennet's pin money was doled out in very small instalments by men with very firm countenances.

It was primarily to silence Mrs. Bennet that he asked Mary if she would play the pianoforte for them, but this request significantly brightened the countenance of his sister-in-law, and she rushed across the room and seated herself at the bench. It was not a particularly enjoyable performance – there was a pedantic air to Mary's playing that made him miss Georgiana's lighter touch and greater skill. However, Georgiana had always had the benefit of expert instruction, Darcy thought, and he determined Mary should be offered the same; he would see if he could engage Georgiana's old master, for his new sister.

Having the guardianship of a very musical sister for many years had left Darcy fairly well-versed on the subject, and he recognised her sonata as

Mozart. When she finished, he affirmed with her that he had been correct, and asked if Mozart was a favourite of Mary's, learned he was, and conversed with her for some time on various composers, speaking of his sister's favourites.

He had often wished Georgiana was settled nearer, although less so now that Pemberley was not so empty, and should be filled with his child in the next year. He wished for it again presently, for he thought Georgiana and Mary might have been able to form a friendship over their shared interest in music. If simply speaking of it with him had lightened Mary's usually dour face as much as it had, surely a friendship with a young lady her age would be far more beneficial for Mary.

Darcy glanced at Catherine, his other new sister, wishing he could attempt to engage her in conversation as he had Mary, but he realised several things upon looking at her. The first was that she was looking at him rather critically, and he could not imagine why. The second was that he realised he knew absolutely nothing about what she might like to converse on. He had always thought of her as one of the silly sisters, but upon reflection, he realised that neither she nor Mary seemed to be very silly now. Perhaps it had only been the youngest sister, Lydia, who could be categorised as such, and even she sounded from her letters to Elizabeth as though she had matured, having had to learn to economise as a soldier's wife.

Neither of the two remaining Miss Bennets seemed particularly happy here, he realised, and he determined he must do what he could for them – Elizabeth wished to invite them to Pemberley, and he thought a season or two in town could also be of great benefit, particularly if their mother remained at Longbourn. Their presence might benefit him, as well: while having these two young ladies about would not be the same as the sister he had known all his life, it would be good for him to help look after Mary and Kitty, in addition to his own child.

Thinking of his own child returned his thoughts to that child's mother, and he returned his gaze to her, finding her no better. He felt the ache of worry for her, and wished he had thought to hide the letter as soon as he had seen it. He had thought it better to give it over to her rather than deceive her, but it was a reminder of something she had not wished to be reminded of, and a confirmation of her most terrible suspicion.

It was Kitty who finally asked her sister if anything was the matter, and Elizabeth claimed fatigue and said she thought she would retire early. Darcy longed to go up with her, but felt he should remain a little while longer, so as to be polite to the Bennets. He found himself wishing he had departed with his wife, however, for not ten minutes after Elizabeth had gone up, Mrs. Bennet asked Mary to play them another song at the pianoforte, and sent Catherine upstairs to fetch her mother's needlework from her apartment.

"Oh, I am glad we find ourselves alone, Mr. Darcy, for there is something I wish to speak with you about," Mrs. Bennet said, as though this had not come about as the result of her own machinations.

The last thing Darcy wanted was to have a tête-à-tête with his mother-in-law when his mind was strongly on his wife's welfare, but he saw no way to avoid it, and waited as Mrs. Bennet asked:

"How is Lizzy doing, as your wife? I know she can be impertinent – she is not always as dutiful as she should be. I have tried to get her to see how she ought to be, but – "

Darcy could listen to no more, and interrupted her. "Madam, you insult me grievously."

"Insult you? How did I insult you?" Mrs. Bennet said, in a panicked tone. "I assure you it was not my intent!"

If Mary had overheard, she made no indication of it, and Darcy was again forced to interrupt Mrs. Bennet – who had descended into profuse apologies, all the while insisting she had no idea what she could have said to insult him.

"You seem to think me incapable of judging for myself what I wish for in a wife, and you insult the choice I made."

"Oh no, no," Mrs. Bennet said. "Lizzy can be a good sort of girl, when she endeavours to – "

"I love Elizabeth as she is," said he, firmly, "and I will have no insults to her and no attempts to change her. This house remains hers and I cannot control whether she continues to allow you to stay here, but any further word from you on such subjects and I assure you, you will never be allowed to set foot within Pemberley, even to see your grandchild."

Mrs. Bennet gaped at him, her mouth opening once, twice, three times, but no sound emerged. She barely croaked out a good-night to him when he announced his intent to retire. Kitty came in, then, dropped a work-bag on the sofa beside her mother, and said she thought she should retire as well, and would walk up with him. He offered her his arm to go up the stairs, but she halted firmly in the landing, saying, with the critical look returned to her countenance: "What happened to Lizzy? She was so anticipating your arrival, but something clearly happened. She is as she used to be."

"She – when we were going through the trunks in the attic, she had a rather unexpected reminder of her first marriage," Darcy said, feeling suddenly as though it was of the utmost importance to defend himself to this young lady.

"So all is well, between the two of you?"

"Yes, generally. I worry over her reaction to that reminder."

"But you still love her? You shall still look after her?"

"Yes, Catherine. I will do both as long as I live."

Kitty looked relieved. "Good. She is usually so much happier when she is with you – at least she was, when we saw her at Pemberley. I could not bear to see her returned to how she was before."

"I promise you, I could not bear to see it either. I will return her to Pemberley as soon as it can be done, if this house is too much of a reminder," he said, and then thought to add, "and I would like for you and your sister Mary to join us there, for a long visit. Perhaps in the spring or summer?"

"I would like that very much," said Catherine, brightening for the first time since he had arrived at Longbourn.

Darcy offered her his arm again, and they separated in the hallway, Darcy very desirous of seeing how his wife was faring. The master's dressing-room at Longbourn was a little space scarcely bigger than a closet, and it was in this room that Darcy rang for Mason, and, when his valet arrived, told him to work quickly. When Mason had finished and Darcy went into the bedchamber, however, he found his wife was not there.

He was required to quell an undercurrent of panic, upon seeing this – his pregnant and very beloved wife was not where she ought to have been at this hour of the night – for a few moments of rational thought gave him a good sense of where she might have gone to. Longbourn was of an age that the back staircase was for the use of both the family and its servants, but Darcy encountered no-one as he went down. The door to the library was closed, but a faint glow from within told him he had been correct, and he knocked softly, then opened it.

She was wearing her nightgown and dressing gown, and sitting in one of the armchairs before the fireplace with her knees tucked up nearly to her chin, staring into the fire. That she had rang for someone to light it meant she intended her time here to be of some duration, he thought.

"I just wanted to ensure you were well," he said. "I will leave you, if you wish to be alone."

"No, come in," she said. "You are always welcome here."

Darcy closed the door behind him and brought the other chair nearer hers, laying his hand upon her shoulder and saying simply, "Elizabeth."

She was silent in response, and Darcy followed her gaze to the fireplace. It appeared she had not had a servant light the fire, and had instead made it herself – the books he had retrieved from Collins's trunk earlier that day were burning within the coal grate.

"You have learned something horrid about your wife, now," said Elizabeth, laughing bitterly. "She is a burner of books."

"I will presume you had a reason."

"If you consider spite a sufficient reason, then I suppose I did. Those books were part of my required course of reading. I was not even allowed in this room for a very long time – not until I had finished all of the books on the list. And even then, I had to arrange a convenient time for me to take out a book, and could not choose anything too *frivolous*."

"Oh, my poor Elizabeth," he murmured, too shocked to say more.

"I hated him for it while he lived, and yet now in a way I am glad. This is the one room in the house where I hardly remember him – my memories of my father are far stronger here. And I have memories of you from this room, too. Not – not what we did here earlier," she said, colouring slightly, "but when you would come to meet with me here. You always listened to me. You always treated me as an equal."

A man had better listen to the woman he was desperately in love with, Darcy thought, but it was not the right thing to say at such a time. Instead, he asked quietly: "Is it very painful, for you to return to this house?"

"Much more than I expected," she said. "I lived here for a year, after his death; you would think I would be better able to manage having returned. To have been away, though, where everything is new and wonderful, and then to return and see what you found today – it has all been a very painful reminder."

"Do you wish to leave for Pemberley tomorrow?"

She nodded, tearfully. "I suppose if there is one good thing about your finding the letter, it is that it frees me of any mixed emotions over his death. I am free to think he deserved it, now."

"I rather thought he deserved it before, for treating you as he did."

"The worst things he did – so far as I was concerned – were perfectly within his rights as a husband. The estate had already been doing poorly, and he would not speak of it to any of us, but I know he struggled over how to manage it. He was an incompetent man, who took control where he could get it. I had thought I would at least have control over the household, but the more I argued with him over what should be done to the estate, the more he tightened his control there, and I found my mother, who would wheedle and flatter him as I would not, given responsibilities that should have been mine. Before his death, he mandated that he must approve any expenditure on the household greater than five pounds, that I wished to make."

"Five pounds? That is inconceivable."

"I believe it is especially so for you, my love, for you are generous, and have the income to be generous. Most people do not have your disposition, combined with your income."

"That should not prevent them from allowing their wife to take her proper role in the household."

"My role in the household was to make shirts – and breed. That became clear to me, over time, that my purpose was to breed an heir, and I was failing at it."

"Through no fault of your own," he said, longing to touch her belly, to reassure them both of the child growing there, but he could not with her legs tucked so tight against it. He ran his hand back and forth across her shoulder, instead, wishing to soothe her.

"True – if only I had that proof back then. I wanted a child so badly, both because I knew it would make things easier for me, but more because I wanted the love of a child. I have wondered if that would have been taken from me as well, though – if I would not have been allowed my proper role as a mother."

There could be no greater cruelty, he thought, than doing such a thing to a mother, and he could only be thankful she would never experience that with their child. It pained her to speak of all of this, he knew, but he was glad she did; he could only help her in the future if he better understood her past, and she had been reticent about sharing more of it since they had married.

"I am surprised he left the estate to you, given how little he thought of you."

"I have wondered over that myself. Perhaps deep down he did understand that I was capable of more than he allowed, or perhaps he simply did not think to update his will, later in our marriage. The entail had ended, so I am not sure he had any alternatives that would have been deemed acceptable by society. He was certainly eager for me to produce an heir, so he could pass the estate to his own child."

One's will was not the place to be considering society, Darcy thought, for society would matter little upon its coming into effect. Perhaps, though, the sway of society had been stronger on Collins's will than it would have been on other men's, and Darcy wondered whether Elizabeth owed her ownership of Longbourn, in part, to the influence of his aunt. They sat in silence for a while, then he asked, softly, the thing that most pained him to think about: "Did he ever strike you?"

"Once. He spoke of sending me back to town, to visit with another accoucheur, and I said maybe it was better if I did not have an heir, for the estate would be so deeply in debt by the time the child came of age that it would be a burden to inherit. He hit me across the face – I think it surprised him as much as it surprised me."

Up until now, Darcy had maintained a strong mastery over his temper, but this was too much. He stood and strode over to the window, quivering with rage, and flung open the curtains he had closed earlier that day. He knew himself to be in possession of this strong temper, but the thought of being so overcome by one's temper as to strike a woman – to strike *Elizabeth* – was the most abhorrent thing possible. His hands clenched into fists, and in that moment, he wished Collins was there so Darcy could strike him in retaliation. Yes, Collins had entirely deserved his death, so far as Darcy was concerned.

He heard Elizabeth approaching behind him. She must have sensed how this had angered him, for she wrapped her arms loosely about his chest and said, "It was just the once."

"Once was too much." Her embrace had worked, for he felt the anger leave him, replaced with an overwhelming grief for her, for everything she had suffered, including that. He turned, so he could wrap his own arms around her, and they stood there before the window, embracing.

Quietly, she said: "What I cannot help but dwell on is, what if he had not died? What if I had remained married, and you had joined the party at Netherfield? We might have met as acquaintances, and I never would have known all my life could be."

"I think – I think if I had come here and seen you in such misery, I would have attempted to convince you to run away with me, and if I had, once the damage had been done, to persuade him into a divorce, funded by myself."

She looked at him sharply. "You would have exposed yourself to that much scandal, and expense?"

"To get you out of that marriage, and to right the wrong I had committed, yes. I have not always been all that I should have, as a man," he said. "After Charles checked me – after I lost you – I spent a great amount of time in self-reflection, and I came to understand something: nothing is more important than love, and family. Society may hang itself, if it prevents my being with you."

"Society was no obstacle, thankfully, although I am very touched by what you say."

Indeed, it had been no obstacle, for the story amongst the ton had, as expected, been that he had married an heiress. Darcy returned his mind to her earlier question rather than this, however, mulling it over.

"I suppose an annulment might have been possible. I believe you were not of age at the time you married, and I must presume your father would not have left you to the guardianship of Mr. Collins – perhaps one of your uncles. Did your guardian consent to your marriage?"

"No, neither of my uncles did, although my uncle Gardiner was in Bristol for his business when my father died. It all happened so quickly, guardianship was never discussed," she said. "I was old enough, though, when I consented to the marriage. I did not know all that it would entail, but I was fairly certain I was condemning myself to a lifetime of unhappiness."

"That would not have prevented my attempting to use it as a means to end your marriage."

"You know a lot about these matters – divorce, and annulment. I never thought over whether one of my uncles should consent to my marriage."

He sighed, and realised there was something he should have told her of, but it had never come up in conversation. "I once had to consider what I would have done to get my sister out of an elopement."

"Georgiana! She did not elope, did she?"

"No, not in her present marriage. When she was fifteen, though, George Wickham very nearly persuaded her into an elopement. His aim was her dowry. I was fortunate to intervene at the time that I did, for if I had not, I would have been chasing them to Gretna Green, and if that had not been successful, then seeking an annulment on the grounds of my not having given consent."

Elizabeth's countenance showed every bit of shock that such a revelation could engender. "You know he did persuade Mary King into an elopement, do you not?"

"I saw the announcement in the papers, but did not realise that had been the means of it, although I suppose I should have. I hardly know whether to be relieved for my sister, and for you, or saddened for the poor young lady."

"For me?"

"I believe you once liked his company."

"A very long time ago, but I do not think I would ever have been tempted by him into matrimony, although he did succeed for a time in poisoning my mind against you. He told me a very elaborate story about how you had withheld the Kympton living from him, leaving him to make his own way in the world, despite the wishes of your late father."

Darcy had not thought about George Wickham for a very long time, but found the man's name still provoked a deep inner anger, made all the worse for Wickham's having slandered him to Elizabeth; he had already made enough mistakes of his own in the past, without Wickham telling lies to further tarnish his character. "How did you come to know it was a lie? I can hardly imagine him developing a conscience and determining to tell you the truth, and there was no one else in the neighbourhood who knew the particulars of our history."

"I realised it when Mr. Althorpe tried to do the same and convince me of how you mistreated your servants, when I had already seen you do the opposite. I saw what had happened in the past for what it was."

Darcy took a deep breath, and exhaled. He had already lost his temper once, and did not want his anger towards Wickham to influence how he spoke to Elizabeth, particularly on this night. Even if she *had* received the letter, her opinion of him at that time had been influenced not only by his own behaviour, but also her belief that he was a selfish, spiteful man, to withhold what his father had promised.

"I did offer him the living, upon its becoming vacant, but he had no intent of becoming a clergyman," he said. "Wickham asked for alternate compensation, I gave him three thousand pounds, and when he had wasted all of that away in idleness and dissipation, he tried to replace it with Georgiana's inheritance. I am surprised you never asked me of the truth – I would have told you at any time."

"I wish I had asked you directly back then, but once I came to realise it was a lie, the details behind it mattered little to me," she said. "Now you know better why I might not have chosen you, if I had received your letter."

They stood there for some time longer, loosely embracing. Darcy thought he should suggest they go upstairs and attempt to sleep – this had already been a wearying day for her, without speaking of such things – when the last remnants of the books burning in the fireplace shifted and fell through the grate with an ashy thud, leaving the room dark save their two candles.

She sighed. "We should go up, if we are to leave tomorrow."

Darcy took up his candle, and she hers, and they made their way up the creaky old stairs and into the bedchamber. Elizabeth halted, when they were halfway to the bed, laid her hand on his arm, and said, "Fitzwilliam, I don't want to – I don't want to have marital relations tonight. Please – not in this room. I hope you understand."

"Of course. I did not think you would desire it tonight, regardless," he said. "I loathe the thought of what you endured here."

Darcy stared at the dark, sombre bed where his wife had suffered every night, and thought that if there had been an axe in the room, he would have been strongly tempted to begin chopping it apart and feeding it to the fire, just as she had done with the books. They approached and climbed in; Darcy felt a momentary strangeness at occupying a dead man's place, but then it passed. He laid on his back, and was glad to see that she came over to him and laid her head down upon his shoulder, as she usually liked to do.

"Elizabeth, why did you never change rooms? You are the mistress of the house – you have a right to sleep in whichever one you wish."

"I had no choice. It would have been admitting weakness to everyone in the house that I could not bear to remain in here."

"Then lay the blame on me, and say I do not like it. The windows *are* full east – it must be terribly bright in the mornings. Let us take up one of the others across the hall, when next we are here."

"Thank you, my love. That is a very kind offer to carry the blame, and I shall take it. My mother, certainly, would like the olive branch if I were to give her these rooms back," Elizabeth said, and then grew more serious. "Fitzwilliam, I am sorry."

"Sorry? Whatever do you have to be sorry over?"

"It cannot be easy to have such a wife as me," she said. "I have healed so much. *You* have healed me so much. I have a philosophy that I try to maintain – to think only of the past as its remembrance gives you pleasure – but sometimes the past still catches up with me: not the pleasant memories, but the worst ones."

"Elizabeth, do not ever feel you must apologise for that again. I love you. I wish I could describe better how very much I love you – I have never been good at speaking of such things – but I believe you know."

"I do," she whispered.

Darcy wondered what his wife must have been like during her first marriage, if she had been brought so low by mere memories. He thought, remorsefully, that if he had asked her properly, she would never have been like this. But tonight was not a night to speak of his own guilt; she knew of it already, and she had reassured him over it, and he would recall those reassurances to mind once he had done what he could to soothe her.

"I want for you to heal, Elizabeth – I want to help you heal," he said, "but I do not think you can expect it to happen all at once, or in a perfect manner. It will bring you low sometimes, I think, and when it does, I will be here. And in time, I hope, it will fade."

They would both fade, he hoped: his guilt and her pain. Darcy kissed the top of her head, and they settled into silence.

Elizabeth seemed drained by their discussion, and fell asleep quickly. Darcy was not long to follow her, but he woke in the middle of the night, and found she was already awake, lying there very quietly with her head on the pillow, looking at him.

"Are you well, my love?" he asked.

"I am," she said. "I had a bad dream, but then I woke, and you were here."

"Do you have such dreams frequently?" he asked, concerned, for she had never mentioned them before.

"I used to, but I have not for some months. Sometimes I even have good dreams."

"Is there anything I may do for you?"

"Just be here," she whispered. "Just be here with me."

If she woke again, Darcy did not know of it, for he forced himself to remain awake until he could see she had returned to slumber. and then he slept deeply until, as he had predicted, a rather severe sunrise imposed itself on them. It was not a day to be lingering in bed, however; Elizabeth was so ill as to need to void her stomach, something that had happened very nearly every morning of her pregnancy. He attended her as best he could, rubbing her back and sending for tea and toast to try to help settle her stomach, but generally he felt helpless. She was carrying their child, but had all the burden of it.

Over breakfast, which Elizabeth took very little of, the rest of the family were informed that the Darcys would begin their journey north that day, rather than staying a few more days as had originally been planned. This prompted a goodly degree of upheaval, and frantic summoning of servants. Such chaos was needless: Mason and Rachel Lawson – now promoted officially to the role of Elizabeth's lady's maid – had already begun packing the trunks, and Darcy had sent Tom to the White Hart to order post horses for the first stage.

Darcy went down to the stables, to see the waggonette loaded with those trunks and items that would not fit on the chaise. It would be pulled north by his own horses, with ample stops for them to feed, water, and rest.

He was a little surprised to find Elizabeth had followed him thither, and then recalled what else was to go with the waggonette. The pony phaeton had already been placed atop it and tied down, and by the expression upon Elizabeth's face, she seemed to think Chip should have been given this conveyance, rather than being tethered behind the waggonette.

"Good morning, my little Chippy," she said, feeding him apple slices from her hand and then, when these had been finished, scratching him behind his ears. "Mr. Darcy, are you quite certain he will be able to keep up? He is so much shorter than the horses."

"You are shorter than I, and yet you have no difficulty walking Pemberley's grounds with me," he said. "The pace will be slow, and they will stop frequently. The horses *are* pulling the waggonette, while Chip has no burden."

She still looked dubious.

"We shall pass them on the road, and you may see for yourself how he gets on," he promised, patting his own horses and then nodding to his under-coachman, John, on being informed that the waggonette was loaded and ready to depart. He stepped aside as the team made their start, and walked with Elizabeth into the yard to watch Chip following behind them with no difficulty. Tom, who was to be the waggonette's outrider, followed after on Archer, but Darcy waved him over to where they stood.

"Tom, take particular care of Mrs. Darcy's pony. I suspect he has become the most valuable animal in my stable."

"Oh aye, sir. Mr. Rodney already tole me. An' gave me these." Tom lifted the flap on his saddlebag to show a great quantity of apples.

Darcy shook his head in mock displeasure. "See that you keep a few for yourself and John."

"Thank ye, sir," Tom said, and trotted off, to catch the waggonette.

"I am going to have to plant more apple trees at Pemberley, I see," he said.

She laughed. He was glad she was laughing again. "You know, your man never did send me an invoice for Chip and the phaeton."

"Oh, he was always intended to be a gift. I understand men are supposed to buy gifts for their mistresses."

"And their wives," she said, smilingly.

"Yes, of course, particularly their wives," he said. "You seem better, my dear. Are you feeling better?"

"I am feeling much better, of all the things that afflicted me last night, and I shall be even better when I am returned to Pemberley," she said, taking up his hand. "Come, Mr. Darcy, let us go home."

EPILOGUE

October 12, 1822

"Faster, mama, faster!" exclaimed the little girl seated beside Elizabeth in the pony phaeton.

"Chip can only go so fast, sweetling," Elizabeth said, looking up ahead to where her husband and son were trotting, Mr. Darcy on one of his hunters, and James on his own pony, the present delight of the boy's existence. "We shall catch them eventually."

Father and son slowed to a walk, and it appeared the boy was being gently corrected on some aspect of his horsemanship. Elizabeth was glad of it; after having lost her first husband in a riding accident, she had feared greatly losing her second, most beloved one in the same manner. She still fretted every hunting season, but over time she had come to accept that his skill was exceptional, and his manner on a horse was never risky. Now, he would ensure his son developed the same skill and caution.

The riders reached the clearing where a very fine nuncheon had been laid out, handed off their mismatched mounts to the grooms assembled there, and stood waiting as Chip trotted into the clearing and Elizabeth brought him to a halt. Tom took hold of the pony's ribbons near the bit, although they all knew this to be unnecessary, and Mr. Darcy handed his wife out of the phaeton before picking up his daughter and swinging her about in that dizzying manner she enjoyed very much.

"And how was your drive, my little Jane?"

"Slow! Papa, I want a pony, like James. I don't wanta go slow with mama."

"Then who will ride with your mama in the phaeton, sweetling?"

"Edward can ride with her! Then I can ride my pony with you and James. May I have a pony, papa? Please, please, may I have a pony?"

Elizabeth sighed. She had suspected this day was coming; Jane was not much younger than her elder brother had been when he first learned to ride, and she had long since entered the phase where she wished to do everything he could. And Elizabeth did not like leaving her younger son behind in the nursery, anyway, so perhaps it was time for another of her children to graduate from sitting beside her. Darcy looked over to his wife, and she gave him a resigned smile.

"Very well, Jane, we will begin looking for a pony for you," he said, leading her over to where the nuncheon had been laid out. "It will be more difficult for you to learn, however, for you will have to ride side-saddle, so it will be some time before you are done riding with your mama."

"Why does Jane hafta ride side-saddle?" asked James, who had taken an inquisitive turn at the age of three, and remained thus at six. Elizabeth had been touched at her husband's suggestion that they name him after her father, but while he might have shared his namesake's curiosity, he was far more talkative and active than it seemed James Bennet ever could have been, even as a child.

"Do you remember when we talked about the differences between boys and girls?" Darcy asked, and when the boy nodded, he continued, "Because ladies wear dresses, they cannot ride astride like you and I."

"Why doesn't mama ride side-saddle?"

"Because she prefers to drive."

The boy nodded again, and made for the cakes and tarts, before he was directed that he could not begin his nuncheon with them. Seeing that his sister had already started on the plate of fine, ripe slices of pine-apple, and that these seemed to be allowed, he joined her.

Elizabeth seated herself beside her husband and said, "I hope they leave a little for us, and later I want to hear more about this conversation about the differences between boys and girls."

"Thank you, Mrs. Darcy, for desiring I relive the mortification. And if they eat all of the pine-apple we shall just send someone to the pinery for more, although I fear someday this family is going to eat all of the fruit on the estate."

Elizabeth chuckled. "At Pemberley, never!"

"Why does Jane inhawit Longbourn and I inhawit Pemberley?" asked James, the lower part of his face covered in pine-apple juice. "Is it because she's a girl and I'm a boy?"

"In-heir-it," Elizabeth corrected him firmly, but gently. "And yes, my messy boy, it is because your papa and I decided before you were born that Pemberley would pass through the male line – through the boys – while Longbourn would pass through the female line – through the girls."

"What does Edward in-heir-it?"

"There are only two estates," Darcy said. "So Edward will have a career, in the law or the clergy, I hope, so his mama does not worry over him too much, and I am sure we will all be very proud of him."

"But I won't have a career! Will you be proud of me?"

"You and Jane will learn about managing estates, which is not a career, but it is very, very important," Darcy said. "Many people will depend on you for their livelihood, and of course we will be very proud of you."

"What if New Baby is a girl? Will she have a career?"

"Girls are not allowed to have very many careers," said Elizabeth. "So if New Baby is a girl, she will have a dowry – she will have money we give her, that she can live on. Or if she falls in love, she can marry, and she and her husband can share the money."

"I want a dow-y!" exclaimed Jane.

"Longbourn brings in three thousand a year, sweetling, and it is worth more money than your sisters's dowries would be."

"But I want a hus-bind!"

"You may have a husband and have Longbourn, Jane," said Elizabeth. It was much too early to be telling her daughter that she would have to be very careful to choose the right husband, with such an inheritance to her name.

"Oh! Good! I am going to have Log-bourn and a hus-bind and a pony!"

"Just like her mama," Darcy murmured to Elizabeth, as the children returned to the pine-apple slices and the two of them made their own selections. They were allowed only a little time to eat before James asked:

"What's the clergy and the law?"

Elizabeth smiled as her husband, who had proven even more patient since he had become a father, explained the professions as best he could in a manner that could be comprehended by young children. She felt suffused with the contentment that seemed now at the core of her life, to be seated here in this beautiful place with her beautiful husband and some of their beautiful children. She did wish her whole family could be together, but it had become apparent that there would always be a younger one in the nursery; even though she had nursed Edward for longer than his elder brother and sister, it had only delayed the creation of "New Baby," the family moniker for the child she now carried, for a little while.

They spent almost all their time at Pemberley, now. Over the years, their visits south had dwindled, and now they only managed occasional trips, to town and then to Longbourn on their return, and they had not even done this since the birth of their third child. Elizabeth had hired a competent steward all those years ago, however, and Mr. Moseby sent her copies of the estate's book periodically for review. He was not supervised so closely as he had been in the beginning, for Elizabeth had long since come to trust his judgment. It had been the three of them together – Mrs. and Mr. Darcy, and Mr. Moseby – that had seen the estate to its present income, through expansion, improvements – of which the most dramatic was that of Mr. Wendell's field – and better enforcement of all that had not been enforced under the two previous incumbents. Jane's inheritance would not be so grand as her elder brother's, but it was far more than most young ladies could expect.

In the beginning, Mary had ably overseen Mr. Moseby's work, between visits to Pemberley and town, but she had, surprisingly, been the first to leave her household responsibilities. Her time with her elder sisters and brothers, and her friendship with Georgiana – returned to England with her family, thankfully – had been most beneficial, and it had pleased Elizabeth to see how Mary had flourished. None of them had expected her to make a romantic attachment, but Mary had indeed done so. She had married, was quite in love with her husband and her first child, and had been, unsurprisingly, a shrewd manager of her household accounts.

Catherine had remained hesitant of the marital state, but in her own visits with her sisters and brothers, she had come to see that if Elizabeth could find such happiness with a husband who thoroughly loved and respected his wife, Catherine should seek the same. She had eventually found such a man for herself, and was now most happily married. Catherine's wedding had been followed by another surprise: Mrs. Bennet had announced her intent to wed a retired colonel of the regulars, a widower like herself. They had settled together in Bath, and either the waters or her second marriage seemed to have done much to improve Mrs. Thompson's nerves. She treated Elizabeth more respectfully, now, although as this had begun well before her marriage and merely improved since, Elizabeth could only attribute it to her mother's having been allowed to take back more of her old role.

Just when it had seemed Elizabeth would be required to find a tenant for the house at Longbourn, however, she had found a more benevolent use for the house. While Ensign – now Lieutenant – Denny had been fortunate to retain his place in the retrenching of the army following Waterloo, Lydia had found herself in the family way and no longer able to follow the drum. Elizabeth had invited her to live at Longbourn, rent-free, and as Lieutenant Denny had managed to return home on leave and make himself a father again since that time, Elizabeth suspected the Dennys's finances would have been far worse if not for the savings this gratis home allowed them. Elizabeth had not suggested that Lydia take up Mary's place in overseeing Mr. Moseby's work, however: while Lydia, far more practical now, might have been capable of it, she was far too harried in what she already had to manage, with two children, no nurse, and an oft-absent husband. Elizabeth continued to pay for those servants required to run the house, but she had left a nurse to Lydia's discretion – and funds – and Lydia had opted to economise.

Elizabeth's favourite among her sisters was still Jane Darcy's namesake, and she now lived within two hours' drive of Pemberley, a drive made with great frequency by the Bingleys and the Darcys. Visits to Clifton House were only occasionally marred by the presence of Caroline Althorpe and her husband, and it had to be said that both members of that couple were far more pleasant together than they had ever been apart. They might have been even more pleasant, if the wish of both for Mr. Althorpe's childless elder brother to find some manner of dying and leaving him the viscountcy ever came to pass, but at present the viscount was somewhat grudgingly said to be in excellent health. However, the Althorpes's eldest son – an exceedingly healthy boy, for having been born so prematurely – did stand a chance of inheriting the viscountcy, so long as his uncle remained childless.

The Bingley children – Charles now had two younger sisters, and one younger brother – enjoyed playing with their cousins, and the adults still delighted in the ties of family and friendship that held them together. Sometimes, Elizabeth caught herself wondering if perhaps any of the boys and girls would someday shift from childhood companions to lifelong companions, but she always required herself to stop. Her children would all have the luxury of choice – a choice she had not been allowed, after her father's death. When she and her husband did pass – events she hoped would come far in the future – her children would know only the sorrow of losing their parents. They would not be required to make any difficult decisions. They would not be required to sacrifice their own happiness for the security of their brothers and sisters. They would know security, and – she hoped – happiness, all their lives.

The children's faces were wiped clean, the family regained their horses and phaeton, and they all returned to the house, Elizabeth walking the children up to the nursery to be reunited with their brother and nurse. She spent some time there with little Edward, watching the delightful cavorting that a boy of his age could make about a room, before he tired and was put down for his nap.

Elizabeth left the nursery and aimlessly made her way back to the other side of the house, contemplating something that had been on her mind since she and her husband had made a decision the evening before, and this was that the decision had been wrong. It had begun with a proposal of his, that they go to town before the birth of New Baby, one Elizabeth had seen little appeal in at first. Tied to Longbourn during her marriage and widowhood, she had thought town an appealing place, but enough time there early in her marriage had shown her that it held an undue proportion of stifling society and stifling air, neither of which could be endured for long when all the superior qualities of Pemberley beckoned. She had listened to his proposal, however, and he had supported it with a very good reason for going to London: although they both preferred this idyllic family life in the country, it was important to maintain their connexions in town, for their children's sake. Someday, James, Jane, and Edward would be introduced in society, and these connexions would determine their future acquaintances.

In addition to being for the ultimate benefit of her children, Fitzwilliam's proposal had been entirely attuned to what his wife would prefer. Being in the family way, she would not be required to participate in the season at its regular pace – only the most appealing invitations would be accepted. They would remain for only a few months, leaving before the noxious air turned her desperate for the country. And when they left town, they would let a house in Richmond and retire there, rather than making her travel back to Derbyshire dangerously near her confinement.

Everything else within the plan Elizabeth was still very much for; it was the house in Richmond that troubled her, for Longbourn would have been the logical choice. It was near town, and already under her ownership. If Elizabeth had thought Lydia would be overwhelmed by the disruption, she might still have favoured letting another house, but based on her sister's last few letters she thought Lydia would have gladly welcomed a resident nurse and other children to occupy Thomas and little Lydia, as well as the companionship of other adults.

The Darcys had never stayed at Longbourn for more than a few nights, however, since that first disastrous return, and Elizabeth could only presume her husband had proposed taking a house in Richmond to prevent an extended sojourn there. She did not fault him for seeking to protect her; she did, however, need to decide whether she still required that protection.

Elizabeth turned into the next hallway and smiled faintly, wondering if perhaps her path through the house had not been so aimless as she had thought, for she was entering the hallway she had first stayed in, all those years ago. She had made good on her intent to leave the room of her early residence as it was, and she opened the door almost expecting the scent of roses to greet her. It did not, but her memories arose regardless. There, on that chaise and in that bed, her future had been decided – her most beautiful future – and her first son had been conceived.

Contemplating this, the site of her most precious memories, Elizabeth found some of them still breathtakingly vivid. Particularly when she considered them from this room, there were certain moments from that night that seemed as though she had left a little part of herself within them; she had but to think of them, and she was there again. These memories, however, were still strong within her even outside of this room, roused out occasionally by a kiss or a caress or a more substantial act by her husband that reminded her particularly of that night.

Her worst memories, the ones that belonged to Longbourn, *had* faded, just as Fitzwilliam had said they would. Elizabeth reached for them now, sought them out in a way she had never done, and what she could remember did not trouble her in the way it used to. Not when so much had passed since – the majority of it wonderful. Her second marriage had not been entirely perfect, of course, but what imperfections it held were trifling. And she had been promised a beautiful future, not a perfect one.

"Elizabeth?"

She was startled from her reverie by the sound of her husband down the hall, calling her name.

"I am in here," she called out.

This was not the first time Elizabeth had come to this room to reminisce for a few minutes – once, when he had gone to town to attend to some business without her, she had sat on the chaise for better than an hour. It was the first time she had been discovered, however, and she blushed as Fitzwilliam entered.

"I wondered where you had gone to," he said, and glanced about the room. "Ah – am I interrupting your reminiscences?"

"You could not interrupt them when you are so much a part of them." Elizabeth smiled, and he needed no further invitation to come to her, to draw her into his arms and kiss her very thoroughly, very differently than that first hesitant kiss they had shared very near this location. Yes, Elizabeth thought, she was ready to go to Longbourn; ready to prove to herself that she was fully ensconced in this second marriage and no longer afflicted by the first.

"Were you feeling nostalgic, or is there a particular reason for your reminiscing?"

"There was a reason," Elizabeth said, softly. "I have been thinking, about what we decided last night."

"Do you wish to have the child here? If you are more comfortable at Pemberley, we may remain here and go to town some other season, when it is more compatible with your health."

"No, I do still wish to go to town for this season, when my *health* will allow our absence from those events we dislike," she said, giving him a shrewd look, then continuing: "It is the house in Richmond that I wished to reconsider. It seems needless to let a house there when I own a home in Hertfordshire that is just as convenient a distance from town."

"I had thought you would not wish to return to Longbourn for such a long stay."

"Perhaps a few years ago, I would not have been ready, but I believe I am, now. And I think Lydia would benefit greatly from having us there for a few months."

"As much as I appreciate how well your younger sister has matured, I would never be in favour of anything that benefits her at the risk of your composure, particularly so close to birth."

"I know, and it is good of you – as always – to think of it. It has been so long, though, and you were right, that the memories would fade."

"Have your memories in this room faded?" he asked. "Because mine certainly have not. Even now, I feel as though I can recall every moment of that night."

"I believe that is my philosophy at work – to think only of the past as its remembrance gives you pleasure," Elizabeth said. This philosophy had been often repeated, both to herself and to him, whenever either of them seemed poised to descend into remorse over the past. "I did learn one important thing, during that awful time at Longbourn – how to take pleasure in the smallest things: the first spring roses, the last of the apples in winter, going to Netherfield to visit Jane. When you have so little to be happy over, you learn to be happy over the little things."

"And now?"

"I still carry that with me, even though I have so much more. I think that is why it was so overwhelming with you, that first night here. When you are accustomed to smaller pleasures, and expecting something unpleasant, to suddenly have this tremendous, beautiful thing instead, it made me understand how much more there could be to life, and that I could have it with you."

"Have you had it, Elizabeth? Are you well and truly happy?"

"Oh, you need not ask that question! You must know I am, a hundred times over," she said. "And that is what I have realised: I have gathered up so many wonderful memories in these seven years, that there is hardly room for the bad ones. They have been crowded out of my mind, I think. I will only know for sure if we do go to Longbourn and stay there for some time, but I want to know. I am ready to know."

He kissed her again, quickly, but with such an intensity of emotion as to communicate far more than what he said, which was simply: "Then we shall stay at Longbourn, and you shall know."

It was nearing time to change for dinner, and he offered her his arm silently, to go down to their chambers to change. Elizabeth closed the door behind them, and the click of finality that signalled the room's return to being preserved for posterity broke – at least for Elizabeth – the spell of seriousness that had attended her reflections. She felt her spirits lightening, and as they descended the stairs, recalled a more recent memory that lightened them still further.

They entered their apartment through Elizabeth's very finely redecorated mistress's chambers, and she halted in the doorway to their shared sitting-room, clasping his hand so he could not leave so soon.

"I shall not let you go so easily, Mr. Darcy," she said. "You must tell me of the differences between boys and girls. Do not think I have forgotten about that."

He groaned. "I was not yet ready to be explaining such things."

"You do very well with his questions, though. You are exceedingly patient."

"You should have seen how patient I was when he asked why mama had mountains, and he and Jane and I did not."

"Mountains?"

"Mountains," he said, cupping one of her breasts in his hand, then sliding his hand down to her belly, only slightly thicker at this point in her pregnancy, "and he can recall when there was an even bigger mountain here, as he will no doubt observe again."

"Oh!" This prompted quite a fit of laughter, both in its inherent humour and in what his reaction must have been, to be asked such a thing by his son.

"I explained the differences between boys and girls and men and women, and how only women can have babies. And because mama is a woman, she would need her mountains to nurse New Baby."

"Are you going to continue to call them mountains?"

"I would rather that, for now, than have my son going around talking about breasts or bosoms."

"Oh my, I had not thought about that."

"You had better begin thinking about it, for clearly he is."

"I can hardly wait until he is older, if he keeps on this way."

"I most certainly can. I can just hear him asking about brothels and courtesans and mistresses."

"I am glad you shall be the one to have to explain such things, and not I. But what will you tell him, if he asks if you ever had a mistress?"

"That I had a mistress once, but only until I married his mother."

"Oh! You scandalous, horrid man!" she cried, teasingly.

"Yes, I was absolutely scandalous," he said. "Sneaking around in the hallways at night, to share her bed."

Elizabeth chuckled. "Giving her positively unbearable looks at the dinner table, and in the drawing-room."

"Oh, but if you only knew what I was thinking when I gave you those looks."

"I have had seven years to understand fully what you meant by those looks," she said.

"May I presume, then, that you understand the one I am giving you now?" he asked, with a very deliberate look in her eyes.

Elizabeth blushed, and recalled those days before her marriage, when she had crept through these very rooms to meet him in his dressing-room and steal a kiss before dinner. They had time and privacy enough for far more than a kiss at present, but they had done a goodly amount of experimentation in the culmination of urgency, in their younger days, and had found they preferred this way of going about things, of teazing each other during the day, allowing desire to build, and then enjoying a wonderfully leisurely night of the marriage bed.

"I understand you perfectly, Mr. Darcy, and I promise you the enjoyment of my mountains *and* valleys tonight," she said archly, rewarded with a low chuckle from him. She was still occasionally struck with how handsome he was, and found herself once again enlightened with this thought as he gave her a very particular look, then left her to go to his dressing-room. When Elizabeth had first seen him again at Netherfield, she had thought he looked older than his years should have allowed. Now, with his hair gaining its first flecks of grey, he somehow managed to appear younger. The difference was happiness, Elizabeth thought; nothing could give a countenance the appearance of youth quite like happiness.

Smiling, she turned back into her own dressing-room, where she caught sight of her reflection in the looking-glass, and knew that this was true.

February 18, 1823

Deep into the night at Longbourn, Fitzwilliam Darcy awoke. He fully expected, upon doing so, the sight that had often met him at such hours early in his marriage, that of his wife lying there, silently awake and waiting to return to slumber after whatever had disturbed her in the night. He expected it still more now, with her belly grown so large that it would not at all have been unusual for her to struggle with sleep, even within those most comfortable environs of Pemberley.

Yet she was still sleeping, nestled amongst the various pillows she had positioned to increase her comfort. It *had* been a busy day, getting the children settled into the nursery and reintroduced to the playmates they had not seen in some time. And following that, Elizabeth had still insisted on a walk; she liked to walk as far as she was able, even now. It helped her sleep better at night, she said, and it seemed tonight that the walk had indeed proven beneficial.

Although he understood why she had wished to do so, Elizabeth's determination to return to Longbourn had worried him, particularly at such a time. Darcy had quietly made inquiries on available houses in Richmond, while in town, and he had been entirely prepared to let one if Longbourn troubled his wife. She had seemed completely at ease all day, however: happily pointing out all the features of the scenery she had forgotten during their walk; greeting Mr. Moseby with praise for his work and a promise that he should have more of her time in the coming days; and cooing with Lydia over the items purchased for New Baby's layette while Elizabeth had been in town, with a great many gifts for Lydia and the Denny children given over in the process.

Then in the evening, they had retired to this room, one across the hall from the master bedroom that had so plagued Elizabeth – now the residence of Lydia, who presumably had no reason to be troubled by it – and here Elizabeth still seemed at ease. There were so many ways in which Darcy found his wife handsome, but there was a particular beauty to her in this state, sleeping peacefully, her belly large with their child. He felt an overwhelming swell of love for her, to watch her thus.

Love, and regret. Darcy was not a firm believer in ghosts, but he wished now that whatever spectre of Mr. Collins remained in the house had heard Elizabeth's laughter earlier in the day, had heard the playful sounds of all the children she had borne.

He felt his old recriminations begin to come to mind, but required himself to stop. *Think only of the past as its remembrance gives you pleasure*, Elizabeth would have said, had she been awake and able to hear his thoughts. And there was so much within the past to treasure. Darcy could still recall the old, selfish days of his former existence, and every time he did, he silently thanked Charles for prompting him to change.

It had done him much good to gain the care of a family, to have those whose welfare he would always put before himself. To have children: delightful, precocious children who must be loved, guided, and educated. To have a wife, whose happiness was his own surest path to happiness. He had known before he married her that he would have given anything to further Elizabeth's welfare, and now he felt this same fierce protectiveness over his entire family.

Men less happy in marriage than him might have said he had given up too much, might have missed those old bachelor pastimes he seldom participated in, now. Darcy had lost love and then regained it, though, and suffered excruciating doubt before he had done the latter. He knew full well that to receive the love of such a woman was worth far more than what he had given.

Beside him, Elizabeth still slept, and he gazed at her in sleepy contentedness: mistress of Longbourn, mistress of Pemberley, wife of a man still most ardently in love with her.

AUTHOR'S NOTES

With Gratitude

This book would not be what it is without the numerous readers who gave feedback from the very beginning, when it was a nascent story not even half its present length, to the time when it was nearing publication. While there are too many to be listed individually, you all have my utmost thanks, and my hopes that you have enjoyed the finished story as much as I enjoyed making it better as a result of your feedback.

Timeline

Readers of my Constant Love series who pay close attention to the dates may be thrown by the timing of this story. This is because that series was moved forward a year from when the events of *Pride and Prejudice* are commonly thought to have been set, while this story was placed within the usual timeline.

Terminology

In this time when the recipient paid for the cost of a letter's delivery, a Member of Parliament could "frank" a letter, so that it would be delivered for free.

"Ribbons" were a term used at the time for the reins of a harness.

"Nuncheon" was a precursor to "luncheon."

Per the *1811 Dictionary of the Vulgar Tongue*, the insult given to Elizabeth by Mr. Boyce was every bit as horrid as it is today.

I had feared "Chip" sounded too American, and was considering changing the pony's name, but the *1811 Dictionary of the Vulgar Tongue* indicates that "chip" was already in use at that time to refer to a child, as in "chip off the old block." It seemed appropriate, therefore, for a pony, although I think we can presume the pony came with that name, and Darcy did not rename him as such.

"Sweet oil" is another term for olive oil, and was used for a number of medicinal purposes at that time (it is still sometimes used as a remedy for earaches, today). In Elizabeth's case it would have been used as a lubricant.

Collins's Death

Elizabeth's mourning would have begun in July of the previous year, and readers familiar with the hunting season may have noticed that this is too early for Collins to have died in a regular hunt. He would have done so during a "cub hunt," which could take place as early as July. In the cub hunt, younger foxes were culled, and young hounds trained before the full hunting season. In Mr. Collins's case, a man who was never a skilled rider would have been still more out of practise to be hunting at this time, and readily enough unhorsed.

Longbourn

There were two ways in which Longbourn's entail could have ended – either because it expired with Mr. Collins's generation (they were commonly put in place for a number of generations, and required members of multiple generations to renew them) or because there were no remaining male heirs. Either might have applied in this case, since Elizabeth did not have a son and we know of no other male cousins, but because the latter would have required a search for extant male heirs, I went with the simpler option of the former.

Elizabeth's reference of Longbourn bringing in three thousand a year in the epilogue is, perhaps, overly optimistic, even if the estate had been severely mismanaged, as Britain suffered an agricultural depression through much of the span of time between the end of the last chapter and the epilogue. However, because I have chosen to focus on that in other works, and because I wanted to end on a higher note, I am operating on the presumption that additional land acquisition (backed by Pemberley's resources) combined with better management could have done it.

Black Walnut

I had been familiar with black walnut as something dangerously toxic to livestock, but on further research I found it can also cause toxicity in soil. Presumably Mr. Wendell had continued to plough the field, distributing the toxins from his trees over the years, and unknowingly making the problem worse.

Black walnut is much more common in North America, but during a tour of Marble Hill House outside London, our guide mentioned that there was a black walnut tree on the grounds. There was, as Darcy indicates, a desire to try "new world" plants in English soil, and I presume the Marble Hill tree was one such attempt, as the grove beside Mr. Wendell's field would have been.

Bow Street Runners

By this time the famous Bow Street Runners had received regular government funding for many years, and were no longer reliant on rewards from the government and private citizens. However, I presumed it still likely that – for the right contribution – they could have been diverted, officially or unofficially, to briefly work on an unexceptional arrest for debt.

Precedence in the Ballroom

Although I have not been able to find a source that states this explicitly for private balls, I have assumed they were like public balls, where the order in the line of dancing was determined by the lady's rank. Ladies, however, who joined a set late were required to join at the bottom of the line, regardless of rank. The rules for the balls at Cheltenham's Lower rooms, which John Feltham lists in *A guide to all the watering and sea-bathing places...* are typical:

"VIII. That a reasonable interval shall be allowed between dances for ladies of rank to take their places. Those who stand up after the dance is called must go to the bottom for that dance; after which, should they wish to take precedence, on application to the Master of the Ceremonies, he will give them their place."

Sex

In the Georgian era, there was a substantial chasm between the expectations of propriety in a young, unmarried woman versus those of a married woman, or widow. While an unmarried woman could not be alone with a man without a chaperone, once she had provided her husband with an heir, a married woman (or a widow) could carry on an affair with little damage to her reputation, so long as she was discreet about it. As in everything, a man could get away with being less discreet, regardless of marital status. This is succinctly demonstrated in an entry in the *1811 Dictionary of the Vulgar Tongue* for a "slice": "to take a slice; to intrigue, particularly with a married woman, because a slice off a cut loaf is not missed."

Ultimately, this was much more about property rights than the morality that came to play in the Victorian era. Young women were expected to come as virgins to the marriage bed (while their husbands could have had far more sexual experience without being judged for it) because this was a better guarantee that their husbands' heirs were in fact parented by their husbands. For this same reason, widows – like Mrs. Bennet and Elizabeth in this book – were expected to mourn for a full year after their husbands' deaths, to ensure they were not carrying a child. Widowers – particularly those with children who needed the care of a mother – could remarry much more quickly without any judgment by society.

Elizabeth's proposal to become Mr. Darcy's mistress for a night, therefore, was risqué and therefore surprising to him, but did not result in outlandish behaviour for a widow during this time.

Pornography, Positions, and Terms

Darcy's early understanding (even before embarking on his research) that there are some nuances to female pleasure would likely have come from an illicit reading of John Cleland's *Fanny Hill* – perhaps filched from a dusty corner of Pemberley's library, or passed around during his school days. If it had not been in the library, the illustrated 1766 edition would certainly have been among the books he acquired and made a study of, and would have been the source of his idea to use the pillow on their wedding night.

While an untranslated copy of the *Kama Sutra* could perhaps have made its way back from India and into Darcy's collection, it was not translated and distributed more widely until later in the nineteenth century. It's more likely that he acquired and took inspiration on positions from *L'arétin Français*, with its exceedingly provocative illustrations, and perhaps even from Thomas Rowlandson's caricature prints and similar publications.

During the seventeenth and eighteenth centuries, writings regarding sex for women underwent a change, from indicating that they did gain pleasure from it to indicating that it was something to be endured, rather than enjoyed. This accounts for the opinion of the accoucheur Elizabeth sees, although Jane's first-hand experience indicates otherwise. Darcy might, then, have either acquired or dug up from that dusty corner of Pemberley's library a copy of Nicolas Venette's *Conjugal Love Reveal'd (Tableau de l'amour conjugal),* which indicates the earlier theory of a woman's pleasure, and also goes into some discussion of sex positions and the role of the clitoris. These, of course, are the (in)famous books that survived, but I expect there were others available then that have been lost to time.

The position they use on that first night was kneeling lotus; readers are left to their own adventuresome googling if they wish to see it in more detail.

As for the terms used, I went with what I thought would be both historically realistic, and realistic for Elizabeth and Darcy to have picked up and use in internal thought. This meant leaving off such period delights as "venerable monosyllable," "Miss Laycock," "shaft of delight," and "nature's scythe." Again, adventuresome googlers can look up the Gizmodo article, "Two Timelines of Slang for Genitalia, from 1250 Through Today," for links to more of these terms.

Common Licence and Diocese of Chester

Mr. Darcy would have gone to Chester to get a common licence, which would allow the couple to marry on any consecrated ground without waiting for the banns to be read. Before the Diocese of Derby formed in 1927, Derbyshire was, in essence, split between Chester and Lichfield, and I've opted to put Pemberley within the Diocese of Chester.

Further Reading

Research for these and other items within this story owe a particular debt to: *1811 Dictionary of the Vulgar Tongue*; *Sex in Georgian England* by A.D. Harvey; *Governing Pleasures: Pornography and Social Change in England, 1815-1914*, by Lisa Z. Sigel; *In the Family Way: Childbearing in the British Aristocracy, 1760-1860* by Judith S. Lewis; *Beau Brummell: The Ultimate Man of Style* by Ian Kelly, from which I drew the anecdote of sex workers being employed at fabric shops, which were the lone female domain amidst the shops catering to men's fashions in the West End; and *Georgian London: Into the Streets* by Lucy Inglis, from which I drew the detail of the pornographic shops in Holywell Street.

ABOUT THE AUTHOR

Sophie Turner worked as an online editor before delving even more fully into the tech world. Writing, researching the Regency era, and occasionally dreaming about living in Britain are her escapes from her day job.

She was afraid of long series until she ventured upon Patrick O'Brian's 20-book Aubrey-Maturin masterpiece, something she might have repeated five times through.

Alas, her Constant Love series is only planned to be seven books right now, and consists of *A Constant Love, A Change of Legacies*, and the in-progress *A Season Lost.*

She blogs about her writing endeavours at sophie-turner-acl.blogspot.com, where readers can find direction for the various social drawing-rooms across the Internet where she may be called upon.

Made in the USA
Columbia, SC
05 July 2018